Happily Ever After in Bliss

Other Books by Lexi Blake

ROMANTIC SUSPENSE

Masters and Mercenaries
The Dom Who Loved Me
The Men With The Golden Cuffs
A Dom is Forever
On Her Master's Secret Service
Sanctum: A Masters and Mercenaries Novella
Love and Let Die
Unconditional: A Masters and Mercenaries Novella
Dungeon Royale
Dungeon Games: A Masters and Mercenaries Novella
A View to a Thrill
Cherished: A Masters and Mercenaries Novella
You Only Love Twice
Luscious: Masters and Mercenaries~Topped
Adored: A Masters and Mercenaries Novella
Master No
Just One Taste: Masters and Mercenaries~Topped 2
From Sanctum with Love
Devoted: A Masters and Mercenaries Novella
Dominance Never Dies
Submission is Not Enough
Master Bits and Mercenary Bites~The Secret Recipes of Topped
Perfectly Paired: Masters and Mercenaries~Topped 3
For His Eyes Only
Arranged: A Masters and Mercenaries Novella
Love Another Day
At Your Service: Masters and Mercenaries~Topped 4
Master Bits and Mercenary Bites- Girls Night
Nobody Does It Better
Close Cover
Protected: A Masters and Mercenaries Novella
Enchanted: A Masters and Mercenaries Novella
Charmed: A Masters and Mercenaries Novella
Treasured: A Masters and Mercenaries Novella, Coming June 29, 2021

Masters and Mercenaries: The Forgotten
Lost Hearts (Memento Mori)
Lost and Found
Lost in You
Long Lost
No Love Lost

Masters and Mercenaries: Reloaded
Submission Impossible, Coming February 16, 2021

Butterfly Bayou
Butterfly Bayou
Bayou Baby
Bayou Dreaming, Coming December 1, 2020
Bayou Beauty, Coming August 2021

Lawless
Ruthless
Satisfaction
Revenge

Courting Justice
Order of Protection
Evidence of Desire

Masters Of Ménage (by Shayla Black and Lexi Blake)
Their Virgin Captive
Their Virgin's Secret
Their Virgin Concubine
Their Virgin Princess
Their Virgin Hostage
Their Virgin Secretary
Their Virgin Mistress

The Perfect Gentlemen (by Shayla Black and Lexi Blake)
Scandal Never Sleeps
Seduction in Session
Big Easy Temptation

Smoke and Sin
At the Pleasure of the President

URBAN FANTASY

Thieves
Steal the Light
Steal the Day
Steal the Moon
Steal the Sun
Steal the Night
Ripper
Addict
Sleeper
Outcast
Stealing Summer

LEXI BLAKE WRITING AS SOPHIE OAK

Texas Sirens
Small Town Siren
Siren in the City
Siren Enslaved
Siren Beloved
Siren in Waiting
Siren in Bloom
Siren Unleashed
Siren Reborn

Nights in Bliss, Colorado
Three to Ride
Two to Love
One to Keep
Lost in Bliss
Found in Bliss
Pure Bliss
Chasing Bliss
Once Upon a Time in Bliss
Back in Bliss

Sirens in Bliss
Happily Ever After in Bliss
Far From Bliss, Coming 2021

A Faery Story
Bound
Beast
Beauty

Standalone
Away From Me
Snowed In

Happily Ever After in Bliss

BLISS
COLORADO

Nights in Bliss, Colorado, Book 11

Lexi Blake
writing as
Sophie Oak

Happily Ever After in Bliss
Nights in Bliss, Colorado Book 11

Published by DLZ Entertainment LLC

Copyright 2020 DLZ Entertainment LLC
Edited by Chloe Vale
ISBN: 978-1-942297-45-1

Sign up for Lexi Blake's newsletter
and be entered to win a $25 gift certificate
to the bookseller of your choice.

Join us for news, fun, and exclusive content
including free Thieves short stories.

There's a new contest every month!

Go to www.LexiBlake.net to subscribe.

Acknowledgments

While I was writing this book, I had to stop sometimes and just sit and enjoy the moment because I'll be honest, I wasn't sure I would get to write this book. I wasn't sure I would ever be able to come back to this place again. I won't go into all legalities of the corner I was in regarding the Sophie Oak books, but I found myself walking a tightrope and had to choose to move on from these worlds I loved so much. Flash forward to a book conference in Orlando a couple of years ago and I meet an attorney who happens to live in my city and who thinks she might be able to help me out. I was reluctant because I didn't want to make waves. Waves can crash into a person and take them under. Or, she pointed out, you can ride one and it can take you all the way to shore. It was my choice. I could accept the situation or I could try to change it.

I am eternally grateful that I made the right choice.

We so often make choices in order to keep peace—oftentimes to our own disadvantage. We don't advocate for ourselves because we've been taught that's arrogant or unbecoming. It's fitting then that my first trip back to Bliss is a book about Nell. Love her or hate her, she doesn't back down.

To all the romance authors out there - your work is important. Fight for it. Believe in it. Do not let others tear you down. Someone somewhere needs to hear your voice, needs the particular story only you can tell. Ride the wave and if you fall off, get back up and try again.

This one is for Margarita.

Prologue

Bliss, CO

He'd done it. The wait was over and there was a ring on his finger that he would never take off again.

Something settled deep inside John Bishop's soul. Something he'd never imagined he could have. Peace. Love. This feeling was beyond anything he'd felt before and it was all because he'd gotten one petite woman to say I do.

"It was such a beautiful ceremony." Nell walked into their suite at the Elk Creek Lodge still wearing the cream-colored flowy dress she'd gotten married in. The dress was like the woman herself, ethereal and lovely. Her hair was down and pretty white flower petals still clung from the wreath she'd worn. "I wish Laura had come."

Laura Niles was new in town, and there was something dark about the woman that made him curious. He didn't think she was dangerous. Not to Nell's health, but she was proving resistant to forming friendships. She'd holed up in a cabin and rarely came out unless she was working a shift at the Stop 'n' Shop. He watched his wife, a delicious sense of anticipation starting to thrum through his veins. "I don't think she's interested in making friends, baby."

Nell stopped and frowned. "Everyone needs friends."

He could argue with that notion. He'd held himself apart for so long that he'd almost forgotten what it meant to need others. It wasn't that he hadn't been fond of some of the men and women he'd worked with over the years. He'd liked many of them, but he'd had to balance his affections against the reality that any of those people could be lost at any moment. The work he'd done for the CIA had been deeply important and very dangerous. He'd been responsible for protecting an entire country, and that meant he or anyone he worked with could be cut loose at any time.

But not now. Now his wife was the only one he needed to protect. Now he had one mission in life and that was to take care of Nell Flanders.

She twirled around, taking in the big room that served as the bridal suite. "I'll get through to her eventually. Holly is going to help me. You'll see. We'll get the new girl involved in some fun activities and soon she'll be our new best friend."

Holly Lang and Callie Shepherd had served as Nell's bridesmaids during the ceremony. He'd wanted to elope, but Nell had put her foot down. She'd been more than happy with a simple wedding, but it had to include her friends. Her family, as she'd put it.

Nell didn't share an ounce of blood with the people of this town, but they'd all shown up for her. The owner of the diner had provided a vegan feast, though Stella and her cook had to figure out how to make a vegan cake. Holly and Callie and Teeny Green had helped sew Nell's wedding dress. Mel had ensured the wedding was free of all alien influence, though he hadn't been able to promise a Sasquatch-free ceremony. Apparently it was high mating season and Sasquatch males were attracted to the flowers Nell had chosen to carry.

And the Harper twins and Stef Talbot had given him a long talking to about what they would do to him if they ever found out he'd hurt Nell. He'd sat at the bar at the base of the mountain and nodded gamely, promising to never cheat on her and hopefully looking properly intimidated. His history professor persona was good cover for the fact that he could take out the three of them and not have his heart rate tick up.

The good news was he never intended to cheat on his Nell, and they'd made it through the whole ceremony without a single attempted kidnapping by a Sasquatch.

"I have no doubt." He sat back and watched her, patient because he knew how this evening would end. It was good to be patient, to revel in the idea that he knew exactly what tomorrow would bring. It would bring a tofu scramble and a nature hike, and at some point in the nature hike, he would fuck his lovely bride with the blue sky above them and nature all around.

He liked Bliss. It was odd because if he'd been asked where he would retire he would have said a city. Well, he would have said a casket because he'd never thought he would live long enough to retire, but if pressed he would have said New York or London. Certainly not this tiny piece of paradise where he'd discovered the world wasn't as cruel as he'd believed.

He'd thought briefly about taking her out of here. It would be easier to get her to focus exclusively on him if she wasn't surrounded by the familiar. He could do it. She was in love with him, and if he asked her to leave this place, she would.

But that had been John Bishop thinking, and he was Henry Flanders now. Henry Flanders loved Nell so much he would fit himself into her life. He would give her the best he had and share her with her friends because it would make her happy. Henry Flanders had started volunteering around town because he loved how Nell's eyes softened when he helped.

John Bishop was starting to recede, and Henry Flanders was taking his place. It was a good thing. He liked Henry Flanders quite a bit.

He also liked that Henry Flanders could be the nice guy around town and a dirty Dom when they were alone. Nell's Dom.

"Show me your breasts."

She stopped and faced him, her eyes lighting with anticipation. "I've missed you."

He felt his lips curl up. He smiled so much around her that at first his face had ached because he almost never used those muscles. "You have no idea how much I've missed you this week."

He'd stayed at the naturist resort high on the mountain where he'd first met the lovely Nell Finn. His former Army CO Bill Hartman ran the Mountain and Valley Naturist Community. Six months before, John Bishop had needed a place to think and Bill had provided it. He hadn't

15

imagined it would come with a whole lot of naked people and the one woman who could change his whole world.

Nell started to slowly bring the straps of her gown down, fully exposing her soft shoulders and the graceful line of her neck. "I never would have imagined you would be so old fashioned."

She didn't imagine many things about him, and he intended to keep it that way. "I wanted tonight to be special. I wanted to spend the week thinking about our marriage and how much I want to commit my life to you."

It wasn't a lie. He'd wanted the week away from her to give her one last chance to think about what she was doing without sex blinding her. The sex between them was the absolute best of his life, and as she'd been a damn virgin when he'd taken her, it was the best of hers, too. He wanted her to go into this marriage knowing it was truly what she wanted. He hadn't needed the week, but he had spent the whole time thinking of her.

He'd thought of the people he'd left behind. It hadn't been fair since he'd had balls up in the air, but someone would take over and the United States would go on like it always had. The country didn't truly need John Bishop, but Nell needed Henry Flanders.

And god he needed her.

She'd stopped and her eyes shone in the soft light from the lamps. "I love you, Henry."

He liked hearing his new name. He didn't have some great dream to hear the name John from her lips. He was Henry now. Nell's Henry.

"I love you, too." He'd never thought he would say those words. Never. "Now show me your breasts. I loved our wedding, but I've been looking forward to this since the day I met you. Tonight you're truly mine. I'll share you with the rest of the world during the day, but when we're alone you belong to me."

She let the gown fall to the floor. "There's something I should tell you. Something I probably should have told you before we got married."

He smiled. If anyone else in the world had said those words he would have gone on edge, ready for a blow. But this was Nell and any confession from her would likely be about some ridiculously minor infraction she perceived she'd committed. "What is it?"

She hadn't worn underwear to her wedding. When that dress had hit the floor she'd been gloriously naked, and she was such a sight for sore eyes. And sorer cock. His dick had gotten hard the second her skin had come into sight. His organic cotton slacks were getting far too tight.

"Remember when I was writing that thriller about the Dust Bowl?" Her eyes had gone wide and she bit her bottom lip.

She was trying to use sex to get him in a good mood. He could have told her he was always in a good mood around her.

"Yes. I believe you told me you put that aside." He intended to encourage her to finish it. She was a talented writer and telling stories gave her pleasure. She should pursue her dreams.

She nodded and moved toward him. "That one didn't work out. But I wrote another book. A romance book."

He sat up, spreading his legs a bit to accommodate his ever-hardening cock. "That sounds nice. Turn around. I want to see that pretty ass of yours."

She turned around, giving him a spectacular view of her ass. Heart shaped and perfect. She turned her head, looking at him over her shoulder. "It's an erotic romance. And I got it published. And another one, too."

He stood up, a genuine sense of joy going through him. She'd been busy while he'd been gone, and that made him proud. "Are you serious, baby?"

She smiled. "Yes. You're okay with it? I did it under a pen name so no one knows it's me. You're a history professor. It might embarrass you."

He moved to her and turned her around to face him. She needed to understand a few things. It was far more important than getting his hands on her. "I am proud of everything you do, and I can't wait to read your book. I want a copy of it in my hands tomorrow. I want to read everything you write, and I'll be proud to tell everyone I know about my wife, the novelist."

She went up on her toes and pressed a kiss against his lips. "I love you so much and you have no idea how glad I am to hear that." Her nose wrinkled. "But I should probably stick to the pen name since I might or might not have written a couple of the people around me as characters. In ménage romances."

Oh, how she delighted him. "Max and Rye?"

She nodded. "After you left to go back to work, I closed myself up for a while and wrote some books. I thought about how I wanted everyone to find their happily ever afters, and I started with Max and Rye. I had them find a woman in trouble and they all fell in love. I did the same with Callie. I had two men from her past show up and they all worked it out. There's a nice danger element in them. Callie's men were on the run from the mob."

Oh, he could tell her stories. "I want to read that one, too."

Her eyes came up and there was a heat there that let him know she was comfortable now. She'd gotten her terrible confession out of the way. "I want to write one about a Dom. I didn't before because the character was too close to you, and I thought it would hurt too much."

He stared down at her. "I was stupid to leave, but I needed to tie up a few loose ends." Like his untimely death. Like walking away from everything he'd ever known. Like becoming someone new for her. "I won't ever leave you again, Nell. I'm here and I will be your family for as long as you allow it."

"That will be forever, mister."

Forever was exactly what he had in mind. His past was behind him, but the future suddenly looked bright. He kissed his wife and let his hands find her. It was time to show her everything he could give her.

He was a new man and he would never look back again.

Summer

Chapter One

Bliss, CO
Six years later

Henry Flanders was a happy man. Sometimes it was hard to believe he'd once been someone else. That was what it felt like. That time when he'd been known as John Bishop was so far from this place in the mountains, from the woman humming in the kitchen as she made bread. The sound of some opera played through the house. He wasn't a huge opera fan, but Nell loved it, so he'd grown accustomed. He was fairly certain it was *La Bohème* she'd put on as the soundtrack for her kitchen time.

"We're almost out of maple syrup."

For her vegan bread. He knew her recipe by heart and though she enjoyed making it, he'd learned how to make it as well. That bread was comfort food for his wife. He wanted to ensure she wouldn't have to go without it when she was heavily pregnant and didn't need to stand on her feet for the time it took to knead the bread. He moved in behind her, putting his hands on her shoulders and bringing their bodies together. He breathed her in. She was his oxygen. "I'll put it on our list. I'm going into town tomorrow. Teeny called. My shipment came in."

He'd gotten into woodworking lately. It was soothing. He found he enjoyed the satisfaction that came with making something with his own hands.

He wanted to make their baby's crib, wanted to lay their sleeping child in something he'd created out of wood and love. His Nell thought he was making a present for the upcoming wedding of their friend Wolf Meyer, and he was. The lazy Susan would be embellished with the Meyer name, proclaiming the family was established this year. It would be a lovely present, but the true reason he was spending money on the new table saw was the gift he wanted to give to her.

"That's good. Though I think it's a lot for a saw." She turned her head slightly so he could see her nose wrinkle. "You don't think it's an indulgence?"

He kissed her cheek. "I think I will make many lovely things with reclaimed wood." She would be horrified at the thought of chopping down a tree. And honestly, he'd come around to her way of thinking. They lived in a magnificent forest. There were plenty of opportunities to use wood that would otherwise rot. "One day I'll be good enough to make our furniture if we need it. And we've got the money. The new book sold well."

She cuddled back against him. "Yes, it did. It was fun to write. I hate to admit it, but I do enjoy putting my characters in situations I would never want anyone in. I never imagined I would enjoy writing spies so much, but you do impeccable research. I suppose it's the history professor in you."

The history professor had never existed. The spy was the man who seemed so far away. Except when he and Nell were working on a new book. "I do like to research."

He didn't have to for the series Nell had recently been writing. She didn't realize how close to the truth she was about him.

But that truth was in the past, so it didn't matter. He was a man who built things now, and one of those things was a beautiful future with his wife.

And kid. He was going to be a dad. He felt a loopy grin cross his face. And then fade because it wasn't the first time he'd been here.

She turned, keeping her floured hands down and away from him. "Don't."

He lowered his forehead to hers. "I'm just worried about you."

He felt her head shake slightly, though because he was against her it felt like she was nuzzling him. That's what Nell did for him. She took something that was naturally a negative and made it warm and fuzzy. "It's not the same this time. We're past the first six weeks. This one is going to be okay. I feel it deep inside. When I was picking herbs this morning, I felt the sun on my face, and I swear a butterfly landed right on me. My mother used to tell me that when a butterfly landed on me, it was the pixies telling me everything was all right."

Her mother had deeply believed she'd come from another plane of existence. He'd only known Moira Finn briefly, but he'd heard Nell talk about her mother often and the challenges of growing up with a woman who perceived reality differently.

Once he would have simply called Moira Finn insane and thought the best way to deal with her was to force her to acknowledge reality. But he'd grown to learn reality could mean different things to different people if one was open minded. If thinking their unborn child was blessed by pixies made Nell more confident after two miscarriages, then he would thank the pixies.

Did they drink cream or something? Or was that brownies?

He knew too much about faery creatures, but then Nell had written a romance featuring a faery prince and a human woman, and it was his job to do all the research she needed. It was their secret—the fact that she wrote erotic romance.

And their baby was their secret. For now.

"I'm glad to hear it." He glanced up and saw someone moving across the lawn. His first instinct was to wave at Logan Green and point him out to Nell. Logan was staying at that monstrosity of a cabin Seth Stark had built, along with Seth and Georgia Dawson. Watching those three work through their problems had been deeply entertaining for him and Nell. The last few days they'd sat on the front porch at night and listened in on the relationship drama.

Sometimes it was good to know his wife was human. Oh, she might have shaken her head and said they shouldn't find someone else's troubles entertaining, but she hadn't gotten up from her chair. She'd let him rub her feet while Georgia proved she could yell really loud.

Yes, he would have pointed out to his wife that Logan was coming over, except Logan didn't go for the front of the cabin. He moved toward the rear, and he stopped twice as though trying to ensure he hadn't been followed.

Henry's primary instincts took over, the ones he'd buried deep when he'd left his old life behind—the ones that told him trouble was coming.

Every instinct he had told him something was wrong.

He forced himself to move away from Nell and kept his expression as calm as possible. "I just think you do too much. Between all the housework, the writing, and everything you've done to help with the wedding, you need to rest more. And you haven't been eating much."

He walked out of the kitchen and into the small room at the back of the cabin where they did much of their work. They had two desks set up on one side. One for him and one for her. Her desk overlooked the backyard, with their vegetable garden and a view of the Rio Grande. Much of the money they'd made over the last couple of years had gone into their cabin and their property, though Nell had protested no one should own land.

He'd pointed out that if the land was for sale, who knew who could buy it? Potentially someone who would pollute or overfish or do something terrible with it. When she'd thought about the possibilities, she'd decided it was best to own the land she wanted to steward. Now they quietly owned one of the larger tracts in Bliss.

Logan moved across that land they'd purchased, and there was no mistaking the glint of metal in his right hand. Logan was dressed in the khakis that marked him as a deputy with the Bliss County Sheriff's Department, though no one thought he would be working there for much longer. He'd been fighting the idea of being in a relationship with Georgia, of sharing her with his best friend, Seth, on a permanent basis, but there wasn't a person in Bliss who thought Logan would win that fight.

However, it looked like there was another fight entirely playing out at that big cabin of Seth's.

Henry watched as the door to the back of Seth's cabin opened and a large man stepped out. He was muscular and packing. There was a gun in his shoulder holster.

A chill crept up Henry's spine.

"I'm better." Nell had gone back to her bread. "You worry too much, Henry. It's perfectly normal. I'm actually quite hungry now."

She hadn't been for the first few weeks. It was one of the ways she'd known to take a pregnancy test.

He moved to the screen door, going light on his feet so Nell might think he was at his computer. She wanted her new hero to be a former Interpol officer, so Henry was busy pulling together all he could about the international agency. He could have simply sat her down and told her that he'd worked with them many times and they were difficult because they had all sorts of rules that tripped up an agent.

"I don't know. I think you should see Caleb." Logan was right in front of him now, and Henry put a finger to his lips, silently asking for quiet. If Logan had come running, he would have brought Nell into the conversation. He would have had Nell call the sheriff.

But he hadn't. Logan had snuck up, and he clearly had his radio. So he didn't need someone to call the sheriff. He'd likely already done it.

That meant he needed help, and not from Nell. Not from Henry either.

He needed John Bishop. There were only a few people in all the world who knew his secret, and one of them was Seth Stark. If Seth was in trouble, he would have sent Logan for him.

"I need some rest. That's all," Nell continued. "Caleb would try to prescribe things, and you know how I feel about big pharmaceutical companies."

If he didn't distract her, she would hear Logan, and then he would have to make decisions he wasn't ready to make. He'd been able to deal with that man from Gemma's past quietly, though he knew Caleb Burke had questions about the way the man had died.

Henry had split the man's spine at the top of his neck. It was a neat and bloodless kill, one he'd perfected over the many years he'd worked for the CIA.

"They're not all bad." He said the words to get a specific reaction out of Nell, knowing she wasn't even halfway through her kneading process.

"Not all bad? I recently read an article about this terrible

24

company," she began.

She would be at least five minutes. It gave him the opportunity to slip out on the deck. "What's going on? I caught you running across the yard with a gun in hand about thirty seconds ago and then that big guy stepped out onto your porch. Have you called Nathan?"

His gut was in knots. Why now? Why was everything seeming to come to a breaking point right as he and Nell had managed to make it past that first awful six weeks of this pregnancy. He'd felt like someone was watching him, like something was bearing down on him.

Nell was going on about some pharmaceutical company with a German-sounding name as Logan leaned in. "Yeah, though I think this is your problem. You tell me something and you tell me now because my partner and my wife are being held by some sort of drug lord. Did you work for them before you came to Bliss?"

Now his gut took a deep dive and he felt bile at the back of his throat. And he knew why he'd felt eyes on him. The cartel. They'd found him? "They're from a cartel?"

It was his worst nightmare. The Agency finding out John Bishop wasn't dead was only his second worst-case scenario. The cartel was the worst.

How the hell had they found him? How had they figured out he wasn't dead?

Did they know about Nell? That was the real question that went through him. Was he about to cause the death of the most precious person in the world to him?

"I could be wrong. They could be mob. They could be a traveling circus. I don't give a shit because they're going to kill my people and I think they're here for you. So I'm going to ask the question and you're going to answer. Are you on the payroll?" Logan asked the question low, his tone hard. It was the tone of a man who thought he might be about to lose everything.

Henry knew the feeling. He forced his panic back down. There was no place for it here. If the cartel was at Seth's place, then he needed to be cold as ice. He could make this work. After all, Seth had known who he was for years. Seth had kept his secrets. Logan could keep them too.

Or the time had come and he had decisions to make.

"No. The cartel was the target. If it's who I think it is, they were mixed up with a terrorist cell. I was CIA and then I wasn't. Damn it. They're supposed to think I'm dead." Telling Logan was all right. Especially since if the cartel had Seth, Logan was about to find out how good he was at killing.

It was odd because there was no anxiety about what he was about to do. He knew how to kill quickly and quietly, and cartel assholes were fairly easy to take down. They only tended to know how to shoot things, and he didn't intend to even let them know he was there until it was far too late to pull the trigger.

"They seem to have caught on." Logan's gaze went back toward the cabin as though he could see it. He couldn't. Not standing here. "Nate's on his way, but I don't have time to wait so I need you to get your freak on. You owe Seth. You owe him, Henry. And you damn well know it."

He owed the whole town of Bliss, and that meant he couldn't hesitate. He nodded Logan's way and walked back into his cabin, into the place where he was happy and safe. It was the place where he lied to his wife so he could stay happy and safe.

Was it the place where he would lose her?

Henry moved to his desk. It didn't have the view Nell's had, but it did have a view of her, and that was all he needed. He loved to watch her while she typed away at a story about true love sprinkled in with lessons on recycling and tolerance. And anal sex. He rather thought that was why they truly sold. His wife had a deliciously filthy mind.

God, he loved her, and he would do anything to protect her. He opened the drawer to his desk and found the knife he kept there. His sweet wife thought he kept it around because he was learning to whittle. The only reason she thought that was because she'd likely never seen a knife that was meant exclusively for killing. He didn't have time to go for the guns he kept stashed away. The knife would be quieter, and if he needed a gun, then he would take one off a dead cartel guy.

He could make this work. She didn't have to know.

"Hey, baby, Logan's here. He says there's a problem with the plumbing. I'm going to check it out. You knead your bread, okay? I wouldn't want to ruin it. And I'll turn up the music. I know you love this aria." He used his mouse to pump up the volume on the opera that was playing through the cabin. It might mask the sound of gunfire.

Might.

"I could come and help." She was looking over at him with the most adorable Nell expression. He'd cataloged her expressions over the years. She had twenty different smiles and only two frowns. One of those frowns was on her face now. It was her slightly disgruntled frown.

"No, baby, you stay here. It's just a little wet work. I'll be back in ten minutes." He took her in for a second. She was the light of his life. "I love you, Nell."

He forced himself to go outside and prayed he could pull this off.

An hour later he'd taken a shower and changed into some of Logan's clothes, tossing his own in the trash because they'd gotten covered in blood. Luckily his clothes were interchangeable, and Nell rarely noticed what he was wearing so long as it was sustainable and organic.

He forced himself to move across the grass, feeling almost like he was outside his body, like he was a robot moving only because he had the programming that forced the action.

Like he used to feel every single day of his life.

Seth was going to live. Georgia had been spared the worst of it. Seth had taken the pain for her, and he'd even had a smile on his face at the end because he'd known he'd gone through the fire and come out of it with everything he could have wanted.

Henry feared his fire was about to begin.

Henry, I respect a man's privacy. You know I do, but if something's heading into my town, I need to know.

Thirty minutes ago, Nate had asked him about the possibility of the cartel returning to look for Henry as they'd stood in Seth's living room surrounded by dead bodies.

Hell, sheriff. Hell is coming to Bliss, and I invited it in.

It had been explained to him that the man who'd shown up hadn't been sure Henry was in town. He hadn't reported back to his boss, and wouldn't because everyone was dead. Still, he had to figure that at some point the cartel would catch on to where he was.

Should he leave?

Nell rushed out onto the porch, only stopping when she saw him walking up. She put a hand over her mouth and then ran to him, throwing herself into his arms. "What happened? I got a call from Laura. She said there was trouble at Seth's."

He wrapped his arms around her. God, he couldn't leave this woman. "It was okay. Logan took care of it. I'm sorry. I didn't take my phone with me and I had to help with the cleanup. I had to change. I got...I got some blood on my clothes." At least he didn't have to lie about that. "Seth is all right."

Nell's face turned up and there were tears in her eyes. "They were coming after Seth because of all that money he has. I've told him it would be better to donate it."

Nate was giving him some time, but the sheriff wouldn't keep quiet forever. For now Nate was allowing the idea that they weren't sure why the cartel had shown up. They were going on the theory that they were after Seth for either money or data. Seth Stark was a tech billionaire. He was a good target for any one criminal organization that wanted money or tech. It was a believable story.

But the truth would have to come out. He'd begged Nate to give him until after the wedding. By then they should truly be past the most dangerous time in her pregnancy, and Nell had been so looking forward to the wedding. He wanted a few more weeks before he had to tell his wife everything she knew about him was a lie.

"You're all right?" Nell clutched him close.

He kissed her forehead. "I'm fine now."

He held his wife close because he was on borrowed time. He needed to figure a way out of the trap he was in and fast.

"You're sure you're all right?" Nell asked, her gaze filled with uncertainty.

"I'm fine. Just a little shaken up," he said. "Come on. Let's get you back inside. Are you feeling okay? No cramps?"

She shook her head. "I'm fine. What happened? How close did you get?"

He kissed her again. He wasn't sure what he would do if she lost the baby. He wasn't sure he could survive that because she would blame him, and she would be right to.

How had he ever thought he could get away with it? How had he thought his past wouldn't find him again? After all the blood on his hands, why had he thought he could be clean again?

"Too close," he said, holding her again. "I'm upset, Nell. Would you mind if we sat together for a while?"

"Of course." She gave him a squeeze. "Come on. I've started dinner and I'll pour you some Scotch and we can sit and watch the river."

It was his favorite place to be if he wasn't in bed with her wrapped around him. He loved to sit and watch the sunset with her. "That would be nice."

He followed his wife and prayed he could use these days to find a way to tell her he was a lie.

* * * *

"I heard it was a drug cartel." Holly frowned as she poured a cup of chamomile tea and set it in front of Nell. "But I heard that from Marie, and she seems to think Seth has invested heavily in drug rehab centers and that's why they came after him. I don't think that was it."

Laura patted her infant daughter as she rocked back and forth in the rocking chair that used to be Nell's mother's. "Yeah, I don't think so either. Somehow I don't see a cartel targeting investors in rehabs. Cam hasn't come home yet, so I haven't been able to grill him. I'm so tempted to go to the big house and see if I can pick up any clues. You're sure Henry didn't tell you anything at all?"

Nell took the tea and settled back into her place on the sofa. Laura had shown up with Holly shortly after Nate had knocked and asked Henry to come down to the station house. Nate had explained that they needed to take a more thorough report on what he'd seen now that Seth was in surgery and expected to make a full recovery. Nell had tried to go with her husband, but Henry had insisted that she rest. And Nate had insisted they go to the station rather than taking his statement here. It had been an odd exchange, with some weird tension running between the sheriff and Henry. She'd been glad when her friends had shown up on her doorstep offering to sit with her for a while.

"He told me what he knew," Nell replied. "He was there. He went over to help Logan with a plumbing problem." Except he hadn't taken his tool kit. Had he? He hadn't come back with it. She supposed he could have gone out to his shop, picked it up, and then left it behind in the chaos. He'd seemed so dazed when he'd come home. She looked to Laura. "Why would Nate need Henry to come down to the station? According to Henry, he didn't see much. He was in the bathroom, and he hid there until the shooting was over."

Which also didn't sound like her husband. Henry wasn't a violent man, but she'd never had a question in her mind that he would protect the people around him. She believed in nonviolence, but she wasn't so naïve that she didn't understand sometimes there was no other way. She already knew she would defend her husband and child and friends if she was forced to.

Henry wouldn't hide. He might throw his body in front of something deadly, but he wouldn't hide.

And that meant something was wrong with his story.

Laura patted her daughter, Sierra, on the back as the baby started to mewl. She'd only recently adopted the infant, but she was already settling into her new role as a mom. "I suppose he wants Gemma to take a long statement. You know Nate doesn't love to type."

"Why would he need a long statement from a man who was in the bathroom the whole time? Henry didn't leave the bathroom until it was all over." He'd said he'd had to help stop Seth's bleeding, and that was how he'd gotten the blood on his clothes.

He'd seemed haunted by the whole thing. But Henry had been around blood before. He was always solid in a crisis. Something was different this time. The only other time she'd seen him so shaken was a few months before when Gemma had been in trouble.

Holly sank down beside her. "I think Nate is trying to make sure he gets everything right on this one since he's going to have to talk to the feds. Some of the people who attacked Seth and Georgia were from other countries."

She didn't buy it. Something was wrong, and it made her wonder about the incident that happened before. "Do you remember when Jesse got shot?"

Laura let out a huff. "Who could forget that? Gemma's ex-fiancé comes into town and tries to kill her because he thinks she's working with you on a case that eventually got a presidential candidate taken out of the primaries. No. I don't forget that easily."

It had hit close to home because Nell had been working with the township that formed the basis of the case Gemma's old firm had been working on. They'd been able to prove the EPA investigator was taking money under the table from the corporation that was polluting the town's water table and causing a cluster of cancer cases. One of the primary investors had been a presidential candidate. Gemma and Nell had been able to prove that the candidate had known what was going on. The scandal caused the candidate to drop out.

But not before Jesse had been shot and Gemma and Cade had nearly died.

Holly sat down beside her. "Caleb complains regularly about how he's taken more bullets out of Bliss citizens than all his years in war-torn countries."

Holly and Laura shared a look, one that normally Nell would let slide as her two best friends trying to figure out how best to handle her so she didn't go off on a protest. But this time she rather thought it was about something else.

"How did that man die? Gemma's ex?" She'd heard the rumors and laughed them off. Because the rumor was someone had killed the man who'd shot Jesse and tried to kill Gemma. Because there was only one other person in the woods that night. By the time Nate and Cam had gotten there, the man had been dead.

"He broke his neck," Holly said matter of factly.

Laura said nothing, but there was a tightening around her eyes.

"I heard the words *internal decapitation* used." She'd overheard Max and Rye Harper talking about it at Stella's one morning. And it wasn't like she'd eavesdropped. Max was very loud. "That's when the spinal cord is separated from the base of the skull. It's a rare injury and one that doesn't normally occur from someone tripping and falling. I believe that was the theory Nate put forward."

"How do you know about internal decapitation?" Holly's eyes had widened.

She felt herself flush. Not even her two best friends knew about her writing. They knew she wrote, but not what she wrote and that she'd been published. It wasn't because she thought Holly and Laura would be shocked. They wouldn't. Her best friends would be supportive. But when Henry had started working on the books with her, she'd liked the intimacy of it being only the two of them. They shared so much of their lives with everyone around them that having this part remain private made it even better. Those books contained her secret self, her fantasies and dreams, and sharing them with Henry alone felt right.

Henry didn't actually write the books, but he helped her plot. He did a lot of research and was her first line editor. Henry had read everything she'd ever written.

Henry had been the one to suggest that her spy hero understood the fine art of atlanto-occipital dislocation, more popularly known as internal decapitation.

"I'm doing research for a possible book." They knew she was always planning something.

"I thought you were writing about recycling or climate change." Laura had sat up, shifting her now sleeping baby from her shoulder to her arms.

"I research a lot of things." She researched the things she found interesting and let Henry teach her about things like war and which kinds of guns law enforcement would use. He'd researched everything from how to defuse a bomb to bioweapons. She worried he might be on several watchlists. It was probably a good thing they didn't travel much. "And my research taught me that it requires a good amount of force in exactly the right place to separate the skull from the spine. There's a reason it's rare. It mostly happens in high-speed car accidents."

"Why are you asking, Nell?" Laura asked before she glanced Holly's way again.

It was obvious they'd been talking about this, too. "I think it's odd, that's all. I also think it's odd that Seth had a problem with the plumbing. It was just put in."

"Did he say what was specifically wrong?" Holly asked.

"Plumbing can go wrong at any time." Laura continued to rock. "And it makes sense since you said he hid in the bathroom."

Nell nodded. "That's what he told me. Do you know when the call went in? I can't see the front of Seth's cabin from the kitchen. I was working on some bread and then I answered some email. That window faces the river, so I was utterly unaware anything was going on. Why didn't Nate have his siren on?"

"I think Logan managed to get a call out before he took down the bad guys," Laura explained. "I'm sure Nate didn't want to alert them the police were on the way."

Nell had gone over and over the timing in her head. "I talked to you five minutes before Henry came home. By then he'd helped with the people who'd gotten hurt, and then helped some with the cleanup. He had to take a shower and change his clothes because he got blood on them. And he was only gone for an hour and a half."

"Nell, what are you worried about?" Laura asked, her mouth down in a frown.

She wasn't sure she wanted to admit it, but she needed to talk to someone. "Have you heard the rumors? About Henry?"

Holly sighed. "I've told Caleb he's insane. It's ridiculous."

"He's not the only one," Laura countered.

She'd heard the rumor from Rachel, who'd rolled her eyes and called Doctor Caleb Burke crazy for even hinting that Henry Flanders might be some sort of trained killer. She'd thought Nell would find the idea hysterical, but then Nell heard how the man had died.

Was it merely coincidental that Henry had done a ton of research on internal decapitation for her latest book, and not a few weeks later someone died that way right here in Bliss?

"I've heard Gemma thinks something's wrong with Henry, too," Nell admitted.

Holly reached out and covered Nell's hand with hers. "No one thinks there's anything wrong with Henry. Caleb and Gemma both have vivid imaginations, and neither of them have been here for long. What do you think happened this afternoon? Do you think Henry stormed into Seth's cabin and took them all down? How would he have even known there was trouble?"

But that was where Logan came in. And Seth. When Henry had first come to Bliss, he'd met Logan and Seth. He'd had an oddly close relationship with Seth over the years. Henry had kept in touch with the young man while he'd gone to college and started his incredible business. "Why would Logan come to our door when he could have called? If it was an emergency, calling would have been faster."

"You know how people are around here," Holly countered. "They like to be friendly."

"But he wasn't friendly. I didn't even hear him knock on the door. He didn't come in or say hello to me." It hadn't bothered her at the time. She'd been concerned with her bread and her latest project. She found kneading bread a soothing way to think, and it wasn't until later that she'd been struck by how odd the encounter had been.

"I still don't understand why this is a problem." Holly sat back. "Do you think Henry lied?"

"When he first came to Bliss he was cold." She could still remember how cold he'd been unless his hands were on her. He'd been a bit combative with everyone he'd met in the beginning. She'd known there was a warm heart under all that ice, but it had taken a while to find it. Then he'd left and when he'd come back he'd been a different man, a warmer man. He'd been the man of her dreams.

"So was I," Laura pointed out. "This place has a way of changing a person. Do you think Henry lied to you about who he used to be? Is that what this is about? You've heard the rumors and you're worried they're true?"

She couldn't help but think about it. "I don't know."

"I'll have a long talk with my husband," Holly promised. "He's always paranoid, but he usually manages to keep it to himself. If it helps, Alexei teases him about it. He thinks it's completely ridiculous, and he was in the mob for years. If Alexei can't tell who's dangerous and who isn't, then no one can. And Gemma literally worked with murder lawyers for years and didn't see it. I think Henry is fine."

Holly wasn't telling her anything that hadn't gone through her head. He hadn't given off signals anyone had picked up. She knew Stef had vetted him.

Why was she even thinking these things? And why hadn't she confronted Henry with her questions?

"I hid a lot of things about my past when I got here," Laura admitted. "It certainly didn't make me some kind of killer."

Nell shook her head. "I didn't say he was a killer."

"Then what else are you worried about?" Laura sometimes got a look in her eyes that reminded Nell she'd worked for the FBI for years before she'd come to Bliss, though she hadn't admitted that for a long time.

"I've never met any of Henry's old college friends. With the singular exception of Bill, I've never met anyone who knew Henry before. He talks about some people he knew and they sound interesting, but he's never offered to go see them or bring them to Bliss." She'd known he didn't have any family, that he'd been raised by a single mom and she was gone. No siblings or cousins.

"Not everyone is close to their work friends," Holly pointed out. "And it's easy to fall out of touch when there's so much distance. Caleb doesn't have any friends from his days in Chicago. Alexei has a cousin he talks to quite a bit, but that's about it. All of their friends are from here now."

"It's pretty much the same for Rafe and Cam," Laura agreed. "Rafe tries to reach out to his family, but I don't think it's going well."

"I'm sorry to hear that." Laura had explained that Rafe's family was very old fashioned, and they were giving him trouble about his unorthodox marriage. They didn't consider it a marriage at all. "That has to be hard on Rafe."

"It is." Laura looked down at her sleeping child. "We thought his mom would bend when we adopted Sierra, but apparently she's only interested in children who have her blood. I don't know. Family can be overrated. Sometimes it's good to make a family on your own, to choose the people who stand beside you. I think that's what Henry's done. He's incredibly devoted to this town and its people."

He was. Henry was always the first to volunteer. Was she looking for trouble where there was none?

"The rumors are getting to you," Laura said, not unkindly. "My question to you is does it matter?"

Holly frowned Laura's way. "Of course it matters. I would be upset if people were talking about Caleb and Alexei around town."

"They're always talking about Caleb." Laura shook her head. "But it's not the talk that bothers her, not really. Nell's dealt with rumors all her life, but something about this one is getting to her. It's the idea that Henry might have a darker past than he's been willing to talk about. Does that matter? If you found out Henry wasn't who he said he was, that he might have hidden something about his past from you—would that change how you feel about him?"

It was time to level with her closest friends. It had been so hard to not talk to them, but she could now. "I love him. I'll always love Henry. I'm having his baby."

Laura's eyes widened, and Holly went still.

"Nell, are you serious?" Laura managed to get to the edge of her seat without waking the baby.

She hadn't told anyone because she and Henry had decided to wait a while longer, but she needed to talk to her friends about this. "We've been trying for over a year. I've had a couple of miscarriages."

She said the words simply, and this time they didn't bring immediate tears to her eyes. She'd cried so much over those two losses.

"Caleb didn't tell me." Holly's eyes filled with tears. "Does he know?"

Even in Bliss there were HIPAA rules, and Caleb followed them. The doc was awfully good at keeping his mouth closed. Even around his wife. "Of course. We went to him both times. It was very early on in both pregnancies. So early that he thinks I might not have been pregnant at all the first time."

But she had been. She'd felt it.

"Why didn't you tell us?" Laura held Sierra close.

There had been so many reasons. "It wasn't that I didn't want to. You were getting married. At first I didn't want to take attention away, and then I didn't want to make anyone sad. It's a happy time."

"It can be both." Holly moved closer to her. "It can be happy for us and we can still mourn with you. That's what it means to be sisters. Like Laura said, sometimes we put together a family out of the people we love. Laura and I don't have any family left. Not the blood kind, but you two are my sisters and that means we don't hold things back. Not for anything. I would rather have postponed the wedding than have you go through that alone."

"But she wasn't. She had Henry," Laura said quietly. "Haven't you noticed how close he's stayed to her the last several months? He's hovered even more than usual, and he's been...sad."

He'd been mourning, too. Now he worried. Another reason to think something had been odd today. She'd offered to go with him because he didn't like to leave her alone. But he'd told her to stay.

"We've both had a rough time, but he's been amazing through all of it. Now we're pregnant again, and Caleb says everything is going well and I feel different this time. I'm further along than I've ever been. I think the other reason I didn't want to tell you was that I've always said I wouldn't have kids."

She'd been rather arrogant, thinking she didn't need the things other people seemed to. She'd proclaimed to all who would listen that she wouldn't contribute to the world's overpopulation, and yet here she was putting herself through great heartache for the shot at overpopulating with one more kiddo, one who looked like Henry.

"Oh, sweetie, you can change your mind." Laura reached for her hand. "There's nothing in the world that I want more than for you to have this feeling I have when I hold Sierra. If you want it, there's nothing better in the world. And I'm so glad you and Henry get to have this together."

Holly reached out, too, putting her hand over Laura's and completing their trifecta. "You should know that I'm taking fertility treatments because we've decided we would like to have a kid. Just one. Caleb is unconcerned with passing on his genes, so Alexei and I are trying and Caleb is playing fertility god for us."

"He doesn't care?" Laura asked.

"He's Caleb. We know we're only going to have this one shot, and he wants Alexei to take it. He says there are too many Sommervilles in the world already. He's gotten closer to his brother, but he still worries about the rest of his family. They can be overbearing, and they put far too much faith in genetics." Holly shook her head. "But that doesn't matter. I think about how amazing it would be if we all had kids close in age. It would be so nice for them to have cousins to play with."

Now the tears did show up. They made their appearance as the sweetest vision hit her. All her life she'd been that weird kid with the single mom who thought she was a refugee from a faery plane. She'd had no family and few friends. As much as she'd adored her mother, the idea that her baby could have cousins pierced through her.

If there was one thing Bliss had taught her it was that families could be made through love and choice and pure will.

"I would love that so much," she said.

The door came open and Henry was there alongside Cam, who'd

likely driven him back since Nate had taken him to the station.

Henry's eyes went wide at the sight of her, and he visibly paled. "Nell?"

She stood because she knew that look. She'd seen it on his face twice recently, that helpless look she'd never seen before and now seemed too familiar. "I'm fine, Henry. I'm good. I just told my best friends about the baby. I know we decided to wait but..."

Her explanation was lost as Henry crossed the distance between them and hugged her tight to his body. "I was so worried. When I saw you crying..."

He took a shaky breath and she could feel a fine tremble go through him. He'd thought she'd started bleeding because that was how he'd found her twice before.

"I'm fine. I'm good, and so is the baby." They'd been through a lot in the past couple of weeks. Why was she pushing for more? Henry didn't lie to her. Even when it hurt. He would do it gently, but he told her when her culinary experiments didn't go well or when a particular color wasn't the best on her.

He was so worried. That was why he seemed off. He was worried about her and the baby, and he'd been through something terrible. She was awful for thinking differently.

"Nell is pregnant?" Cam was a big presence in her living room. "I thought they were all about overpopulation..."

"Cameron Briggs," Laura began.

"I meant congratulations. That's awesome news." Cam reached down to take his own baby. "Come on, Sierra Rose. Let's get you home now that everything's been sorted out. Seth has come through the surgery and everyone's fine. We've survived another Bliss disaster. Holly, will you be all right driving home?"

Holly patted Nell's back before she joined Laura and Cam at the door. "I'll be fine. Since we moved down the river, it's so much quicker to get here, though I do miss the valley. Nell, call me tomorrow and we'll talk some more."

"Or we can meet for lunch," Laura offered. "The special at Stella's tomorrow is eggplant parmesan, and I happen to know that Hal is doing one up with vegan cheese in case you come in."

Henry had moved to her side, though his arm was around her.

"That's thoughtful of him."

"I'll see you there at noon." Now that the news was out, she could talk about it. She had a million questions to ask about pregnancy. She could ask Holly and Rachel and Callie and Jen. Beth McNamara had recently had a baby girl. They were having a baby boom in Bliss, and she could be a part of it all.

Henry hugged her tight as the door closed behind their guests. "You're really all right?"

This man meant the world to her. He was her everything. Pregnancy was making her paranoid, and he'd had a rough day. She held him close. "I'm perfect, and so are you. We're all fine. I hope you don't mind me telling Holly and Laura about the baby. I needed to talk to some women. It's not that you…"

He interrupted her with a kiss and then let her go and locked the door. "I'm happy for you to have some women to talk to. You need your friends." He stopped. "I want to upgrade our security. What happened at Seth's made me think. I know we're in a small town, but with Seth close, we might have to worry about people who want to steal from him."

"If you think so." She wanted him to be comfortable. If a few locks could do that, then she could handle it. "How did it go with Nate?"

"Good, but he wanted to be thorough. Logan couldn't talk for long because he needed to be at the hospital. The same was true for Georgia, so until tomorrow I was pretty much the only one he could ask questions of. I'm sorry I left you here alone. It's why I called Holly and Laura to see if they would come by and visit you."

Of course he had. He always thought of her.

She forced those silly questions out of her mind. Henry was the best man she'd ever met and he wouldn't lie to her. She wasn't going to insult him by asking.

"I kept some dinner warm for you." It was time to take care of her husband. "And I kept a second plate for me." She winced. "I ate earlier, but I'm so hungry these days."

"Then let's get you some food. I could definitely eat." He took her hand and led her to their kitchen table.

She sat beside her husband and let all of her worries go.

It was the next morning when she went out and found his tool kit sitting on his table in the shop. It hadn't been moved in days. She could tell from the slight dust coating it.

It was later that day, she found the guns.

Chapter Two

"What do you mean you found guns? Where did you find guns?" Holly asked, leaning across the table.

Laura's eyes had gone wide, too. "Like on your property?"

"What's wrong with your property, Nell?" Stella Talbot walked up with a pitcher of water in her hand and started to fill all their glasses.

She might be ready to bring her best friends in on her worries, but she wasn't ready to alert the whole town, and that's what would happen if the rumor started going around. It wasn't that Stella would mean to spread a rumor. She would inevitably talk to her husband, Sebastian, about the problem, and then Sebastian would ask Stef who Henry was—because he was still learning the town. Stef would go to Jen, Jen would mention it to Rachel, and Rachel wouldn't want Callie left out. From there it would grow to Blissian proportions, and Henry would be in league with the aliens or something equally ridiculous like he was some kind of secret spy.

"Nothing at all." Nell gave Stella her brightest smile. "Although you know I don't believe anyone can truly own property. The land is alive, too." She saw the minute Stella's eyes went from concerned to slightly dead inside. Sometimes her lectures could be excellent deflection. "Did you know that Aspen trees have a sort of collective consciousness?"

Stella finished with her task. "That's so interesting. I'm glad to know there's no trouble after what happened with Seth yesterday. Craziness, I tell you. I was worried it might have spilled over to you since you're so close to their cabin. We went by the hospital and he seemed real good this morning."

"I'm glad to hear it. We're going to visit him this afternoon." She'd made muffins to take over to their cabin, but Georgia and Logan had stayed at the hospital with Seth. She'd left them on the table. She had a key since she and Henry took care of the place when Seth was in New York.

She'd stood and looked down at the rug and the blood stains on the floors. She'd seen bullet holes and wondered how on earth Logan had taken down so many men on his own.

If she'd been writing it as a scene, her editor would have told her it wasn't realistic unless the hero was some kind of supernatural creature.

Her husband was her editor. Had her husband helped Logan with more than his plumbing?

"I hope we're not going to need another town hall. I'm too busy with the wedding and all the parties that go along with it," Stella admitted. "Jen's got a caterer for her party, but Mel insisted that I make food for something called a Meeting of Men. I'm fairly certain Mel intends to explain to Cassidy's grown sons what happens on their wedding night. That requires a lot of sandwiches. And I'm supposed to sneak beets into something the bride eats in case she won't comply with something called a beeting ceremony. She didn't spell that out. She's talking about the vegetable, right? Cassidy's not going to beat up the poor girl, right?"

"It's merely a ritual in which the bride proves herself free of alien influence," Nell explained. Cassidy Meyer had some firmly held beliefs about otherworldly visitors. Personally, Nell believed that the universe was a big place and all should be welcome. She'd told Cassidy that, and it was lucky Nell enjoyed beets because she pretty much had to eat them regularly around Cassidy now. "Don't worry. I'm sure anyone marrying into Wolf's family will be a deeply tolerant woman. I'll make sure to send some food along."

She always tried to make sure Henry had options when he went to parties where the majority of the attendees would be meat eaters.

Which was all the parties he attended with the exception of their monthly vegan cooking class.

Stella's expression softened. "Don't you worry about that, honey. I've got Henry covered. It's not any trouble to make sure all my friends get fed properly." She shrugged a single shoulder and reached up to pat her blonde hair. "It's what I do. I'm a natural caretaker."

Stella joked, but it was true. "Thank you so much. He will appreciate it."

If he was still around and she hadn't buried him in the backyard.

Had she just thought that?

Stella walked away with their lunch orders and Holly leaned back in, her voice low. "Guns? Are you sure they're real guns? Maybe they're like toys or water guns or something. Men can be weird."

"I know what a gun is, and these are real." She'd had guns pointed her direction more times than she would like to count. She'd also been pepper sprayed once, and she swore it hurt less than finding those guns. "They're not hunting guns, either. I thought about the fact that maybe Henry used to hunt, but they were handguns. They're semiautomatics, and one of them has a suppressor."

Holly's brow rose. "What's that?"

Laura was staring Nell's way. "It's what laypeople call a silencer. I find it interesting that Nell knows what a gun enthusiast would call it. Did he have any ammo?"

"A couple of..." She'd been about to say magazines. "Boxes. They're the clippy things."

Laura still looked suspicious, but she seemed to let it pass. "Okay, so where were they?"

"Two were in his shop, and one was in the back of the closet under some old textbooks. I went out to his shop because I'd cleaned his pliers. He'd gotten them all filthy working on our septic system. I went back to put them up on his tool wall and that was when I noticed his tool kit."

"Did he have it with him when he came back from Seth's?" Holly asked.

"He didn't. And before you tell me maybe he grabbed it this morning, he didn't. I went over there early to drop off some muffins. I checked the bathroom and it wasn't there. Also, it looked like he hadn't touched it in a couple of days. I put his pliers up and that was when I noticed there was something behind the organizational wall."

"I understand how you found the guns in the shop, but how did you find the one in your closet?" Holly asked.

"Because Nell is exactly like the rest of us and she went crazy-ass paranoid and tossed her whole house," Laura replied.

Nell bit her bottom lip and sighed. "Not the whole house. Just the parts I don't regularly see. Like his side of the closet and his desk. Maybe I went through his wallet."

There had been nothing special in his wallet—a couple of pictures of her, his driver's license, two fives and a ten, a library card.

But then she'd found the small case under an old blanket at the very back of his side of the closet. It had been locked but she'd quickly figured out the combo. Their anniversary.

"Why haven't you asked him?" Holly took a sip of her water. She seemed oddly flustered, as though she was as shocked as Nell herself. "I'm sure there's a reason. He came from the city. He's probably had those guns for years, and honestly, Bliss can be dangerous at times."

That had also gone through her head. "He's always been so in sync with me when it comes to gun control."

"He's got them hidden and or locked up. It sounds like they're under control." Laura had never seen her point on guns, but then Laura had actually been held hostage and tortured by a real serial killer, so she had her reasons.

"Honestly, my views have changed a bit over the years. I suppose I was influenced by the fact that my mother kept many weapons in our house at one point. She had several swords, a mace, knives, and some weird-looking thing she always told me was a sonic weapon I should never touch." The weapons her mother had hidden all over any place they lived had been one of the reasons Nell had spent time in the foster care system. When her mother had regained custody, she'd gotten rid of all of them, but Nell would still find odd knives under her mother's pillow. And bits of wrought iron sometimes.

"Was it because she was worried the bad faeries would come and take you?" Holly knew the story.

Nell nodded. "According to the state's psychiatrist, my mom was the victim of a violent incident that her mind couldn't process, so her brain created a more comfortable backstory. She believed she was a Fae royal who had to flee her home plane when her evil cousin killed her nice cousin and took over. It was why we couldn't have cats. They're familiars to hags and sent to spy on us. We couldn't have dogs because she was allergic. But we had lots of swords."

"I don't think Henry keeping a couple of guns around for protection is the same thing," Holly said gently. "Why don't you ask him about them? You're going to have a baby in the house."

"Were they loaded?" Laura asked.

"No, but the magazines were close at hand. It wouldn't have been at all hard to…" Nell stopped.

Laura pointed her way. "I knew you knew more about guns. What the hell is going on? Last week you left a bunch of notes at my house about how to defuse a bomb. What are you planning, Nell? I know you're upset about the practices at the new water treatment plant in Alamosa, but you can't blow it up."

They thought she was going full-on anarchist, blow everything up? It was good to know she could still surprise someone. So many people assumed she would be nonviolent—likely because she preached nonviolence—and she'd found that made many of them think she was weak.

She'd once lived in a massive tree for two weeks in order to save it from being turned into someone's mulch. There were no bathroom breaks when protesting. She wasn't weak.

"I'm not blowing anything up. I'm merely researching for my book." The one her friends thought she'd been writing for years.

Laura's eyes narrowed. "The book about the Dust Bowl? You needed modern-day bomb technology for your romance about the Dust Bowl? You know that happened in the last century."

Laura seemed to be zeroing in on her secrets. The last couple of weeks her friend had asked some incredibly specific questions that made Nell think Laura was suspicious. It should be annoying, but it was kind of a fun game. The good news was she had a creative imagination. "There's now a time travel element. I finally figured it out. It's what's been missing all along. You see, there's this odd artifact in the barn and when my heroine touches it, she meets her own great granddaughter, who also happens to be a bombmaker."

She saw the minute the light in Laura's eyes died. Score another one for Nell. Sometimes she thought her superpower was being able to drain a person's will to live simply by talking.

It was kind of a sucky superpower.

Henry always listened to her. He never zoned out or shut her down no matter what she was talking about. She could be talking about the most boring aspects of public policy and Henry would stare right at her and ask intelligent questions.

"All I'm saying is it seems to me Henry's being responsible. Yes, he should have told you he had the guns, but you can be hard to talk to about these things," Laura said with a sigh.

Her heart ached. "Henry's never found it hard to talk to me."

"I have to think there's a reason." Holly sat back. "How much do you know about who he was before he came to Bliss?"

She'd thought about this all morning. "I thought I knew a lot. Like when we're talking it feels like he's told me things, but I look back at the conversations we've had about his past and I realize he always deflects. I know he's an only child and he doesn't know who his father is. His mom died when he was young, but he doesn't like to talk about that. He went to college and discovered a love of history and that's about it."

"Have you ever read anything he's published?" Laura asked, seemingly diverted away from the other mystery.

"Of course. He's got a bunch of papers he published on his computer. He didn't bring the copies of the journals with him. He had a roommate who threw them out. He thought they were supposed to be recycled with the other paper products." She'd thought about trying to hunt down copies for their anniversary. It might be a good project.

"That's sad." Holly waved at someone walking in.

"It's weird." Laura nodded, greeting someone behind Nell. She leaned in. "Rachel's on her way over. Nell, I think you should talk to Henry. You have to be open and honest about what you're worried about."

"I'm not truly worried about the guns. I'm worried about the lies. He lied by omission, and I worry he's lied about other things," Nell admitted.

"Would it change how you feel about him?" Laura asked, her voice low.

That was the question she didn't want to ask at all. "I think I need to consider that. I need some time before I confront him. It could be pregnancy hormones."

"Who's got pregnancy hormones?" Rachel Harper stood at the head of the booth, her strawberry blonde hair up in a ponytail. "Because I'll trade stories with that lady. The best way to deal with hormones is to follow all your homicidal impulses."

Laura had flushed and Holly's mouth closed.

Rachel's face lost its snarky look. "I'm sorry. Is it a secret thing? I won't say anything. I promise."

Should she tell Rachel? If she told Rachel everyone would know, and she'd wanted to wait for a while longer. Telling Holly and Laura was one thing, but…

"It's not a secret that Alexei, Caleb, and I are trying." Holly gave Rachel a bright smile. "But I'm not pregnant yet. Although I am full of hormones." Holly gave Nell a wink. "I've already told both my men to buckle up because being pregnant can make you do crazy things."

Like suspect her husband was anything but prepared for trouble that might come their way. Henry was a good man. He'd proven it to her over and over again.

She would find those journals for him. She would replace something he'd lost and she would forget about accusing him of something she was sure he hadn't done.

"Well, I hope it works and soon. I would love to have another pregnant lady to hang out with." Rachel's hand went to her barely there belly. "I'm almost sure this one is a boy, and I fear for my sanity. Now I came over to let you know we're moving book club out to Jen's because I have feelings about this one. Deep, personal feelings."

Nell had missed the last two book clubs. They were held on a monthly basis, and every month one of the ladies picked a book to read and discuss. "Why would your feelings mean we need to change locations?"

Laura snorted slightly. "I was wondering if you would pick up on that."

Rachel's hands went to her hips. "Laura picked a book called *Her Two Cowboys* by the romance author named Libby Finn. It's a ménage where this dipshit chick thinks she can handle her stalker with kindness or something, but then she finds these twin cowboys in a small town and falls for them. It's a good book and that woman's mind is filthy, but damn, the heroine could be a little more trusting, you know. It's ridiculous that she won't tell the sheriff the mob is after her. Also, those two men are so much smarter than my husbands. But seriously the fact that the heroine accidently ends up kissing the wrong brother is silly. You can always tell."

Yep, she would be missing book club again. She was totally skipping out because while she had a thick skin, she did not need to hear about all the ways she'd gotten it wrong. She got enough of that off the Internet.

Everyone was a critic.

"Have you read that one, Nell?" Laura had that suspicious gleam in her eyes.

Nell put on her blandest smile. "I tend to stick to nonfiction and the classics, but you know I would never judge anyone on what they read. You should read what makes you happy."

"Nonfiction texts about climate change make you happy?" Holly asked.

"Only in that knowledge makes me happy." Though she had to admit that sometimes ignorance really was bliss.

She needed to back off. If Henry felt better with protection around the house, then she wouldn't cause a fuss. Of course when the baby came, they would have to talk about better hiding places.

She could imagine Henry's face when he realized she'd known about them all along. It would make him think twice about keeping things from her.

As for whatever happened at Seth's cabin, she would drop that, too. Henry seemed haunted by whatever he'd done. He would talk to her when he felt comfortable enough to. If he'd had to do something terrible to protect their friends, then she would help him get through it. Henry was a gentle soul at heart. She simply had to be patient and he would open up to her.

"I find it interesting that the cowboys are named Mac and Ty," Laura pointed out. "That seems like too close to be a coincidence."

Well, she couldn't simply call them Max and Rye. That would

have outed her quickly. The fact that the heroine was named Rene was pure coincidence. After all, she'd written it before Rachel had ever come to town. And she thought it was awfully judgmental of Rachel to condemn her poor heroine's trust issues. "You think someone wrote that book who knew Max and Rye? Someone wrote their love story with Rachel? That would be so interesting."

She wouldn't lie outright, but she could hide behind a wall of wide-eyed naïvety.

"It was published before Rachel came to town, but those brothers are awfully close to Max and Rye," Laura pointed out.

Rachel laughed. "Mac and Ty are much smarter. They figure out Rene's problems way before she's willing to talk to them. See, that's why we need to move the meeting. Max is fine being known for his hotness, but Rye thinks he's an intellectual. I don't want to hurt his feelings."

"Because he'll spank you silly," Holly pointed out.

Rachel grinned. "In that case maybe I *should* have it at my house." She winked. "There's Callie. See you guys there?"

"I'm looking forward to it." Holly gave her a wave and her eyes lit up. "Lunch is here. I'm starving. I kind of hoped the fertility treatments would suppress my appetite and I could lose some weight before I gain a bunch, but it hasn't."

Stella set the plates down in front of them, and Nell found her appetite was back as well.

"I'm hungry, too." It was good to let go of her suspicions. "And forget about the stuff I said before. Laura's right. I'm being paranoid. Eventually I'll talk to him about the guns, but I'm letting it go for now. He seems shaken by what happened to Seth and Logan and Georgia. I'm going to be supportive."

Laura reached out and put her hand over Nell's. "I think that sounds like a Nell thing to do." She sat back. "But I'm still going to figure out who Libby Finn is. I think you know her. I think you've been feeding her stories for years."

"I would never feed someone stories about my hometown." Not a lie. She would, however, write them herself. It was good to know Laura wasn't as close as she thought she was. "Holly, tell me all about your fertility treatments."

Nell worried about the chemicals, but if Holly thought this was the best way to take her shot, she would be supportive. It was the theme of the day.

Holly started to tell her all about it and Nell settled back.

Everything was going to be okay. She just had to believe it and it would happen.

* * * *

It was all going to go to hell. He could feel it. He needed to hold out a bit longer. Wolf Meyer's wedding was soon and then...

Then he might not make it to his anniversary. Maybe he should wait for that. Perhaps celebrating their anniversary would soften Nell up. He could plan something lovely—picnic under the stars with chocolate-covered strawberries and her favorite salad. He could gently make love to her and then when she was satisfied, slip in that "hey, I used to be a CIA operative and I killed a whole bunch of people but they'd all deserved it."

He hoped.

Yeah, that was going to go over like gangbusters.

"Henry, you okay?" Seth Stark was the one who wasn't okay. He was hooked up to a whole bunch of machines that monitored his every bodily function.

Henry had dropped off Nell at Stella's and then made the drive to the hospital in Del Norte, where Seth would be laid up for at least another day. He'd texted and been told Logan and Georgia were downstairs in the cafeteria.

Henry sank down on the chair next to Seth's bedside. "I'm fine. I just wanted to talk to you alone. Does Logan know everything?"

Seth's eyes closed, and he took in a long breath. "I'm sorry about that. He doesn't know everything, but he knows enough."

Henry had told Logan the basics, but he needed to know if Seth had filled him in on the rest. "No. Don't be. I'm only asking because I need to know how much to tell him. He should know what's been going on for the last several years. Seth, I should never have put this on you."

Seth's eyes came open and he winced as he turned a bit Henry's way. "I didn't actually tell him, you know. He figured it out. He's smarter than he thinks he is. You should know that Georgia figured it out, too. The man kept talking about John Bishop, and it wasn't so hard to connect those dots. Outside of Logan, you're the person I'm closest to in Bliss. Logan remembers what you were like when you first came to town. I think everyone else has forgotten."

He was the monster who'd smiled enough that people had forgotten how sharp his teeth were. "There are some new people who have suspicions. I probably shouldn't have killed Gemma Wells's ex-fiancé the way I did."

Seth's lips kicked up slightly. "Ye old internal decapitation?"

"Force of habit." He cringed even as he said it. A man's habits shouldn't include a favored method of murder. He didn't want to be this man. "Are you feeling okay? I know how the cartel treats people it wants information out of."

He'd been on the receiving end more than once.

"It was awful, and now my future wife knows exactly how serious I am about her. She knows I'll do anything to protect her, even take a beating." Seth always found a way to look on the bright side of a situation. "It's weird. I think it was way harder to sit there and let them beat on me than it would have been to do what you did. Not that I could have. Really it was best that I was the one tied to a chair."

"You did everything perfectly. You gave Logan time to come get me." He didn't want Seth to think for a second he'd been less than heroic. "I was proud of how you held up."

"Thanks. I knew Logan would save us. It was good to have faith. I haven't always had it, you know." Seth turned serious. "But you didn't come here to recap yesterday. We need to talk about what's going to happen."

It was exactly why he'd come here today. Seth had told him a little, but he'd been in pain and then on drugs. "How bad is the situation?"

"The cartel definitely knows you're alive. According to the man who tortured me, they found a…somebody who worked at a bar."

Henry nodded. "Yes, there was a man who owned a bar in Bolivia. He was paid to tell the police what we wanted them to hear. I worried that there would always be rumors. So the cartel knows I'm alive and they connected me to you."

"They've gone high tech. They managed to find the number of the phone you used shortly after you died. You called me," Seth explained.

Guilt threatened to eat him alive. "Like I said. I shouldn't have brought you into this. You were a kid."

Seth snorted at the thought. "If you hadn't called I would have tried to track you down. I was completely fascinated with you. You underestimate my stubborn will. In the months you were gone, I'd already managed to put some stuff together about you. I had a whole file."

His heart clenched. "That could have gotten you killed. You're lucky you didn't get the Agency on your doorstep. They don't like having their operatives looked into."

"Hence it was good you decided to come back and you needed my help. You should take it again now because if you don't, I'll try to do it all myself, and it could go poorly. I had Logan bring me my laptop and I did some investigating this morning. This Jones guy, he was looking for information. I have no doubt if he'd found you, he would have taken you in," Seth explained. "But he clearly didn't want to be wrong. I think I've managed to trace him back. I checked his phone records. He's had no communication with his employers in the past week. He was a guy looking to move up in his organization. He wanted to walk back into the office with you as an offering."

"So Jones knew where to look, but no one else knew what he was doing." He went over the possibilities in his mind. "I assure you if the cartel knows I'm alive, they've got feelers out. If they're looking, eventually they'll find me."

"Jones got lucky. I can hide you. He didn't know the name Henry Flanders. He was only here in town because I was. I think it's time for John Bishop to resurface."

He knew Seth wasn't talking about him going back into business. "I take it you mean to put some rumors on the Deep Web? Maybe fake some pictures of me in another country. If you do that I'll have more than the cartel looking."

"The Agency?"

Henry sighed and sat back. "Yes, though I suspect they're already looking. I assure you the Agency still watches the cartels, especially the ones that work more closely with jihadists. If the Agency knows I'm alive, they will want answers I'm not willing to give them. Or they might simply send someone to kill me."

And Nell could be caught in the crossfire.

"Let me poke around a bit," Seth said. "I have a lot of government contacts. I also have contacts that I probably shouldn't. Don't do anything right now except watch your back. If someone has eyes on you, anything out of the ordinary could tip them off."

He wasn't wrong about that. "I'm out of practice."

"Then let me help you. Unless you want to reach out to old friends. How about that guy in Dallas? The one you said I should work with when I had that corporate spy problem."

Seth had been the only one he could talk to over the years. "Taggart. He thinks I'm dead. Ian is oddly the most reasonable of my former…students. I worry I would be dragging him and his family into something they shouldn't be involved in. He's got kids now. I think it best I leave him out of this. I'm going to do some research."

He'd already decided to do it the previous night. He'd gotten next to no sleep, merely sat in bed watching Nell and wondering if he was going to lose her.

He needed to get a lay of the land. He'd completely washed his hands of everything having to do with the cartel when he'd walked away. It hadn't been hard. It wasn't like he'd made friends there, but he had felt guilty for leaving a few people behind. Taggart had left the Agency around the same time and he'd done well for himself. Tennessee Smith was another of his trainees, and even he'd left the Agency after some time. Kayla Summers was the one he felt the most guilt over.

"I can help you with that," Seth promised. "But first you have to decide what you're going to do about Nell."

"I'm going to tell her."

A brow rose over Seth's eyes. "When? I think it needs to be soon. It was an easy secret to keep when it was only you and me who knew. As soon as I can get out of this bed, I'm going to take Logan and Georgia to New York. I have some things I need to do there. I want you to think about coming with us."

"That would only put a target on you. And I think you're right about not doing anything out of the ordinary. My Nell getting on a private jet would be out of the ordinary." She didn't like big cities. She was a country girl at heart. Though maybe if he took her somewhere like New York, she would be forced to cling to him.

He hated this. He hated the way his skin felt too tight, like that bastard John Bishop was trying to get out, wanted another taste of what he'd had the day before. Like his old life was a shark that had merely dove deep and now was resurfacing to feed again.

"I want you to stay out of this, Seth." He already had too many people to worry about. He'd sat with Nate Wright and Cameron Briggs the night before and told them everything he knew about the possible danger that could come to Bliss.

"Like I said, I'm already in it, and it's hard for me to stop once I've started."

"You have a family now, too." He couldn't risk any more people than he already had.

"Yes, he does, and this family sticks together," a deep voice said.

God, he was out of practice if he hadn't even heard the door open. He turned and Logan and Georgia had apparently cut their lunch short. Henry stood and faced Seth's new family. "You should, and I think New York is a good place for you right now. I don't want you to have to go through anything like this again."

Logan merely smiled.

Georgia strode in and took her place at Seth's side. "Well, I thought it was exciting. And I was good. I'm thinking seriously about a job with the CIA."

Seth groaned. "You would bedazzle the whole place."

Georgia's shoulder shrugged. "Shiny objects distract people. I suspect they work on spies too. After all, my boobs distracted that jerk long enough for Logan to save the day."

Logan's jaw tightened. "He's lucky he's dead because I would very much like to kill that fucker again. Henry, I didn't get a chance to say thank you."

Henry shook his head. "No need. You wouldn't have been in danger without me."

"That wasn't what I meant," Logan corrected. "I meant thank you for taking care of Seth all these years. You've been more a father to him than his own."

"Because my own is an asshole," Seth offered.

"You kept up with him even when I didn't, and I appreciate it. Seth brought us all together, and you had a part in that," Logan continued. "I understand that you feel guilty, but I also understand why you did what you did. You fell in love with Nell and you had to get out in order to be with her. You changed your whole life for her. I get it. I admire you for it. But it's time to tell her."

"I don't think that's going to go well." Georgia almost always said what other people were thinking.

"She will understand." Logan moved close to Georgia. "If there's one thing I know it's that Nell loves you. She'll be okay."

"I think Henry should count himself lucky that Nell doesn't believe in violence." Georgia frowned as though she couldn't quite believe the "everything's going to be all right" bit.

He didn't believe it either. "I'm going to talk to her, but I would like to push it off a little if I can. If we've got some time, I'd like to get through the wedding before I talk to her. I know I have no right to ask…"

Logan held up a hand. "We're not going to say a thing. This is between you and your wife. And Seth here tells me you probably have time. Nate's got to be ready, though, and that means telling some of our citizens. Cam's got to know. So does the mayor. You have to bring in Stef at some point."

The wedding was only a couple of weeks away. "I need to process this and figure out how fucked I am."

"We also need to be on the lookout for new people hanging around town," Seth pointed out. "If your old bosses figure out what the cartel did, they'll likely send someone in."

Henry nodded. "I'll be on the lookout. I know there are a couple of new hires at the lodge, and I think River Lee hired some guy from Canada."

"And the blonde," Logan added. "Though I think she's been here for a while. Name's Heather and she's from California. Nate says she's been helpful. River's been struggling since her husband walked out."

He'd met the bubbly Heather a couple of times, but she showed no real interest in him. She talked to Nell at length about granola and the best storage techniques. He hadn't met River's other hire at all.

"I need some time. That's all. After the wedding, I'll sit her down and tell her. Until then, I'm going to figure out how to protect her. I worry if she knows and I don't have a plan, she'll come up with one on her own," he admitted.

"Or she'll kick you out and throw, like, tofu at your head," Georgia said under her breath.

"Hey. Give him a break." Seth reached for her hand. "He's been like a dad to me."

Henry felt the need to point out a few facts. "I am not old enough to be your dad. Could I be like a kindly big brother?"

Georgia's lips quirked up. "I don't know. You have serious dad vibes. But I'm on Nell's side here. And I think she's hiding some serious rage under all that happy-earth talk."

He was okay with having dad vibes. He wanted to be a dad, wanted the chance to raise a child with the woman he loved.

Would she still love him when she knew who he was?

"I'll look into things from my end," Seth began.

Henry opened his mouth to argue, but Logan stopped him.

"He's going to play it safe, Henry, but Seth can't leave you alone in this," Logan said. "He wouldn't be able to live with himself if he did. Do you have what you need to protect yourself and Nell if something goes wrong?"

He'd checked his stash before dawn, making sure everything was still stowed away. "I've got some guns, but I can't keep them too close or she'll find them and she'll have questions I'm not ready to answer. I would walk away, but if they find me, they'll be able to find her. They'll be able to figure out she's my weakness and they'll use her."

Georgia held up a hand. "Oh, that is the wrong thing to do. I know I said I was on Miss Nell's side, but I wasn't telling you to leave. That would be a mistake. You need to stay and grovel. Like really grovel. Buy her things she likes."

He wasn't sure that was how to get to Nell. "I don't think I can buy social justice."

"I don't think Georgia understands Nell." Logan glanced at his girlfriend with an affectionate grin. "Nell is from Bliss and she can't be bought with Chanel. But she is a reasonable woman. She'll be upset, but then Henry's going to explain to her how much he loves her and how she changed him and she'll understand."

"She will, you know," Seth added. "I've known Nell for a long time, and she's got so much compassion for the world around her. She's going to be fine."

His wife *was* a reasonable woman. She was tolerant and accepting. She was open hearted and loving.

"You two are crazy. She's a woman. His ass lied, and she will not be happy about it," Georgia said with a shake of her head.

He had to pray that Logan and Seth knew his wife better than Georgia did.

The three of them started to argue about how to best deal with a woman's fury, and Henry glanced down at his watch. It was almost time to pick up Nell from Stella's and head home. She was planning on writing this afternoon, and he would use the time to start to figure out how to get them out of this situation.

A plan. That was all he needed. He would formulate a plan and have something to tell her when he...told her. That would make her feel better. They would get through the wedding and it would put her in a better mood. Weddings always reminded Nell of love and commitment. She would be upset with him, but Logan and Seth were right. She would be okay.

He would make sure of it.

Chapter Three

"The wedding was beautiful," Nell said, and she felt the smile slide over her face. The wedding of Leo, Shelley, and Wolf had been lovely, and it had bolstered her. The words Lexi O'Malley had said the day before still had the power to move her to tears even in the middle of the farmer's market that was held once a month outside the Feed Store Church.

Marriage, family, life, they're all hard and require work. Happily ever after is a choice we have to make every day. You think you're making your choice today, but I challenge you. I challenge every single one of us. Start each day by choosing. Skip the good morning and say something infinitely more important. I do.

"I heard it was lovely." Belinda Ellison had a small stall where she sold the extras she had from her large garden. Belinda used no pesticides and had very earth-friendly gardening practices. Nell always purchased from her. "Though it's so sad about Hiram."

Another thing that could move her to tears. This morning the announcement had gone out that Hiram Jones, the long-time mayor of Bliss, had passed at the age of ninety-seven. He'd lived a good life, but it was hard to let go of anyone.

"It is," Nell acknowledged. "It's hard to go from a wedding to a funeral in the course of a few days. We'll miss him terribly. He was a good neighbor and a good friend."

She glanced over and saw Henry looking through the late-summer strawberries. It would be fall soon and she would switch from strawberries and melons and zucchini to pumpkin and apples. She would make Henry's favorite soups and they would watch the trees change as they waited for their baby.

He looked up as though he knew she was watching, and his expression went from bland to soft and affectionate.

She chose him. She'd been silly to even question him. He'd given up his career for her. He loved her. He was exactly who he said he was. Her lover. Her husband. The father of her baby.

"Did you hear the rumor that they stored him in the freezer at Trio?" Belinda asked.

That made her laugh. "That is nothing more than Zane Hollister trying to create urban legends about his bar."

It was ridiculous to think they would store poor Hi in a freezer. Caleb had a perfectly good facility for those who had passed. Didn't he? Surely he did.

"I also heard that he died while...well, while having fun, if you know what I mean." Belinda started packing up some red bell peppers Nell intended to use in a stir fry.

She seemed to be through with morning sickness, and she had a big appetite. She'd felt bad when she'd realized she'd eaten most of the hummus at her table at the reception the night before. Somehow she'd managed to eat the big bowl without really thinking about it. Henry had simply found her another and a big plate of celery sticks to go with it.

"Having fun? Like he was working a puzzle or something?" Nell gave Belinda her best blank look because she knew exactly how Hiram had died, but she wanted to make Belinda say it.

It was a little mean, but it was also the tiniest bit fun. And honestly, the valuable tasks sex workers did should be normalized. Older people needed human touch, too, and if they happened to enjoy being in a sex swing when they got it, Nell couldn't see how that was a bad thing.

"He was..." Belinda finished placing the peppers in the bag Nell had brought. "Yes, I think it was something like that."

She took the bag with a grin. "Hiram always liked to have fun. You have a lovely day, Belinda."

She took her peppers and strode over to the juice bar that Teeny and Marie ran on market days.

"Nell, honey, how are you feeling? I heard you were under the weather." Teeny didn't have to ask what she wanted. She immediately started making an alien influencer. It was beet, carrots, and strawberry juice. Her favorite, and it had the added joy of letting Cassidy Meyer know she was alien-free for at least the next week.

"I'm good." It was such a lovely day, and with the beauty of the wedding and the emotions of Hiram's passing, she felt like sharing her news. It was time. Henry had told her this was her choice and that when it felt right she should tell their friends. "I wasn't sick. I'm almost twelve weeks pregnant."

Out of the corner of her eye she caught Henry talking to the man selling blackberries. Her husband was so gorgeous in his khaki shorts and T-shirt. Even his big feet were sexy in sandals.

She was starting to get horny. Like really, jump-her-husband horny, but Henry was treating her like a delicate princess who couldn't possibly be touched or she might break. She wanted to play.

Teeny had stopped and her eyes went wide. "Are you serious, honey?"

Tears pierced her eyes. How could she go from crazy horny to super emotional in a single second? Teeny calling her *honey* made her miss her mom. "Yes."

When her mom had passed she'd found Teeny and Marie and Stella had filled that void. She would always miss her mother, but she was so grateful for the women who stepped in and provided her with their loving care.

Teeny came around the bar and opened her arms. "I'm so happy for you and Henry. Oh, I love seeing all these babies. I'm so glad our Bliss family is growing."

She hugged Teeny, sniffling because she was right. This was their family. All of Bliss. "Thanks. I'm happy about it. I told a few people, but I'm ready for everyone to know now. Henry and I are excited."

She was starting to think that all Henry would ever do is worry. He'd seemed so distant in the last few days. She was scared that what had happened to him at Seth's cabin was affecting him more than he was willing to admit. Between the guns and the odd silence that at times sat between them, she'd been thinking they might need to go to counseling. And not the kind Mel proposed where they would sit in a sweltering tent until they got so hot they simply blurted out whatever they needed to say so they could leave.

Teeny beamed at her as she moved back behind the bar. "I'm thrilled. It's going to be so much fun watching all these babies grow up. We're going to need a school soon."

She'd heard there was already a plan in place to pit Stefan against Seth in a war to see who could spend the most on a school. She was going to have to watch that because some of the things kids needed couldn't be purchased with cash.

Although now that she actually had a kid on the way, she was thinking a school might be a good idea. Despite the baby boom, the class would still be very small and likely multigrade. They would need to integrate technology, but they would be small enough that they could often enjoy the outdoors.

Would Henry teach history?

"Here you go, sweetie." Teeny placed the glass in front of her. "It's on the house, and I promise I'll let Cassidy know you drank every drop, though after what she did at the wedding, you should be safe for a while."

Cassidy had sat outside the chapel with shots of beet juice for everyone she hadn't tested at the various parties. For anyone who refused to take the beet, Mel was there with his handy Detector 6000.

"Thanks." Nell moved to one of the standing tables that dotted the "food court" part of the farmer's market. Besides Teeny's juice bar, there was a baked goods stand with coffee and tea, and a place to get handmade sausages.

Which did not smell good. No. They did not.

She needed more protein. She would stop by the stall where they sold legumes and beans.

What if her baby liked meat? What if she was giving birth to a ferocious carnivore?

She might have to learn how to cook it. It sent a shiver down her spine, but she had to let her child decide what was important to her.

"Hello, ma'am. Do you mind if I join you?"

She turned and there was a man standing at her table. He was probably a bit over six foot and dressed like a tourist in jeans and a T-shirt, though he was wearing all black and it was a warm day. He was likely from a big city where they didn't have to worry too much about outdoor activities. He had a cup of coffee in his hand, one of the dark roasts from the smell.

It was odd because there was an open table. River Lee stood at one, drinking coffee with her hiking guide, Heather Turner, but the third was empty. Still, it could be hard to be alone in a new town. "Of course."

He set his coffee down. He had dark hair and eyes and a scar on his face that ran across the left side of his jaw. "Thanks. It's a nice day. My wife is roaming the stalls but I strained my calf on the golf course yesterday."

There was a new course outside of town. She didn't like it. She wasn't sure why they had to use so much water in order to prove someone could put a tiny ball in a hole on perfectly manicured lawns. It would be more impressive to do it on real land. Still, she gave him a brief smile. "I'm sorry to hear that. Are you staying here in Bliss?"

"We rented a cabin in Del Norte," he replied. "It's nice and quiet. It's also got a kitchen, hence our trip out here. My wife is all into this organic stuff."

Good for his wife. "She's lucky. We only have this market once a month."

"Yes, we're definitely lucky," he said with a nod. "This is a nice town. I looked into it a bit when she wanted to come here. I was downloading directions, you know."

She wasn't sure why he'd had to download directions. They were right off the only highway that connected Bliss to Del Norte. "Of course. You wouldn't want to get lost."

"No. I'm not all that into nature, but I will admit it's pretty. So do you and your husband live around here?"

He must have seen her wedding ring. "Yes, we've been here for a long time. Well, I have. My Henry and I got married almost six years ago. He's been here ever since."

"He's not from Colorado?"

She shook her head. "No. He was born in Ohio, but he was working as a college professor in Washington State when he came here for a vacation, met me, and moved here six months later."

She didn't mention the whole "he left her alone for those six months and she hadn't thought he would ever return" part.

"That must have been a big change," the man said.

"He fit right in." When he'd come back to her, he'd embraced the whole of Bliss. It made it easy to remember how naïve he'd thought she was, how he'd initially been cold. He was so warm now.

"Well, I've heard this is the place to be. I read something about that tech guy building a big cabin out here. The one from New York. Read about it on the plane. Can't remember his name, though."

"Are you talking about Seth?"

He pointed her way. "Seth Stark. That was it. Yeah. Read he spent some time out here. I work in the tech sector, so I hear about him all the time."

But he couldn't remember Seth's name? Something was off. "What's your wife's name?"

He took a long drink and then smiled again. "Susan. We're from Houston. How about your husband?"

"Henry. Henry Flanders. And I'm Nell."

"Dave Smith," he replied smoothly. "I'd love to meet your husband. I spent some time in Washington State, too. Does your husband golf by any chance?"

Oh, that was not happening. "No. He's more of an intellectual."

She often invited new friends over to dinner, but something about the man put her off. She wasn't sure what it was, but there was definitely some instinct telling her it was time to find a way to politely exit the conversation.

"Hey, Nell. I was looking for you. I needed to ask your opinion about the zucchinis." River walked up with a smile. She was a sweet-faced woman with dark hair that was cut in a bob that hit right past her jawline. "I was going to make your muffins. I don't want to overbuy. Could you help me?"

Women always seemed to know when their sisters needed a hand. "I would love to. Please excuse me, Mr. Smith. I hope you enjoy your day."

"I will, Ms. Flanders. I think I'll enjoy it very much," he replied.

"Okay, Heather was right," River said with a shake of her head as they walked away. Nell placed her glass back on the bar for Teeny to wash. "She thought you needed some help. That dude was creepy."

He kind of was. She didn't like to judge people, but he'd been rather intense for a man on vacation. "I think he was lonely in a new place. Where did Heather go?"

River shrugged. "That girl is a mystery to me. She's been so great to have around, but she spaces out at the oddest times."

She probably had an artistic nature. Nell herself had been accused of spaciness. "Well, I'm more than happy to help you find the perfect zucchini. I heard there was some lovely okra, too."

She was kind of craving fried okra. This baby was making her crave all kinds of things.

But mostly she craved Henry. If he didn't touch her soon, she was going to go crazy. "How many muffins did you want to make?"

River sighed. "Oh, the muffins were just to get you out of the situation. I don't cook much anymore. It's only me now."

River's husband had left her, and her father had passed after a long illness. Nell was glad she had a friend in Heather. River needed more people around her, and it had been a while since Nell had gone out to River's. She slid her arm around her friend's shoulders. "Well, I'm going to buy some ingredients because I need your rice casserole. I've been thinking about it for days. I'm pregnant, and you can't turn away a pregnant lady."

She was fairly certain River was struggling financially, but she was a proud lady. Nell would simply overbuy, and River would have plenty for herself, too.

"Oh, Nell, that's wonderful," River said, smiling brightly. "What exciting news for you and Henry. You know I always thought you would make great parents. I would love to make it for you. We veggie girls have to stick together."

She let go of her worries again. It was the theme of the month. She let River lead the way and vowed to enjoy the afternoon.

* * * *

64

Henry stepped away from the berry stand and glanced down at his phone. He was waiting on some information Seth was running down for him. Something was happening in Mexico and he was afraid he was putting together threads that he would rather stayed apart.

If he was right, he might need to bring John Bishop out of retirement because his old friends were going to walk into a nightmare.

He could come up with some excuse to travel, deal with the situation, and maybe take a side trip to South America. If the whole cartel was dead, they couldn't come after him.

Then Nell would be safe, and she wouldn't ever have to know anything was wrong.

He'd started thinking more and more like John Bishop. Ruthless. Uncompromising. Out for the best result for himself.

If he was John Bishop, he would have spent the last couple of weeks fucking his wife. He would have put her in bondage and tweaked those rings on her nipples until she cried prettily for him and she begged him to give her what she needed.

John Bishop wouldn't care about how fragile she was. He would only care about branding himself on her and ensuring she understood who she belonged to.

John Bishop was an asshole.

Henry Flanders was the nice man who took care of his wife and didn't burn down the world to ensure she never had to know he lied. Henry Flanders was going to tell her.

Tomorrow. Maybe the day after. Maybe after he figured out what was happening with the Jalisco Cartel and a CIA operative who went by the name Levi Green.

"Hey, Henry." One of the Harper twins strode up. "Did you get the news about Hiram? Got done in by a hooker and a sex swing. At least it was a hell of a way to go."

Ah, Max. The Harper twins were perfectly identical to the eye. Totally different once they started talking. Rye Harper was the former sheriff and a completely reasonable man. Max was amusing. Most of the time. "Sex worker, please. They have dignity, too."

"I heard about the position he was in from Zane, and I don't know there was a lot of dignity to it. Though Hi did die with a smile on his face." Max sighed. "I'm going to miss the old guy."

"We all will." Hiram Jones had been the mayor of Bliss for as long as anyone could remember.

Henry had sat in his office days after what had happened at Seth's. Nate had decided that the mayor needed to be brought up to date on the potential threat to Bliss. Henry had been forced to sit in front of Hiram and admit what he'd done.

Hi had been told that a citizen had lied and now the town was in danger, and all he'd done was given Henry a hug and told him they would get through this the way they always did. Together.

Then Hi had told him to tell his wife.

He still wasn't sure how to tell his wife. What would he do if she got upset and lost the baby? How would he ever take another breath? Caleb said Nell was healthy and sex was fine, that oftentimes women who miscarry have perfectly healthy pregnancies follow and they never knew exactly what went wrong the first time.

"Anyway, I wanted to come over and ask if I can borrow your drill. Mine crapped out and I don't have time to go into Alamosa for a new one. The latch on my barn door finally rusted over and the new one came in. Rach will have my hide if I don't fix it soon. That woman does not understand that preseason football is important."

"Sure. I'll bring it by this afternoon. I'll even help you."

"I appreciate it." Max tipped his hat and started to turn.

"How did you get through Rachel's pregnancy? The first one. I can imagine this one is easier. Were you scared?" The question was out of Henry's mouth and he couldn't take it back.

Max turned, his eyes going wide. "Uh, this is probably one of those times I should call Rye in, but I'm super curious now."

"Can you not be an asshole and just answer my question?"

Max seemed to think about it for a moment. "I think asshole is my default state, but I can put it off for a few seconds since we both know you'll end up fixing that door and I'll drink a beer while I watch you. So, the first time Rach was pregnant I was pretty freaked out. Do not look shit up on the Internet. It will not ease your mind. I don't know who said knowledge is power, but they have obviously never had a pregnant wife. Knowledge is scary as shit. I found it was best if I just let Doc give me a thumbs-up at the end of an appointment." He glanced around as though wanting to make sure no one was listening. "You and

Nell trying?"

Henry shook his head. "Forget I said anything."

"I'm real good at forgetting things. Ask my wife. If you need to talk, I can listen and totally forget until such time as you think it's good for me to remember." Max sighed and patted Henry's shoulder. "When you come over, I'll tell you how I trained Quigley to let me know when Rach's water broke. You need a dog."

Actually, that wasn't a terrible idea. A big nasty dog he could train to protect its mistress. Nell would love that.

Of course she would also love the fact that he'd told Max. He'd promised to keep it private until Nell was ready.

Max pulled his phone out of his pocket and looked down at it. He grinned when he looked back up. "Hey, congrats on the baby, man. Rach says she already knew but kept it quiet. Now I don't have to forget."

What had happened? "Rachel sent you a text?"

"Yeah, she heard it from Callie, who heard it from Marie, who heard it from Teeny." Max's phone buzzed again. "Oh, and it's gotten to Mel. Has Nell recently been probed?"

God, it had been so long since he'd probed her. So freaking long.

"How did Teeny know?" He should find Nell.

Or she'd decided to tell the world and knew Teeny would be a good way to get the word out. She'd been on her way to the juice bar when they'd split up. Teeny was a sweetheart. She wouldn't have started a rumor if Nell hadn't told her it was okay. Well, Nell was in for a whole lot of beets. Luckily he didn't hate them, and they might lower his damn blood pressure since he could feel it ticking up.

You wouldn't be so on the edge if you got dirty with your wife.

You wouldn't be so on the edge if you got honest with your wife.

Yep, he had an angel and a devil on his shoulder, and he didn't want to listen to either one.

Max shrugged. "No idea. She has her ways. But again, congrats, and if you need it, I'll loan out Q when Nell's closing in on the finish line. See you later on this afternoon." He turned and then Max was tipping his hat Heather Turner's way. "Ms. Turner."

The tall blonde gave him a snarky curtsy. "Mr. Harper." She smiled Henry's way. "I love a small town." She had a backpack on her back and carried a small tote filled with veggies. "Hey, I thought you should know there's a weird dude asking Nell all kinds of questions. I don't think he's from around here."

Henry felt his whole body shift into fight mode. "Where is she?"

Heather pointed over her shoulder. "She was at the food court, but I had River save her. I think the guy's still there. Not that it matters or anything. Just thought I'd warn you. I heard some of it. He was asking about Seth Stark. He might be a reporter or something. Nell's such a sweetie. We all have to look out for her."

Henry nodded, but his mind was already running through all the possible scenarios. He moved down the aisle, heading toward the food court that sat in the middle of the parking lot. Up ahead he could already see Nell moving away with River at her side. She was smiling at her friend, and he caught her say something about zucchinis.

Fuck. If he missed the asshole, there would be no way to find him. Bliss didn't have CCTV cameras on every block. They had exactly one, and it had been used to prove to Mel that it had been a hungry bear that had knocked over the trash cans at city hall and not aliens attempting to steal DNA.

It was precisely one of the things he loved about Bliss, one of the things that had kept him safe, but now it could hurt his wife. He brushed past a couple buying potatoes and made it to the small courtyard.

It was empty.

"Henry, such wonderful news." Teeny was smiling brightly. "I'm going to start on a baby blanket as soon as possible. Only organic cotton, and I'll make sure it's sustainably sourced."

He didn't have time to talk about baby gifts. "Teeny, do you know where the man who was talking to Nell went?"

"He seemed rather odd. Asked me if I knew where Seth lived," Teeny said. "And then he didn't even want a juice. A little rude if you ask me. He walked off toward the church. Is everything all right?"

He couldn't tell her that the man might be an investigator for a drug cartel that wanted him dead. He could only imagine the text chain that would come from that admission. "I thought I recognized him from my professor days. I wanted to see if he was an old friend. If my wife asks, tell her I ran to the restroom and I'll be back."

He made his way toward the church in time to see a man dressed in black slip inside. The church kept its doors unlocked during the market to provide access to restrooms, but he happened to know the staff wasn't working today. When he and Nell had a stall earlier in the year, they'd joined with the other sellers to ensure the church was cleaned after the market closed and they locked everything up.

He wanted a look at the guy. He would follow the man into the bathroom, get a good look at his face, and then see what car he got into. It would likely be a rental if he'd been sent to look for John Bishop, but Seth could work miracles if he had a plate number.

He slipped inside the church and the world immediately went darker and colder. The air conditioner was running, giving the quiet space a hum. The bathrooms were to the left, and the feed store portion of the Feed Store Church was in front of him. The lights were out, and he didn't hear footsteps.

He felt that instinct flare up again. It was too quiet. He'd seen the man come in. Unless he'd sprinted down the hallway, Henry should be able to hear him walking.

Cautiously, he stepped into the store. It was the only place to hide quickly.

Why would he hide?

Henry looked around, and nothing seemed to have been disturbed. There were big bags of feed of all kinds and aisles of tools. To his right was a display of various lawn care machines. He'd had his eye on a sweet leaf blower, but he suspected his wife liked the leaves to be free.

It was darker as he moved into the middle of the store.

What was he doing? He didn't even have a gun. He turned, ready to check the bathroom and then get the hell out of here. He would sort it all out later. He could come up with some excuse and have Heather give him a thorough description of the man.

"Hello." The man was standing right beside a big display of bird baths. He held a Ruger in his right hand, pointing it straight at Henry's heart. "I suspect you're the one Jones was looking for. You Bishop?"

Fuck. Henry held up his hands. He needed to get his head back in the game. "My name is Henry. I was just looking around. I don't want any trouble."

But he would have to make some because this man knew his face

69

and if he was allowed to get back to the cartel, all hell would break loose. It seemed someone was looking for Jones and they'd found Henry instead.

"Cut the crap. I've seen your picture," the man said with a sneer. "Fucking Agency assholes have to ruin everything. Jones was being cagey about where he was heading, but when he didn't come back, I checked into things. He came here. I found evidence that he was looking into Seth Stark. Stark is working with you, isn't he? I'm intrigued as to why a billionaire is working with a ghost. Did you kill Jones?"

"I don't know a Jones." It wouldn't work, but he needed time and a whole lot of luck.

The man chuckled, an amused sound, as though he enjoyed this part of the game. "Maybe you didn't catch his name. He would have come through town a couple of weeks ago with some of our associates. Big guys. Big guns. I'm trying to figure out what happened to them because they all went real quiet. Now someone sent all their cell phones to Los Angeles. Imagine my surprise when I get to the place in LA where their signals say they are and all that's there are the phones that some asshole has helpfully kept charged."

That had been his idea. He was certain whoever Seth had given the job to had thought the boss was running some kind of test on the phones and how easy they were to track. It had bought them time because even if he'd destroyed the cells, there would have been a way to track their last known locations. So he'd given them another one.

Henry started to back up. If he wasn't mistaken, he was close to the shovels. They would be one aisle over. He would have one chance. He couldn't let this guy get away. He knew far too much.

He had to hope the other man hadn't had enough time to get a call out. "I wouldn't know anything about that."

The man's hand had the slightest tremor. "We'll see if you keep quiet when I get you back to our base. My boss is incredibly angry with you. You're the reason he's in the mess he's in, and he will cover me in riches when I deliver you to him. I think I'll bring your wife along and see if she can make you talk."

The idea of his sweet Nell under this man's thumb made him see red, and he knew he wasn't going to make it to the next aisle. They were going to do this here and now.

Henry kicked out, catching the other man's hand before he could get a shot off. The gun clattered against a riding lawnmower and Henry took a punch to the gut.

He didn't even feel it. It registered, but not as anything close to pain. That would come later. Adrenaline pumped through his system as he focused fully on the task at hand.

He took another punch, but landed one of his own. The man flew back and his head hit hard against the floor.

That was the moment the knife made its appearance.

His opponent flipped up to standing and rushed Henry, knife at the ready.

Henry moved to one side, letting the heavier man's weight carry him past. He wasn't particularly skilled, but then Henry had found most of the cartel men weren't well versed in hand to hand.

It was a mere moment before Henry had his arm wrapped around the man's neck and heard the crunching sound that let him know his job was done. Nell was safe. For now.

The cartel man slipped to the floor without a sound.

But there was a gasp that let Henry know he wasn't alone. He turned and his worst nightmare was standing there in her organic cotton dress. She was alone and her eyes went right to the body on the floor, the dead body he now had to find a way to make her understand.

"Henry?" Nell looked pale.

"I can explain."

She dropped the bag she'd been carrying and then she started for the floor, her eyes rolling back.

He caught her and realized everything had gone wrong. He felt for her pulse. It was strong. Henry held her close and reached for his cell. He kept this particular number on speed dial.

"This is Wright."

Nell was going to kill him. "Sheriff, I seem to have a problem."

He hoped Zane Hollister's freezer could handle another dead body.

Chapter Four

"I'm fine." Nell said the words, but they felt dull coming out of her mouth. She was back in her cabin but it suddenly felt oddly foreign to her, as though all her familiar things had been transported to someplace new. She recognized the space, but deep inside she knew there was something wrong with it.

"Caleb said you need to rest. He, Holly, and Alexei are in Alamosa for the afternoon, but he can be here this evening. I could call Ty or Naomi." Henry was the most familiar and yet foreign thing of all. Henry—the man she felt she knew better than anyone in the world—was now a mystery. He put a glass of water in front of her. "Caleb said it was probably the heat. He wants you to drink some water."

She didn't need water. For the first time in her life she truly understood why people who got mad thought they could solve their problems with vodka.

"He thinks I passed out from the heat because you didn't tell him the whole story. I can handle the heat. It was watching my pacifist husband murder a man that made me faint." She didn't want to bother Ty or Naomi. Ty was one of the EMTs around town and Naomi was Caleb's nurse. It was her day off and she didn't need to be bothered with taking Nell's blood pressure. Her current health situation wasn't about pregnancy. It was about marriage.

Her marriage. To a man who killed someone.

Henry sank down onto their sofa, the very sofa where he often sat beside her at night, reading a book while she knitted and listened to podcasts or watched a documentary about climate change.

It was the sofa where at least twice a week, he turned from mild-mannered husband to dirty Dom and ordered her to take off her clothes or to drop to her knees and suck his cock.

Well, until recently.

How could she be so confused and mad and horny at the same time? One second she was on the verge of tears and the next she wanted nothing more than for him to take charge and tell her everything was fine, that she hadn't understood what she'd seen and all she had to do was follow his lead.

"Nell, we should talk."

He'd put her off for two hours. Not that she'd asked him anything. She'd come to in his arms. When she'd woken, she'd been on Henry's lap and he'd been sitting on the riding lawn mower that had been on display at the Feed Store Church for over five years. For a second she'd thought it was all a dream, but then she'd realized there was still a body on the floor.

With vacant eyes and absolutely no blood. If she hadn't watched Henry snap the man's neck, she would have thought the man had died of natural causes. But there had been nothing natural about what Henry had done. Graceful, predatory…but not natural.

She stood and paced because she was done sitting still. She'd sat while Henry had talked to Nate and Cam, while they'd closed the building up and taken the body out the back. Nate was talking to Pastor Dennis, who'd been surprised at the fact that someone had died in his church. She'd listened as Nate had covered completely for Henry. "Pastor Dennis thinks that man had a heart attack."

His eyes came up and he watched her carefully. There was a stillness to Henry that belied the look in his eyes. "It was necessary to control the narrative."

She put her hands on her hips, outrage rising. He sounded like people they protested. "The narrative? That wasn't a narrative. That was a murder."

"It was one hundred percent self-defense. I did not attack him. I followed him inside the building to see where he was going. Heather told me he'd been bothering you and he was asking about Seth. When I turned around, he was in front of the exit and he had a gun on me. We fought. I managed to get the gun from him but that's when he pulled the knife. I had to fight for my life."

"Why would he try to kill you? He was a tourist. Did anyone find his wife?" She hated the thought of that poor woman walking around looking for her husband while the Bliss County Sheriff's Office was busy covering up his murder.

Henry sighed. "Honey, there was no wife."

She wasn't sure why or how he thought he knew better than she did. As far as she could tell, she'd had a much longer conversation with the man. All Henry had done was kill him. "He told me he had a wife. He's staying in Del Norte with her. At least he was before you murdered him."

Henry's hands went into fists, but then he took a deep breath and his tone was patient. "He wasn't vacationing. He was looking for me. The same way the men who nearly killed Seth were looking for me."

This was it. This was the moment she'd been dreading since she'd found those guns. Or maybe it went back further than that. Maybe it went back to the second she'd looked into his eyes and known a predator was there. She hadn't been so foolish that she'd believed the Henry Flanders who'd walked into Bliss and challenged her on everything was the same man who'd married her, but she'd thought he'd been hurt in the past and was protecting himself with walls.

It seemed like Henry didn't need walls. He had guns and very dangerous hands. "So you weren't hiding in the bathroom. Logan came to get you, and not for your plumbing skills. Logan knows you're good at killing people."

His jaw tightened and there was a bleakness in his eyes that threatened to break her. "I need to tell you the whole story."

"The story that everyone else already knows?" That was what she'd been stewing over for hours. Nate hadn't looked surprised, with the singular exception that Nell had been there. He'd walked in and sighed and acted like it was nothing more than boys playing games until he'd turned and seen Nell. Nate knew. Cam knew.

Did Laura know? Laura was married to Cam. Had one of her best friends been hiding this massive secret? Had everyone laughed about how dumb the vegan girl was, how naïve she had to be to marry a man and not even know who he was.

He shook his head. "No. Not everyone. Very few people know. In the beginning, it was only Seth, and only because he basically figured it out when I first came to town. Logan didn't know until the other day. We had to bring Nate in. And Cam, of course. Gemma doesn't know. Nate's kept her out of it completely, but I can't keep hiding it now. I have to tell everyone the truth."

"Everyone, including me." She was just a part of the background here. He knew everything about her, all of her secrets. She'd held nothing back, and she was one more person who now had to be let in because he had no other choice.

"I know you're not going to believe me, but I was going to tell you. I wanted to wait until the wedding, and then Hiram died." He frowned. "I would like to point out that I did not kill Hi."

She rolled her eyes. She hadn't even thought of that. But now she could ask the question she did want an answer to. "Did you kill the man who shot Jesse? He didn't trip, did he?"

He hesitated. "Yes. I mean I killed him. No, he didn't trip. We got into a fight, too, and again, he had a gun."

"Well, why didn't you pop out to the shop and grab one of yours?"

His eyes closed briefly and when he opened them she could see the guilt there. "I'm sorry. I didn't think you would find them. When you hear my story, you'll understand why it was necessary to keep them. I'll be honest, over the years I've practically forgotten I have them."

This wasn't about Henry being worried over her. He was worried for himself. "So you've had them since we got married?"

He nodded. "I moved them around from time to time, and then I built the safe into the wall of the shop. You weren't supposed to find them. They were there in case trouble found me. Like I said, I never carry anymore. Those guns have done nothing but gather dust for years."

This was all some kind of surreal dream. Or a joke. It had to be. Except Henry looked so grim.

Henry looked like he had when she'd first met him. Grim. A little dangerous. Deeply sad.

She quashed the sympathy that rose. It was always there, but now she couldn't afford it. Now, if she let that part of herself take over, she would be weak and vulnerable, and apparently she'd already been far too vulnerable to this man. He was her husband and he'd lied. Not about something small like whether or not she looked good in a pair of jeans. He'd lied about the foundations of their life together. He'd lied and turned her into a fool.

She was carrying his baby.

She took a deep breath and forced herself to move forward. "All right. What do you need to tell me?"

A bit of hope lit his expression. "I should have told you a long time before, but I was afraid. Nell, before I came to Bliss I wasn't a history professor. That was my cover. The truth of the matter was I worked for the Central Intelligence Agency."

She stared at him. He couldn't come up with something more interesting? "Sure you did. I'm supposed to believe that you worked for the CIA?" She was back to pacing. "The history professor thing was far more believable."

"I wouldn't have been effective if I looked like James Bond, would I? Most of us are normal-looking people. They teach us to blend in, to be chameleons. I was recruited straight out of the military because I was highly intelligent, showed a moral flexibility, and I had no family. They like that. They like having all of an operative's loyalty belong to the Agency."

"You were in the military?" Her husband? Her antiauthoritarian husband had been a soldier? And a good one, if what he was saying were true. He'd been so good that the CIA had recruited him. Moral flexibility? Her Henry was known for his deeply held beliefs.

How could he be standing here telling her these things? The world she'd gone to sleep in had turned over, and she was in a different place, a colder place.

"I was in the Army. I joined up when I aged out of foster care. I didn't have anywhere else to go. I lied about getting a scholarship. I never applied for one. I knew I wouldn't get to college," Henry said. "I got my degree after. I got it with the help of the man who recruited me. I'll be honest, I don't know where I would have been without Franklin

Grant."

She felt tears pulse. "I don't believe you." Her mind sought any other explanation. She couldn't have been this foolish. He'd left for six months. By the time he'd come back, she'd started publishing. "You found out about my writing career. That's why you came back. You knew I would start making money."

He stood, a grave look on his face. "No, my love. I came back because I figured a way out. I came back because I couldn't go back to being that cold spymaster I'd become. I came back for you and only you. I didn't know you'd gotten published until our wedding night. I was perfectly happy to find a job. I'd already talked to Stella about potentially learning to cook so I could take some shifts for Hal. You asked me to stay with you and be your assistant and researcher."

She'd wanted him close, and it seemed silly for him to sell things at the Trading Post or wait tables at Stella's. There wasn't anything wrong with those jobs, but if they had enough money, she didn't see why he couldn't use his skills in a different way. "So you were never a history professor."

"I've always been fascinated by it. You know me. I read a lot of books about history. Both fiction and nonfiction."

"I know you? I thought this whole conversation was about how I don't know you." She could feel her panic starting to rise. She'd had these moments lately. They'd come from worry about her pregnancy, about being a mom in the first place. When it felt like she couldn't breathe, Henry would hold her and kiss her. He would touch her until she cried out and all the worry seemed to fade away.

She wanted him to touch her now, to tell her this was all some ridiculous joke.

"You know all the important parts of me."

A sudden thought hit her. How deep did her ignorance go? "Do I know your name?"

He went still. "My name is Henry Flanders."

It was obvious she was going to have to be specific. "Is Henry Flanders the name you were born with?"

"It doesn't matter what name I was born with. I am who I choose to be."

She wasn't about to let him off the hook. "I want to know your name."

His jaw tightened. "Which one? The one my mother gave me because my father wasn't around? She named me after the bastard in case he ever came back. She thought it might soften his heart toward me. He never did. Should I give you the name I used as a CIA operative? There were many of those, but Bishop is the one people remember. John Bishop. I've gone as Mr. Black. Mr. White. Really whatever color suited me that day. Mostly I should have used red because that was the color of my world then."

She'd never seen him so on edge. He'd been quietly getting into her space, moving closer and closer with every word.

She was angry with him. Volcanically angry, and yet there was something about this man that called to her. Every time. It was precisely why she'd put up with his moody crap the first time around. She turned her chin up. He towered over her, but she wasn't about to back down. "How many?"

"Names? I told you."

She shook her head. "No. How many people have you killed?"

He put a hand on the wall behind her, caging her in. "Myself or on my orders?"

He was pushing her, and the atmosphere of the room was turning into something…dangerous. "How about you give me a nice round number."

"Hundreds before I met you. Probably thirty or so myself. Many more on my orders, and I can't tell you that every one of them deserved it. I gave my bosses intel that led to bombings of entire cities." He stared down at her. "So here I am, Nell. I am everything you write about. I'm the beast who got tamed by a slip of a woman, who changed his whole being because he fell in love. Are you really going to toss me out?"

She shook her head. "You don't get to do that. You don't get to challenge me like that. I'm not the one who lied. I have never lied to you."

"You never did anything you weren't proud of," he said, challenge plain in his voice. "You never had to completely reinvent yourself."

"Are you serious? You act like I never went through anything bad in my life." There was a tension that charged what little air there was between them. She had to put her hands back against the wall, palms flat against the curve of the logs that formed the cabin. Her breath came out ragged.

He stared down at her and there was more than sorrow in his eyes now. "I'm not saying that."

"But you are. You had it so rough? You think foster care was a breeze?"

"I know it wasn't. I spent my time there, too. My mom died when I was young, and there was no one else to take me in. I moved from home to home. I was that kid who kept his shit in a garbage bag because I didn't have a suitcase."

"You didn't lie about that?"

"I only lied about the things I was ashamed of," he admitted. "This changes nothing between us. Nothing."

How could he possibly say that? "It changes everything."

"I am still the man you love."

She didn't understand how that could be true. "The man I love would never lie to me. Not about something this important."

His hand came up and cupped her breast. "I'm still the man who can make you melt."

God, he was. She knew she should push him away, but it felt too good.

And it might be the last time he ever touched her.

His fingers found the place where the rings pierced her nipples, reminding her of the night she'd had them done. Henry had been with her. He'd held her hand as she'd closed her eyes and hissed at the minor pain. He'd been the one to lovingly take care of them while they healed. And he'd been the one to toy with them and the VCH she'd had done at the same time. He would gently twist them and light up her breasts.

They'll remind you that I'm always with you, love. I'm always thinking about you, and I'm incomplete when my body isn't inside yours.

How many nights had been spent wrapped around this man, so close to him she was sure she would never be alone again? The last six years of her life had been settled, centered around Henry Flanders and the marriage they'd made. There had been none of the terrible uncertainty from before, and now it was all roaring back to life.

He'd lied. He'd had a whole life he'd hidden from her, and she knew she hadn't heard the worst yet.

She couldn't make it through this. Not without the strength she would get from one last time with the only man she'd ever made love with.

It didn't have to be love. It could be sex. It could be a place to put all the awful emotions she was feeling. They needed somewhere to go or she would drown in them.

She lifted her chest slightly, her heart starting to pound.

"If I asked, would you show me your breasts?" Henry's voice had gone deep.

"You never ask." They'd set specific parameters when they'd started their relationship all those years ago. She could stop the encounter at any time, but until she said no, her husband could demand when it came to sex. Henry was so undemanding when it came to everything else. He was sweet, thoughtful, considerate, but when his eyes focused in on her, her whole body went soft and wanting.

"No. I don't. I tell you," he agreed. "Show me your breasts. I was wrong. We don't need to talk, Nell. I need to show you how I feel. I need to remind you why you chose me in the first place."

She'd chosen him because she'd fallen for a man who hadn't existed. She'd married him because he'd been half her soul. But she'd been attracted to him for this. She'd been drawn to his darkness.

It was a huge mistake, but one she seemed incapable of avoiding. Her hands went to the buttons of her blouse. She wanted nothing more than to forget the whole day had happened, to pretend it had all been a bad dream. She would wake up and tell him and he would laugh. He would growl in that oh-so-sexy way of his and roll her over and make love to her. They would start plotting a superhot spy book.

She felt the air on her breasts, the way her nipples had tightened. Her blouse was loose enough that she hadn't worn a bra. Despite the fact that she was barely through her first trimester, she would swear her breasts were already bigger. And they were so sensitive.

Henry dropped to his knees and his hands went to her hips, holding her in place as he leaned over and took a nipple into his mouth. He tongued the ring there, darting around it before gently tugging on it.

Her body went electric, and she didn't care about anything but how this one man could make her feel.

One hand came up to toy with the ring on her other nipple.

He was the only man who'd ever seen her like this, who she'd ever trusted enough to open herself up to.

He switched to her other breast, tonguing it and laving it with affection. She let her hands drift to his hair. So soft. When he'd first come to Bliss he'd kept it short, but over the years he waited longer and longer between cuts, and she liked running her fingers through it.

"Do you have any idea how much I adore these?" He twisted the ring just enough to make her gasp. "I love the fact that you look so fucking sweet and innocent on the outside, but under your clothes you're my dirty girl."

There was nothing dirty about sex, but even she liked dirty talk. She loved it when her oh-so-staid husband spit out the filthiest sex talk. All for her. Henry hadn't so much as looked at another woman since they'd gotten married. He wasn't the kind of man who flirted with other women. He was focused on her.

Or that was what he wanted her to think.

His hand tightened on her hip. "Don't. Don't fucking think about anything but right here and now."

There was the hint of threat to his tone, that stern warning that if she didn't comply he had ways to make her. Again, it was all a sexy game and one that always brought her back to exactly where she wanted to be. In the moment. No past. No future. Just pleasure.

Henry had given this to her. All of her sexuality was wrapped up in him.

What would she do without him?

Henry stood, his hair mussed and gaze dark. "Put your hands on the table, Nell. Palms down flat, and spread your legs for me."

Alarm bells were going off, but she didn't care. She wanted to stay in the moment with him because deep down she feared it might be one of their last. No matter how afraid she was, she wasn't sure that was enough of a reason to let him stay.

Was she going to kick her husband out of the home they'd made together?

His hand found her hair, sinking in and forcing her to look up at him. "Did you hear what I said, Nell? Or do you want me to grab a crop?"

She didn't take the question as a warning. He was truly asking her what she wanted. When she was so wound up she couldn't process her basic emotions, sometimes pain helped her release it. She'd had a therapist tell her once she'd been taught not to be emotional as a child because of what had happened when her mother was taken away. The therapist had suggested a virtual rebirth, group sessions, primal scream therapy.

Henry had taught her what worked for her. A hard-core spanking followed by nasty sex.

She couldn't take the spanking right now. Not from him, and if it couldn't come from him it wouldn't happen. But she would take the sex. Especially the way he was offering it to her.

She pushed past him and did as he'd instructed, pressing her palms flat against the table where they sat and ate and talked and dreamed.

No. She refused to let those memories seep in. This was about getting what she needed. She needed an orgasm. She needed to be in her body and not her head. Just a few moments of respite before she had to make some hard decisions.

She hissed slightly as Henry dragged her skirt down and exposed her to the cool air of the cabin.

"Wider."

She moved her feet out, the waist of her skirt trapping her ankles and giving her the delicious feeling of being restrained for him. She heard the sound of him unbuckling his belt and it clanging to the floor as he moved in behind her.

"God, I've missed this." He gripped her hips and his cock nudged between her legs.

She'd missed everything about this. She'd missed the physical sensations, but beyond that she'd desperately missed being this version of herself. For months she'd been this fragile thing that needed to take care only of the life growing inside her. She'd wanted to be Henry's sub, a sweet thing devoted to bringing her master pleasure and taking it for herself.

He thrust hard inside her, filling her up in a way nothing else ever could. She bit her lip against calling out. The last thing she wanted to do was scare him away. He seemed to have momentarily forgotten she was delicate.

She gripped the table and tilted her pelvis back.

He slapped her ass, sending a thrill up her spine that made her groan.

"Hold still." His voice had taken on a desperate tone.

He was as on the edge as she was.

They were in the same place. He was standing there with her, looking at a future where they weren't together, where his lies had pushed them both over and she hadn't trusted him enough to hold on.

This was why she was happy with the way he'd chosen to fuck her. She wasn't sure she could have handled looking him in the eyes.

"You feel so good." He thrust in and dragged that big cock of his out again. "Not one thing in this world ever fit me the way you do."

He fucked her hard, giving her what she'd been craving for months. She needed this. She couldn't get through the days without this. She held on to the table and rode the wave. When he reached from behind and his fingers found the piercing that sat against her clitoris, she screamed out his name as the rush took her.

She felt him come, his body stiffening and then relaxing.

For a moment there was nothing but the sound of their breathing, the sweet languor of her body after orgasm. It had been so intense, and now the comedown was every bit as fierce as the high.

"Let's go to bed. That's where we need to be." Henry's hand started to move up her body, sliding over her belly. He stopped and suddenly stood up. "Nell, I'm so sorry. Was I too rough?"

She forced herself to breathe. The moment was over, and she was faced with all her problems again. They hadn't gone away and she'd known they wouldn't, but somehow she'd thought if they could connect this way again, things might become clearer.

The only thing that was clear was how her world had turned upside down.

"I'm fine." It seemed to be the only thing she was capable of saying these days. She was fine. She wasn't going to fail again.

God, had she thought that? She hadn't failed. Her body hadn't failed. She wasn't less of a woman. She knew those things and yet there was a part of her that still managed to feel them.

She was going to be alone. She was going to be her mother, all alone and trying to raise a child when the world saw her as something not normal, as something of a fool.

"Baby, I was too rough. I don't know what I was thinking. Hell, I wasn't thinking at all. I was being a selfish ass." His hand ran down her back. "Let me get you in the bathtub. You can soak and I'll call Caleb again."

She pushed herself off the table, feeling infinitely older than she'd been before. She pulled up her skirt, settling it around her again. Normally she would simply walk around naked, but it didn't feel right now. There was a distance between them, and it wasn't all about his lies. It had been growing since before she discovered he wasn't who she'd thought he was. "I'll go take a shower. Don't call Caleb. I'm fine. Every single thing I've read tells me sex is safe during a pregnancy. I'm not fragile." The sound of a knock at the door startled her and reminded her that the world was still turning outside. "I'll be right there."

"Hush. They'll go away," Henry said, his voice going low.

She pulled on her blouse, buttoning it with shaky fingers. "Not if they're looking for you. Isn't that what you said? Those men were looking for you. The one you killed today was looking for you. We'll be lucky if they don't come in with guns blazing."

She felt apart from herself, like she wasn't real. The sarcasm coming out of her mouth wasn't her style and yet she couldn't stop the bitterness from bubbling over.

"Hey, Henry!" a familiar voice called. "Do you answer your phone, man? I've been calling for an hour."

Henry's jaw had turned to granite. "Go away, Max."

"He can't," another voice said. Rye Harper had apparently accompanied his brother. "Rach told us both not to come home until we fixed the barn door. If you'll let us use the drill, I promise I'll make sure it gets back to you."

"Hopefully in one piece." Max's face suddenly appeared at the window, his hand over his eyes to block the sunlight so he could see inside. "Put your shirt on, dude."

"Damn it." A hand came out and pulled Max away. "Never mind, Henry. You two have a good afternoon."

"But he promised," Max was saying. "And Nell's already knocked up, so I don't know what the big deal is."

Well, that had gotten around pretty fast. "What did you promise Max?"

She straightened her skirt. Her body hummed pleasantly, but she didn't think she could stand spending the next two hours with Henry hovering over her, apologizing for treating her like a woman and not some sickly patient. Telling her nothing had changed, and she should ignore the fact that she'd seen him standing over a dead body like a lion looming over his kill.

"I promised him I would help him fix his barn door. But he can do it himself," Henry swore. "We're going to make you comfortable and I'm going to behave like a good husband. I'm going to tell you everything."

She didn't think she could stand listening to him tell her his story either. She needed time. Maybe if he'd been willing to take her to bed and distract her, she might have been talked into it. But she had to process the first blow before she could handle anything more. "Go with him."

His eyes widened. "No. We need to talk. People are going to know the truth soon, and I want you to know first."

After Seth and Logan. After Nate and Cam. After Georgia. Probably some other people. She was far down on Henry's need-to-know list. "I need time to think. I won't go anywhere, and I won't lock you out. But I need a couple of hours before I'm ready to talk to you. Please go with Max and Rye. Give me some space."

He shook his head. "I can't. If I go with them, I'll end up talking to them. See. That's one way I'm not the man I was. I'll be too tempted to talk to them, and I owe you the truth first."

She'd asked nicely. She'd told him what she needed, and now it was time to assert herself. Did he think she'd forgotten how to do this? She'd simply never had to do it with him. She walked to the door and flung it open as Rye and Max were about to get into their truck.

"What are you doing?" Henry moved in behind her, tugging his shirt over his head.

"Helping you out, dear." She stepped on the porch. "Max, Rye, Henry is going to come with you. He needs some advice about how to tell his wife that he lied to her about his whole past and he's some kind of superspy who likes to assassinate people. He killed a man today at the Feed Store Church, but it's okay because he's got law enforcement on his side. So take him away before I go back on my vow of nonviolence."

Rye threw his head back and laughed. "That's a good one."

"What do you think you're doing?" Henry stared down at her.

She stared right back. She hadn't been intimidated when threatened with guns or Tasers, and she'd had her fair share of pepper spray to the eyes. She wasn't going to allow her husband to intimidate her. "You had a problem. I solved it. Now everyone will know and you don't have to worry."

Rye was still laughing, but Max put a hand on his brother's shoulder. "I don't think she's kidding, brother."

Henry wasn't even looking their way. "This is not how I wanted it to go."

That was so sad for him. "Do you not get to control the narrative this way? I'll be honest. I don't care how you wanted this to go down. You can go with Max and Rye or you can go on your own, but I need a few hours alone. If you don't give them to me, I'll pack a bag and leave."

She would almost have sworn she heard a growl coming from her husband.

"Or I can pick you up and take you back inside."

She faced him down. "And then you better hope you don't sleep, Henry. Or Bishop. Or whoever you are."

"You know exactly who I am. I'm your husband and I love you." He backed off slightly. "I'll go with them, but I swear, Nell, don't try to leave. It's dangerous and I'll find you."

She wasn't stupid. If anyone was going to leave, it would be him. This was her cabin. Sure he'd been the one to restore it. He'd been the one who'd learned how to keep up the chinking and make the place safer and warmer in the winter. He'd put the shop together with his own two hands. But this was her home.

She had to figure out what she wanted.

She heard him stalk down the steps.

Nell walked back into the cabin and closed the door. When she heard the truck drive away, she was finally alone.

And finally able to cry.

* * * *

"Henry, I would like to point out that it was Max who was supposed to return all those tools he borrowed from you. I only borrowed that set of wrenches once, and I returned them quickly." Rye Harper kept a careful distance from Henry. Since they'd gotten to the Harper Stables and Henry had made it plain that he was absolutely going to fix the barn door and anyone who tried to stop him was in trouble, Rye had watched him carefully.

Rye was scared of him. Good for fucking Rye because everyone should be afraid of him right now. He was angry. Brutally angry. Angry at himself. Angry at the fucking cartel that couldn't stay away. Angry at the world because Nell was supposed to be his reward. After everything he'd gone through there should be a fucking reward, and she shouldn't be able to change her mind because she'd found out he wasn't perfect.

She'd seen him kill a man. She might never look at him the same way again.

He pulled the old latch off with far more strength than he needed to use and it went flying across the yard, barely missing Rye, who jumped out of the way.

"Sorry." He wasn't really sorry. There was still a part of him that thought if Max and Rye hadn't shown up, he would have found a way to get through to his wife.

"No problem." Rye gave him the same slow nod a man might give a hungry grizzly bear who was slowly walking past him. *Nothing to see here, mighty predator. Just walk on by.*

Max merely rolled his eyes. "It's Henry, Rye. Stop acting like we're in the presence of a serial killer. He's Henry Flanders, and if he was going to kill me, he would have done it a long time ago. Hey, Henry, you going to teach me that neck thing you do? I got a couple of people I could use it on."

At least Max was still Max. He'd taken the whole thing with a shrug and asked Henry if he needed a beer—which he'd turned down.

Nell couldn't drink so he shouldn't either. Even though if he could ever have found solace in a bottle of Scotch, it would be now. But what if she needed him? What if they had to go to the hospital again?

"No, I will not teach you how to kill people." He couldn't imagine taking Max Harper on as a mentee. He'd had enough trouble with young Taggart, and Max was even worse. He set down the hammer. He'd had to use the claw even after he'd managed to get the bolts out. That sucker had taken root and it took force to get it off.

Maybe that's what he should do. He would simply squat in his own home and vigorously protest any attempts at removal. Could one squat a marriage? If anyone could understand the power of protest, it was his wife.

"Come on, Henry. You know how bad it can get around here," Max argued.

Rye stared his way. "So the guy who came after Gemma didn't trip."

He bit back a groan. He should write a full confession for the *Bliss Gazette* and then maybe he could stop answering this question. "No. I killed him because he'd shot Jesse, tried to kill me, and my wife was unprotected at the time. So I took the easy route and severed his spine at the C0-C1 joint, and then I left him on the forest floor because I didn't give a shit."

"See, how do you even find that joint thingee?" Max had the new latch in his hand but seemed far more interested in the conversation than the task that had been of utmost importance a mere hour before. "Do they have a class on that? How did they find you? The CIA, I mean."

The Harper twins were proving the two problems he would have with the people around him. One part would be afraid of him. The other would be frustratingly curious about his past.

"I was in the Army. The Special Forces team I was on worked a couple of jobs with the Agency. They recruited me from there." He hated how grim he sounded. He didn't sound like himself—the himself he wanted to be, the one he liked to be.

Rye shook his head like he was trying to clear it. "You were in the Army?"

Max turned his brother's way. "You forget so easily, man. Do you remember when he first came here? You remember how suspicious you were because he didn't act like a dude who taught history at a sleepy college."

He thought he'd been pretty good with that persona. "You know you're giving in to stereotypes. Exactly how is a sleepy-town college professor supposed to act?"

Rye ignored him completely. "Yeah, but all his records checked out, and Bill vouched for him."

"Of course his records checked out. He's a good spy. He's not a dummy spy. He's got all kinds of ways to fool the system." Max sounded more excited with every word. "See, I don't view this as a bad or scary thing. He's Henry and he's always been the most helpful guy in town. Now he can help me in different ways."

"I'm not assassinating anyone." He knew exactly where Max's brain would go. Oddly, Max's normalcy was helping him calm down. Not everyone would look at him like he was some kind of monster. But he would have to put up with Max's insane requests.

"Now don't say that so fast. We have some obnoxious tourists," Max replied. "Most of them from Texas."

Yeah, he hadn't mentioned that part. "I was actually born in Houston."

Max groaned.

"I thought you were from Ohio," Rye said with a shake of his head.

Ohio had seemed as middle of the road as a state could be. Everyone recognized it, but no one really knew what a person from Ohio was supposed to be. Unlike his home state. Especially in Colorado. Coloradans weren't overly enthusiastic about Texans. Probably because they tended to come in, buy up all the land for their vacation homes, and then generally act like…well, like Texans. "Ohio blended in better."

Rye seemed to still be catching up. "Does Bill know?"

Fuck. He was going to get Bill in trouble. Bill had been his contact here. Bill had built a whole life for himself, and he'd welcomed Henry with open arms. Bill had been the one who'd advised him to choose again, to make the decision that his life didn't have to keep going the way it had gone, that a life well lived was one of conscious will.

He'd found Nell because of Bill.

"Of course Bill doesn't know," Max started.

Rye frowned and looked at Henry, though his expression had gone from wary to slightly excited. Like he'd figured something out. "Bill was in the Army. He was your CO, wasn't he?"

Well, Rye had been the town's sheriff for years. No one had ever said he wasn't a smart man. "Yes."

"Dude, does Bill know how to do all the stuff you do?" Max's eyes had gone wide. "Does he do it naked? Because the naked thing would throw me off. When you think about it, it's probably a good tactic. I would be terrified of a naked man trying to break my neck. And also, he wouldn't have to worry about his clothes. Do you think that's why he opened the naked resort?"

Rye had gotten all the brains in the family.

"Bill was strictly military, though he knew I worked for the Agency. I asked him to keep my secret. It's all on me." He couldn't stand the thought of anyone turning against Bill because of him.

"That's why you came here." Rye's tone had gone so much softer. "You came to see Bill. That's why you go up the mountain and visit him every week. He's your family."

Bill had been good to him over the years. "He was the only friend I could talk to at the time. He's a good man. I hope no one gets upset with him for keeping my secret. I know you're not going to believe this, but I'm no danger to you."

Rye sighed and shook his head. "You're Henry. I'm sorry. It threw me for a loop, but Max is right. I knew something had changed in you when you came back. The first time you were here, there was something dangerous about you. I don't normally run checks on tourists, but I did on you. When you came back, you were a different person."

"Because he fell for Nell," Max continued. "Like how I got so much nicer after we married Rach."

Rye snorted. "Sure you did. You got smarter because you suddenly had a leash." Rye leaned against one of the fence posts that separated the barn area from the big pasture. "I'm sorry if I freaked out. Max is right. Nothing has changed except you'll have some interesting stories to tell over a couple of beers."

"Most of those stories are classified." He had so much to worry about beyond the cartel coming after him. "My whole life before I came here was classified. I didn't exactly resign from the Agency. I wouldn't have been allowed to. I knew too much."

There would have been too many consequences. He wouldn't have simply been allowed to walk away back then.

"How did you get away?" Rye asked.

"Blew up a car. Faked my death." He'd had help, but he couldn't talk about those Special Forces soldiers who'd risked a lot to get him out.

"What kind of car?" Max looked like a kid at Christmas. "How did you blow it? Could you do the same to Mel's old clunker? It's a menace. When you're behind it you get a little high off the fumes coming out of that thing."

Rye nodded. "That's not a bad idea. Mel thinks the fumes keep the aliens away. He'll think they're fighting back. We'll totally get away with it."

If he didn't watch it, he would get pulled into all the twins' plans. "I don't think Nate would like it if we started blowing up things."

Like he'd blown up his marriage.

He heard the door to the house slam open and then Rachel Harper was striding toward them, a baby on her hip and another in her belly. Rachel wore overalls, her strawberry blonde hair up in a ponytail and an expression on her face he couldn't quite read.

"Uh, I might have texted Rachel the news," Max admitted.

Damn. He liked Rachel and she might be about to tell him to get off her property.

"I'm sorry," Max was saying. "If I hear something and don't tell her, she gets all upset with me. I had to. I had to prove my worth."

Rye frowned his brother's way. "Damn it, Max. Did you think about the fact that Henry might not want everyone to know?"

"She has the boobs," Max replied resolutely.

She also never held back her opinion. And she was from Texas, too, so Max was being super hypocritical there.

Rachel walked right up to him. "Is it true?"

God, he hated this feeling, and he was going to have it a lot in the next few days. "Yes."

Rachel handed her baby off to Rye and then crossed the space between herself and Henry. He braced himself for the storm, but she simply wrapped him up in a bear hug. "Oh, Henry. I'm so glad you're safe. Is Nell all right? Did she know?"

He stood there for a moment and then slowly hugged her back. Something eased inside him. Rachel was one of the hard cases. If she understood... "No. She found out today. I'm sorry I lied."

Rachel pulled back and wiped tears from her eyes. "Well, of course you did. You couldn't walk in and announce who you were. I'm sure that was classified, and honestly, even later you had to keep the secret or Max there would have bugged you about assassinating his enemies and Rye would have tried to put you on the payroll when he was sheriff."

"Hey, I would have taken ex-CIA operative over Logan any day of the week," Rye admitted. "Nate got so lucky Cam came to town or we would have the Farley brothers in khakis."

"Is she okay?" Rachel had taken a step back.

She couldn't possibly know how much that hug meant to him. That hug let him know it was still okay to be Henry. Henry was the man who got hugs, who people cared about, who had a place in this town. "No. Nell's devastated, and I'm not sure she's going to let me back in the house."

Rachel's lips quirked up slightly. "Well, I bet you know how to break in, superspy."

There was nowhere Nell could run that he couldn't find her, but there were problems with that scenario. "Shouldn't I honor her wishes?"

Rachel waved that off. "Nah. She's your wife. You can't grovel properly if she won't let you in. And honestly, I'll be surprised if Nell locks you out of the cabin. She'll be mad as hell, but she won't leave you out in the cold."

He wasn't so sure about that. He could still remember how hollow she'd looked when she'd asked him for time. "She wanted to be alone for a while."

"She'll probably need time to process," Rachel allowed. "Give it to her. And when she finally explodes, take it."

"Nell is going to protest you," Max agreed.

"Nell doesn't really get angry. Not at her friends." Rye settled his toddler daughter in his arms. Paige Harper laid her head on her father's shoulder and seemed ready for a nice nap.

Rachel snorted. "Oh, I assure you, she will explode at some point."

"She's a forgiving woman," Max pointed out. "She tells me that all the time. And then she tells me I have to forgive people too."

"Yeah, it's different when it's the one person in the world who's supposed to be safe." Rachel turned back to Henry. "I don't know how it is for men, but sometimes for women it's easier to be angry with that person. You're the person she never has to be fake with."

"I don't want her to be. I'll take all the anger she has." It was her silence that he feared.

"Good. And you need to understand that I'm going to agree with every terrible thing she says about you. If she says you are the worst human being since…whoever Nell thinks is the worst human being on the planet…I am going to agree," Rachel explained. "But when she wants my advice I'm going to tell her that sometimes the past is hard to deal with, and who we used to be isn't nearly as important as who we choose to be."

Rachel had teared up again, and Henry knew what she was talking about. Rachel wasn't Rachel's original name. She'd been Elizabeth Courtney once. "Our situations are not the same. You were hiding from a man who wanted to hurt you. I was hiding from an organization I willingly went into."

"Oh, big bad Henry can't make a mistake?" Rachel's voice was soft, the question not unkindly.

At the time it hadn't felt like a mistake. It had felt like a way out, a way to finally have some power for himself. "I knew what I was getting into."

"Did you?" Rye asked. "Because I think there's probably a big difference between the rah-rah recruitment videos and the real thing. I bet it's not like a James Bond film."

"No, it's not," Henry agreed. "But I take responsibility for what I did. Rachel had a reason to run."

"I don't know. I think it's kind of similar. We both found ourselves in a situation we couldn't live with anymore. We both made choices to change our lives. I became someone different, someone I like. I think you did, too, and you did it for a much nicer reason than I did. You changed for her," Rachel mused. "That's pretty romantic when you think about it."

"I already tried that," he admitted. "And then I was very unromantic and I didn't think about her when…"

He felt himself flush. This is another place where he'd changed from the John Bishop he'd been. John Bishop never flubbed anything. He wouldn't have blurted out that he'd gotten overly emotional and had fucked his wife from behind while she held on to the dining table.

For John Bishop, sex had been a perfunctory thing, a bodily function he had to deal with from time to time. Sex had been a way to clear his head.

For Henry, it was a way to express his soul, to bond with the love of his life.

"Are you talking about when you got all caveman nasty on her? Yeah, we knew what was going on in there." A hint of a smile crossed Max's lips. "Early pregnancy sex is pretty fun."

Rachel's hands went to her hips. "Hey, too much information."

Max waved her off. "Nah. He needs to hear it. It's the only reason he agreed to come out here this afternoon. He wanted to talk about how rough pregnancy is on a man."

Rachel's brows rose above her eyes. "Really? It's so hard on you?"

Max's hands came up as though warding off the inevitable attack. "It is because I love you so much, baby. I worried a lot during the first pregnancy because I didn't know what to expect. And then I read that book and I did know what to expect and it did not help. That book was incredibly graphic."

Rye grinned and patted his daughter's back. "I would not recommend it. But I do understand where you are, Henry. What does Caleb say? Is Nell high risk?"

"He said she's perfectly healthy. He's run all the tests." He'd heard it over and over again. Miscarriages happened for different reasons, and this pregnancy was moving along normally. "He said as long as we're careful we should behave like everything is fine."

"Because it is," Rachel said quietly. "She needs you to be normal. She needs you to be her husband and not her doctor. Caleb knows what he's doing. If he says it's okay, it's okay. Nell isn't going to take any undue risks, but you have to love her enough to know that she's still your wife. Sometimes when a woman is pregnant she ends up feeling like an incubator and not a woman. Remind her she's still everything you want in life, and that includes sex. Max is right. Pregnancy sex can be hot and heavy if you've got the right hormones. It's different for every woman."

Nell hadn't complained. She'd softened when he'd gotten into her space. She'd gone all submissive and warm for him.

Had she missed him as much as he'd missed her? Had she missed those nights when they'd done nothing but lie in bed and talk in between bouts of sex? Something had lit in her eyes when he'd commanded her.

"I don't want to hurt her."

Rachel's expression went sympathetic. "That is an inevitability in a marriage. You can try to mitigate the damage, but when you're as in love with a person as you are with Nell, when you share a life the way you do, you're going to hurt each other. It's in how you handle yourself afterward that decides whether a marriage will survive. I should know. I'm married to Max."

Maybe Max did have something to teach him.

"Grovel, man." Max nodded vigorously. "Sexual servitude works wonders, too. Couple of hours of me putting in the work and she's purring again."

"Well, I wouldn't say that, but groveling does work for Max," Rachel agreed.

Rye shook his head. "Won't work for Nell. I mean you are going to have to grovel, but I get the feeling you shouldn't do it in the bedroom. I think Nell needs something different there."

Max's face screwed into a horrified expression. "Dude, she's like our sister. She doesn't do that stuff. She's very staid and normal."

That brought a smile to his face because Rye was right. "She's a beautiful soul."

With a filthy mind and a need for sexual submission, and he'd been denying her that. He couldn't exactly walk back in and demand that she serve him, but he could work his way back to that relationship.

He could prove she could trust him again.

"I think if you explain yourself, she'll understand." Rachel gave him a friendly pat. "Maybe not today. Maybe not tomorrow, but eventually. Now give me back my baby and I'll whip up a fruit salad to send back with Henry. I promise it will be all kinds of animal-product free. Though you tell Nell if she needs a burger on the down low, I will fix that for her and never, ever bring it up again. Pregnancy cravings are real, and she shouldn't feel bad about them. I'll come by and visit her tomorrow."

He nodded as Rachel took a now sleeping Paige and walked back up to the main house.

He held a hand out. "Give me that latch. I need to get home."

Max handed it over. "All right, but I still think you should teach a class on that easy kill thing. Hey, who'd you kill at the Feed Store Church? Did you kill Dennis? Because I swear it's a travesty that he only gives discounts to people who sit through his sermons."

Henry sighed and got back to the job at hand.

Two hours later he let himself into the house. Nell sat on the couch and it was obvious she'd been crying. His heart ached at the knowledge that he'd been the cause of her tears. But she wouldn't appreciate him pointing it out.

"Hey," he said quietly as he placed the bowl Rachel had sent with him on the table. "How are you? Are you hungry?"

"I made lentil soup." She didn't look up from her knitting. "It's still on the stove."

She'd eaten without him, though it wasn't quite their dinnertime. That made him ache, too. Dinner was when they talked about the day, when they sat together and caught up if they'd been apart, or talked about whatever book she happened to be writing. Sometimes they could be in a room together and Nell was still miles from him.

She would be in her own world and it was safe because he was always here in the real one waiting for her.

Now he was the very reality she was trying to escape.

"Rachel sent some fruit salad."

"That's nice."

"I'm sorry."

She was silent.

He sat on the couch, not quite knowing what to say. Maybe he wasn't clear enough. "I'm sorry for all of it, but I was specifically apologizing for not listening to you. I had a long talk with the Harpers and it was pointed out to me that I'm not being a good partner on a couple of different levels."

She finally glanced up. "Not listening to me?"

"When you were telling me you needed sex."

A fine flush rushed over her cheeks. "When did I say that?"

She was still aware of him, and not in an entirely bad way. "You've told me a hundred different times, and I chose my fear over your needs. You should understand that I won't do it again. All you have to do is give me the word and we'll play. I'll be careful, but I'll give you what you need."

She dropped her eyes back down, but her hands were still. "I'm not playing with you, Henry. I'm angry with you."

She didn't look angry. She looked hurt. Anger would be good, but he might have to wait for it. Rachel was right. Nell needed time to process, and being patient just might kill him. "Doesn't mean you can't use me to get what you need. I've recently been informed that pregnant ladies can have these hormones that make them incredibly horny. I'm the reason you have those hormones. I can be the solution."

She put a hand to her cheek. "Stop. I'm not talking about this."

"Just know that my cock is ready and willing," he replied. He sat back. "Do you have any questions for me?"

Her hands started moving again. "I told you I need time."

"Okay, but we need to talk soon about what kind of danger you could be in." He took a deep breath and decided to ask one more question. "Just one more thing. Do you want me to leave? If you do, then all I ask is that you let me take you to Mountain and Valley. They can protect you there."

She seemed to think about that plan. "That man from today, he was working for the people who are looking for you?"

"Yes. He was from the same cartel as the man who hurt Seth and Georgia," he replied, keeping his tone as even as he could. He wanted to spill everything, to tell her the whole story, but she wasn't ready to hear it.

"But you worked for the CIA."

"At the time I was running a team that investigated narco-terrorist groups in South America."

She turned and he saw the moment curiosity lit her eyes. Nell loved research, adored learning about pretty much anything. She would have a million questions. If she didn't decide to protest him fully, he might be able to draw her back in with info.

Fuck the fact that it was classified. His wife was beyond reproach. Though it might end up in a book. The good news was there were few operatives who followed the world of erotic romance.

She got back to her knitting. "I bet you weren't exactly shutting them down. You know the war on drugs has only brought more violence to the streets of this country. And it disproportionately affects people of color."

"I was really more looking for terrorists," he pointed out.

But she was off, giving him a lecture on how policing morals led to misery on all sides and it would be better to legalize and tax and make rehab and therapy far more accessible.

He sat and listened and found himself oddly soothed.

She finally went quiet after a long time. "You're sleeping on the couch."

He could handle that. "All right."

The cabin fell silent again.

Time. She needed a bit of time, but at least she wasn't throwing him out.

He would take it for now.

Chapter Five

Nell sat in the waiting room of the Bliss County Clinic and wondered if Henry was going to bother to show up. It wasn't a fair thing to think. Not at all. He'd come to every single appointment with her. Every time. He would be here, but usually he drove her into town.

Not today. Today he'd been picked up by Nate for some sort of secret meeting about something she didn't care about at all because she wasn't giving in to her curiosity. What mattered was that Henry had lied to her.

She didn't need to know all the awful details.

She glanced over and the plant she'd brought in many months before seemed to be thriving. Likely because Naomi had joined the practice. It certainly hadn't been Caleb. He barely noticed living humans if they weren't actually on his exam table.

The door opened and Holly rushed in, a big bag of books in her hand. She looked flushed from the afternoon heat, and her eyes went straight to Nell.

A bit of shame flashed through her. Holly was one of her best friends in the world, and she'd ducked her for a solid week using every excuse she could think of. It had been almost a week and a half since Henry had laid out the news that he was some kind of assassin. She'd stood beside him at Hiram's funeral and been surprised they hadn't been inundated with questions since at least half the town knew.

But at some point Laura had found out. Likely because Rafe was the newly appointed mayor of Bliss and he'd been debriefed. Because that was what they did now. From there it had been easy to figure out what had happened. Rafe and Cam had told their wife. Laura had been worried and called Holly. They'd both tried to get hold of her for several days, but she'd simply asked for time and space.

Time and space weren't working with Henry. She found herself getting angrier and angrier. She tamped it down because she needed...

She needed to smash something.

"Hey." Holly slowed down as if she'd run here but now she'd caught her prey and she could take it easy.

Nell hated the fact that she wanted to turn away from this woman, that she wanted to be alone. She wasn't a person who needed tons of alone time. She tended to crave being around groups of people. She gained energy from discussion and debate, from helping people.

She'd barely left the cabin since Hiram's funeral.

"Hey."

The bag in Holly's hand hit the floor with a resounding thump. Holly sighed as she left it there and came to sit on the other side of the couch from Nell. "I went into Alamosa for books. Classes start next week."

Holly was back in college. She was taking business classes so she could run the business side of the clinic someday.

"What are you taking?" It didn't matter, but small talk seemed safe.

"I've got a statistics class I'm nervous about. Especially since I'm not the only one taking it," she admitted with a wince.

"Alexei's taking it, too?" Holly's other husband had been taking classes at Adams State University in Alamosa as well, though he hadn't decided on his area of studies yet.

Holly shook her head. "Micky. I'm taking a class with my son. I feel like such a weirdo."

Holly's son was proof positive that she was awesome. Micky Lang

100

had every bit of his mother's kindness and a wonder for the world around him that always made Nell smile. "You're not. You're brave and strong and you'll teach every kid in that class that they're never too old to follow a dream."

She felt old. Stupid. Maybe that was a better word, though she'd been so tired lately that old felt like it worked, too. She hated feeling dumb, but even more she hated the looks of pity she would get. Like the one on Holly's face now. It was sad when she thought about it because she would tell anyone else to not look on it as pity, to see it for what it truly was—empathy, sympathy, caring.

But she was still a seven-year-old girl watching her mom being carted off to a mental facility, hiding in the corner of her room so they wouldn't take her away. She was still the girl who listened to the social workers talk about how sad it was her mom was insane.

She was thinking more and more about her mom lately. For obvious reasons.

"Are you okay?" Holly asked after a moment of uncomfortable silence.

"I'm as well as can be expected." Nell gave her friend what she hoped was an encouraging smile. She glanced out the window, but still no Henry. "I'm here for a checkup."

No Henry, but there was a gorgeous blonde jogging up the street. Laura wasn't wearing her usual heels. She was in a pair of yoga pants and a T-shirt, sneakers she could easily slip in and out of on her feet. She'd slung a yoga mat over her shoulder. But it was obvious she was more interested in cardio than stretching.

Nell turned back to Holly. "You called her?"

"I texted when I checked the appointments at the clinic for today," Holly admitted.

"Isn't that against HIPAA or something?" She couldn't hide from a doctor's appointment, but she'd thought she could get in and out quickly. After all, it was a weekday and she'd known Holly had to finish her registration and Laura would be at her yoga class in the park. The same yoga class Nell should have been in if it hadn't been for Henry turning her into the town fool.

She could do that all on her own. She was well aware that some of her protests could be seen as less than normal. Mostly the ones that dealt with mime, but it was hard to yell all the time. It was good to change things up.

"I'm the office manager," Holly replied. "Part time, but I do have access to the schedule."

The clinic door opened and Laura walked in, tossing her mat over beside Holly's books. "Thank god we finally ran you down. I've called a thousand times and knocked on your door. Nell, you can't ignore me."

Nell thought she'd done a pretty good job of it. "I'm fine. I needed some alone time. I haven't felt well."

"Really?" Laura stared down at her. She proved that motherhood had nothing to do with the physical act of delivering a baby because she had the mom look down. "You're going with that? You have nothing to say about the whole Henry-used-to-be-a-CIA-operative thing?"

"I don't know that it's anybody's business." She wasn't ready to talk about it. Not even with her friends.

Laura sighed, a deeply relieved sound, and sat down opposite Nell. "You knew. I was so worried that this blindsided you, but if you're this calm, then you knew."

"It's okay." Holly smiled as though she was relieved, too. "I would normally say you should have told us, but I understand why you wouldn't. It's important to keep that particular secret. No one's upset. Everyone will understand you couldn't break your husband's confidence."

"Mel's already bugging him about opening up the 'vault,' as he calls it," Laura admitted. "Apparently Mel believes the CIA has a vault filled with knowledge about alien encounters. He also made Henry take a shot of his special beet-infused whiskey. It's horrible. Seriously, if I was an alien, it would keep me away, too."

Henry hadn't mentioned that, though every time he tried to talk about anything other than what they needed to do around the house, she shut him down. She couldn't listen right now. She was in some kind of purgatory where she couldn't quite tell him to get out and she couldn't do the things they needed to heal the wound.

She wasn't sure the wound could heal.

"I've always known you two had some kind of big secret between you," Laura admitted with a smile. "You're going to think this is crazy, but I decided you and Henry write romantic novels under the name Libby Finn."

Holly rolled her eyes. "Nell wouldn't write romance. I told her. She made me read those books and not one of them talked about recycling. Although some of the characters are oddly close to a few people we know."

"Her latest book was about a woman named Heidi, a doctor named Calvin, and a former Ukrainian mobster named Andrei," Laura said. "She's here in this town. I swear. Or she's someone's sister and hears all the gossip. I would say it's Callie, but Callie can't keep a secret."

Oh, but Nell could. Still, she hadn't even known the biggest secret of her life. "I didn't know. Not until last week. So I take it the word is out to everyone now?"

She'd been hiding from this all week, but it was time to face it. After all, it wasn't like she'd done anything wrong beyond being unable to see what was right in front of her face.

Both of her friends simply sat there for a moment, staring at her like they didn't know who she was.

"You didn't know." Laura seemed to have to say the words in order to believe them.

"I'm not anywhere near as smart as you two seem to think I am," she said with a humorless chuckle. "I had no idea until I watched my husband kill a man."

"Henry killed someone?" Holly's question came out loud, seeming to ping around the room. She flushed and lowered her voice. "I thought that was a joke. I mean, he was CIA, of course, but he worked in an office, right?"

Nell shook her head. "Nope. He was a license-to-kill kind of guy. And he was in the Army."

Holly's eyes managed to widen even further. "He was a soldier? We're talking about the US Army, not some group that calls themselves an army, right? Like Wildlife Warriors? I could see that."

"He was Special Forces. He was so good at it, they recruited him into the CIA." He was everything she'd believed was wrong with the world. Not the idea of a soldier. The world needed soldiers and protectors, but that wasn't necessarily what the CIA did. On the surface, yes, but history had proven the CIA mostly watched out for the

CIA.

Holly turned Laura's way. "You're supposed to be a hotshot profiler. How did you not see this? I am Suzy Sunshine and tend to think everyone is awesome until they prove themselves to be awful. You're supposed to be smarter than me. Smarter than us. You're obviously the brains of our friendship, and you have failed."

"Hey," Laura began and then deflated. "I didn't see it at all. He's good. I should have gotten something off him. I used to find actual serial killers."

According to Henry himself, he practically was one, though all of his kills had been sanctioned by the US government. Or Nate Wright.

Maybe she should protest Nate. It had been a while, and he seemed to have forgotten that there were procedures to be followed.

Henry could have died. It could have been Henry on the floor of the Feed Store Church, his lifeless eyes staring up at her.

"Hey, you just went pale," Laura said.

"I'll get Caleb." Holly stood up.

Nell reached for her hand to stop her. "I'm fine. Rachel's in there right now. At least I think she is. She had the appointment before me. Caleb likes to get all the pregnant stuff done at one time."

Holly sank back down. "I'm so sorry. This has to be hard on you."

Laura had sobered as well. "Are you all right? Please don't give us a bullshit answer. We're your friends. You've been hiding. You need to talk about this."

But if she talked about it, then it would be real. She would have to make a decision, and she wasn't ready for that yet.

"She'll talk about it when she's ready," a deep voice said.

Holly started and Laura turned around to face the newcomer. Henry stood just inside the door of the clinic.

"I didn't hear you," Holly said. "The door makes a noise when it opens."

Henry simply shrugged. "It doesn't have to if you know how to open it."

He wasn't hiding it anymore. There was a difference to her husband that had come in the last few days, some odd meshing of his two personalities. He was still Henry, but sometimes she was almost sure she could see John Bishop beneath that grim expression he wore.

He was here now, staring at her friends like she needed protection from them.

They were likely the ones who needed protection.

"Caleb is running late," she said, trying to tamp down the emotion that flared the moment he walked into any room she happened to be in. Anger always rushed to the surface, but there was something even more dangerous beneath the rage. Curiosity.

She kind of wanted to know this Henry.

He nodded and started to move toward her.

Her friends stood and stared him down.

"Nell, do you want Henry here?" Laura asked.

"I can go in with you if you don't want to go alone," Holly offered.

Something dark sparked in Henry's eyes.

She wished she didn't have such a visceral reaction to that look. A pretty sexual reaction.

She knew how to tame this particular beast. She held out her hand. "Of course I want him with me. This is his baby, too. Come here, Henry. You can wait with me."

The dark look fled and he practically tripped over his own feet trying to get to her. He ignored Laura and Holly, his eyes never leaving hers.

He wore his usual uniform of khakis and a T-shirt, Birkenstocks on his stupid big sexy feet. He didn't look like a man who'd held up the patriarchy and the oligarchy and all the archies with his spy work.

What had he called himself? A spy master? Or did he mean spy Master? Because that could be a book title.

It was the first time she'd even thought about writing in a week.

"Did the drive go all right? I'm sorry I couldn't take you myself." He reached for her hand as he sat down beside her, taking Holly's place.

"It was fine. I can still drive." She almost wanted the predator back. At least the predator didn't look at her like she was fragile and might fall apart at any moment.

Even if that was exactly how she felt.

"Did the talk with Nate go all right?" Nell asked. "Did you find anyone else you need to kill?"

"Nell," Laura started, sounding completely surprised, but then she rarely heard Nell be so sarcastic.

"No, dear." Henry ignored Laura entirely. "I haven't found anyone else I need to kill. Yet. There's a situation brewing out in California that I might have to deal with. I don't know how to though. I have to think about it."

She wasn't sure what that meant, but there wasn't time to deal with it because the door to the exam room opened and Rachel stepped out, followed by both of her husbands.

"You're up, Nell." Rachel had her baby bag slung over her shoulder. "Doc is going to warm up the lube this time. Or else he's going to answer to me."

Naomi Turner walked out of the exam room, shaking her head. "I told him you would care."

"Holly, I'm going to need you to shove an ice cube up the slit of your husband's dick so he knows what it feels like," Rachel ordered.

"Will do," Holly promised, though Nell knew she'd learned long ago to simply agree that Caleb deserved every punishment possible for his fairly wretched bedside manner.

"Why the hell does he need lube?" Henry stood up, his hands fists on his hips and an outraged look in his eyes.

Max nodded Henry's way, holding Paige in his arms. The toddler girl seemed fascinated with her father's ear. "Good for you, brother. I told you not to read those books. You might be the first person to ever take my advice. And the Internet is the worst. Ignorance is the only way to go."

"He's doing a check on my cervix," Nell explained. "It's nothing to worry about. It's not half as bad as a pap smear, but I hope his hands aren't cold."

Henry actually blushed as he obviously figured out what she was talking about. "Oh."

Nell stood because Caleb walked out. "Big bad spy can't handle his wife's cervical exam? If you can't, feel free to stay here in the lobby."

Wife. She caught on the word. She'd married Henry Flanders. It was right there on the marriage license. He'd signed his name. Henry Flanders.

Henry Flanders didn't exist.

She felt tears spring to her eyes, and she turned and walked out. She couldn't do this right now. She couldn't hold his hand and pretend like they were a happy couple waiting on their baby.

What would her baby's name be? Would she go back to Finn since it was a legal name?

She pushed through the door to the clinic and was blasted with late-summer air. It filled her lungs and she could barely breathe.

She needed to go home. She could take a nap and when she woke up there would be dinner to make, and she had a virtual meeting with a group of young activists who needed a mentor. She would make her way through the day and deal with whatever happened tomorrow then.

She had to get home and away from all the eyes on her.

"Nell." Henry jogged up behind her. "Sweetheart, are you all right?"

She was so sick of that question. "Am I all right?"

They'd all stepped out of the clinic, Caleb joining his wife. They were all staring her way.

"Yeah." Henry sounded breathless. "You just walked out. I'm sorry. I didn't mean to talk about…"

"My cervix? You can say it, Henry. God knows your dick has bumped against it enough," she shot back.

Henry's eyes went super wide, and he stared at her like he'd never seen her before.

She'd practically screamed at him.

"Come on back inside," Henry said, his tone so reasonable it made her want to punch his stupid perfect face. "I think Caleb's ready for us."

"Us? There's no *us* here. You're not the one who's pregnant. Oh, I know I've said in the past that we would share this, but we can't. You're not the one who threw up for weeks, and I'm betting your nipples don't ache the way mine do. You're not the one who will soon have Caleb's overly large fingers shoved up your hoohaa." She pointed Caleb's way. "Yeah, I'm talking about you, Doc. I know I said you're good at a pelvic exam, but I was lying to spare your feelings."

This wasn't her. She was nice. She was considerate. And what had it gotten her? A man who lied. A baby she would likely have to raise on her own because she was living her mother's life.

Caleb frowned. "I don't really have feelings."

"Good. Then you won't care when I tell you you're not a gentle doctor," she yelled his way.

It felt good to yell.

"You tell him, Nell!" Max held his fist up in solidarity. "I've had his whole fist up my asshole. He's a sadist."

Paige grinned. "Ashooo."

"Max!" Rachel was yelling now too.

Caleb frowned, his brows furrowing. "It was not my whole fist. Why would I do that?"

"She was sneezing, baby," Max said even as his toddler tried out the new word she'd learned.

"You are scaring the tourists, my love," Henry said under his breath. "Maybe we should go inside and discuss Caleb's poor cervical techniques. Perhaps I can give him some pointers."

She wanted to take the hand he offered. She wanted to be the Nell she'd always chosen to be. Good. Kind. Thoughtful. A woman who put her anger into advocacy, who tried to use the rage every human being felt as fuel to make the world better.

"Are we married?" She wished the world wasn't so watery.

Henry's face fell. "Baby, of course we are. Come here."

He was holding his arms open, offering her the place that had always been safest for her. She could be angry or scared or sad and being in Henry's arms made the world recede. His touch could calm her, remind her she wasn't alone, wasn't misunderstood.

She took a step back because that place had been a lie, too. "Are we legally married?"

He paled.

Well, at least she wouldn't have to divorce him.

"Yes, we are," he said, his tone firming.

"How? You have to use your legal name in order to sign a contract." If someone had asked weeks ago she would have said a marriage didn't need to be legal anywhere but inside the couples' hearts. But now she wanted to know how tied to him she was. How far he'd gone to perpetuate his lies.

That dark look was back. This version of Henry was a lot like the Dom. He didn't like to be challenged. It was one of the things she loved about her Henry. He could be a wonderful partner in their normal lives. They could argue and debate and he never once took it as an affront. But in the bedroom…oh, in the bedroom he was a brilliant caveman, taking what he wanted.

"I assure you my paperwork is perfect, love. You won't find any loopholes to wiggle out of. The marriage is on the books. You are Nell Flanders and you will continue to be Nell Flanders." He practically growled the words and then he seemed to deflate. "Baby, I promise you I wasn't trying to trick you. I wanted to marry you more than anything in the world."

How could she believe him?

"Nell, do you want to reschedule?" Caleb shouted the question across the parking lot.

She glanced around and realized she had far more of an audience than she'd imagined.

"Caleb, maybe we should go inside." Holly had a hand on her husband's white jacket.

She stood there completely frozen in place because she had an appointment and it was about the health of her baby. Henry's baby. But she wanted to go home and lock it all out and pretend it wasn't happening.

She was always assertive, always knew what she wanted and how to advocate for herself to get it.

She was so lost now.

"Henry, I think Nell is going to take this appointment without you." Laura took Nell's hand firmly in hers. "She shouldn't miss appointments, and I'll be with her the whole time. I'll take her for some lunch afterward and I'll drop her back off at the cabin this afternoon."

The look on his face told Nell he wanted to argue, but he stepped back. "Is this what you want…what you need?"

She had no idea, but she wasn't sure she could talk about the baby with Henry, so she nodded. "Do you need the keys?"

He backed away, his face going blank. "I have mine. I'll see you at home."

He turned and walked toward their Jeep.

"Come on, honey." Laura gently tugged on her hand. "Let's get this over with and we'll go back to my place for lunch. The guys are out, and I can make you something nice."

She wasn't hungry, but she followed Laura inside the clinic. She didn't look back.

* * * *

Henry sat in front of his computer, thankful for once to have a problem to work on because if he thought about Nell, he might go fucking crazy.

Think about Nell? He couldn't not think about her, and it had been that way since the moment they'd met.

Are we legally married?

The question had stopped him in his tracks. They'd been legally married, and all the proper paperwork had been filed. He had everything he needed to prove he was Henry Flanders, damn it. He'd made sure of it.

But it was a house of cards, and all it would take was one stiff wind to blow it all apart.

He glanced over at her desk. She hadn't sat there at all this week. She'd studiously avoided her laptop. Apparently she wasn't in the mood to write romantic stories.

Because her own romance had imploded so spectacularly.

He sat back and sighed. What the hell was he going to do? She'd lost her cool earlier today, and that just wasn't Nell. She was serene, even in the face of turmoil.

He heard the sound of a vehicle coming up the drive and stood to greet her. It was still a little early, and maybe that was a good thing. Maybe she'd thought about it and wanted to talk.

He frowned when he realized it wasn't his sweet Nell coming up to the door. It was Stef Talbot.

The door was open, and he could see the big artist plainly through the screen. Stef Talbot was also known as the King of Bliss. This was his town, and he ruled over it more than any mayor ever would, though Henry thought Stef might find Rafe harder to deal with than Hiram had been.

He should have known this meeting was coming. He'd sat across from Stef a few days before when he'd debriefed Rafe after he'd officially taken the mayor's job. He'd made the decision to bring in

Stef and inform him of the situation. Stef hadn't said much at the time, merely asked to be kept up to date.

He should have known Stef would want this conversation to be private. "Come on in, Stef. Nell isn't here, but then I think you probably know that."

"She's at Laura's." Stef stepped inside. "At least that's what I've heard. I also heard about the scene at the clinic earlier today. I thought it might be a good time for us to talk."

"All right." His every nerve was on edge, and he needed to chill because showing Stef Talbot how dangerous he could be wouldn't help his case. "I thought I explained everything during the briefing, but I can certainly answer any question you have."

Stef was a tall man. He had a couple of inches on Henry, and his body was corded with lean muscle. Unlike most men, he didn't find the artist physically intimidating. It was the influence Stef had over the town Henry loved that made him truly dangerous. "I'm afraid I spent most of that meeting in shock. I needed some time to think. You threw me for a loop, Henry."

"You know who I am. You just didn't know who I used to be."

Stef stared at him for a moment. "Did you come to my town to hide?"

There was the arrogant king. He didn't blame Stef. He knew pretty much everything there was to know about his neighbors, and Stef's need to protect the town, to claim it as his, came from his childhood. Stef had been given all the comforts of wealth, but his mother had been completely out of his life and his father had been distant as well. This town had raised Stef, had given him a harbor in the storm.

The way it had for Henry.

"I originally came because Bill was the only person I thought I could talk to." His first instinct had been to tell Stef it wasn't his business and to get out. But that was the Bishop in him. Henry talked his problems through with friends. God, he hoped Stef was still his friend. "I was at a crossroads. I hated what I'd become, but I didn't know what I wanted. The Agency was all I'd known at that point. I went from foster care to the Army to the Agency. When I left, I was responsible for many operatives, many missions. I had power at the Agency, but I met Nell and I realized it was hollow. My power was

111

nothing in the face of her belief. I didn't come here to hide. I came here to find myself."

Stef seemed to take that in. "You love Nell."

It wasn't a question, but Henry found he had a need to answer. "I love her more than I've loved anything or anyone in my life. She's the best part of me, the only part of me I'm proud of."

"All right. I'm sorry to question you. My wife laughed when I asked her what she thought."

"What did Jen say?"

"She said you ate too much tofu to not be in love," Stef said, a smile finally creasing his face. He sobered quickly. "How much danger are we in?"

"If they come, they'll come looking for me. If I can't handle them, then I'll let them take me." He'd gone over and over it in his head. "If I thought they would leave my wife alone, I would go. I can't know what intel they've gathered. If they know about Nell, they'll use her against me."

It was what kept him up at night. The idea of his wife and their unborn child in the hands of the cartel wrecked him.

"Are you working with Nate on a plan to keep her safe?" Stef asked. "Should you two be out here on your own?"

"To be honest, I'm afraid to tell my wife she's going to need security. She's already upset with me." He nodded toward the sofa where his blankets and pillows were sitting neatly folded. "As everyone in town could tell when she screamed about her cervix in the parking lot of the clinic."

That got Stef's brows to rise. "Yeah, that doesn't sound like Nell. I mean, who hasn't heard her yell about female parts, but she's typically upset the patriarchy is trying to control her uterus."

"She didn't want me at her appointment." He couldn't stand the fact that she hadn't taken comfort in him. It had become a point of pride that he was the one she turned to. He hoped Laura had held her hand during the exam. He'd wanted so badly to be in there with her, to ask questions and listen for the heartbeat. He hoped Caleb had been able to find it quickly because she would be worried if he had to search for it for long.

Had he had any right to get her pregnant? To put her through all of this for the simple fact that he longed for a child with the woman he loved.

"I need to know what your plans are," Stef said quietly. "Are you going to take care of this?"

"I'm not sure how. If I turn myself in to the Agency, it leaves Nell vulnerable. If I go after the cartel myself, I leave Nell vulnerable and I probably end my marriage." He might not have a choice. "Part of the problem is how things have moved in the years since I left. I've spent the last week working on putting some pieces together. The cartel I was investigating ended up working with one in Mexico. They're still around, but they've lost some of their power. Something's going on. There are pieces being moved around that I don't like. I'm seeing a pattern."

"What does it mean?"

"It means that my past is coming back to haunt me in more ways than one," Henry admitted. "Some of the last operations I put in place before I came here are unravelling in a way I never intended. I'm not sure what to do about it. I might have to leave for a while. The problem is I don't know if I'll be allowed to come back."

"No one will stop you," Stef replied. "Nell is going to have a baby, and you're the baby's father. I doubt she'll keep your child from you. She might be angry, but she's not vindictive."

"Tell that to my spinal cord," he replied with a sigh. "That couch might have been sustainably built, but it was not meant for sleeping."

"And yet you're still sleeping here when Seth's monster is within walking distance," Stef pointed out.

"I can't leave Nell. She might need me." It was why the thought of taking care of the situation was so distasteful. That and the fact that he didn't want to do that work anymore. He was tired of having blood on his hands.

However, if Kayla Summers was in trouble, he didn't have a choice. He owed her. He'd ruthlessly placed her in danger, and now he might be the only one who could save her.

"I came here to talk to you about that. If you need to leave for a while, Nell can come to the house. I'll pay for round-the-clock protection. I'll call some friends and find a good company to use," Stef offered.

He knew who he trusted. "Use McKay-Taggart."

"I thought you were against that company."

"Only because Ian Taggart was one of my protégés," Henry admitted. "Call him. He's absolutely the best, and he'll have trained the best. He's going to find out I'm alive at some point, though you might not mention you know me. I don't know that Taggart won't be angry. I left everyone when I came to Bliss. I dropped it all."

"Don't do the same thing again," Stef advised. "Don't drop us. It would be a huge mistake. I know Nell."

"Then you should know there's a possibility that she never forgives me. Hell, today she basically said she thinks we're not really married."

"Because you lied about your name." Stef nodded. "I would be worried about that, too. Do you want me to have a lawyer look into it?"

"It wouldn't matter at this point."

"But it will in the future," Stef said. "Your name is on her LLC. You're on all the joint accounts."

Was that why he was here? To look out for Nell. "Yes. I do want a lawyer. Have one draw up a postnuptial agreement. Whether or not our marriage is legal, it's real to me, and any documents like that will give her some sense of peace. If I leave the marriage, I'll leave with what I brought in. Nothing."

When he'd walked away from his old life, he'd walked away from everything. He'd left behind his condo, his car, all of his money. Everything he'd saved and invested. He hadn't touched it because it was more important to maintain the illusion of his death.

"Henry, you've made a lot of money."

"Nell's talent has made a lot of money," Henry corrected. "And she started publishing before I came back. She keeps everything, including the cabin and the land. I won't take anything away from her."

Henry hadn't realized how tense Stef had been until his shoulders relaxed.

"All right. I'll have the documents drawn up. I actually think it could have an impact on Nell," Stef allowed. "No matter what happens, I don't think you should leave Bliss. I know Seth will let you stay in that monstrosity of a house, but there are also some cabins around that you can lease, and there's lots available to build on. You might like building a place for you and your kid."

"I've been wondering if I deserve a kid. Maybe it would be better if I wasn't in his life." He'd never wondered, but was that why his father had walked? Had he known what a shit he was and that any kid would be better off alone than with him? "It's not like I know how to be a parent. My dad walked away and my mom died young."

Stef shook his head. "So did mine. Well, my mom walked away and my dad was absent. And I love my son with every fiber of my being. It's not about what we know or what we've been through. That's the amazing thing about kids. They don't care. All that matters is if you love them enough to be with them. They'll handle a lot of heartache if you share it with them, teach them how to be good humans. I think that's what Nell would call it. You know how to be a good human, Henry."

Nell had taught him. This town had taught him. "I know how to be a bad one, too."

"And that's why you'll be good at this if you choose to honor your vows. Nell doesn't think you're legally married? Show her that her husband doesn't need a piece of paper to do the work of being her husband." Stef stepped back, moving toward the door. "I think that's Laura bringing Nell home. Give me a call and we'll set some things in motion."

"I'll do what's best for Nell. I promise. That's why you came, right? You wanted to make sure I'll do right by a woman you view as a sister." Henry knew Stef tended to view some of the citizens he'd been around for a long time as his family.

Stef turned back. "I did. But I also came because at some point in the last few years, you became my brother, and I don't want to lose you." He turned. "Hey, Nell. I came by to say hello."

"Hi, Stef." Nell walked in, waving behind her. She stopped when she saw him and her purse dropped to the floor. "Henry? Henry, are you all right? Did Stef say something?"

"I'm fine. Why."

"Because I don't think I've ever seen you cry." She rushed to him and threw her arms around him.

There was no way he wouldn't take that. It was too good to be close to her. He was always close to her, and the week since they'd last been together had been one long walk in the desert. He held her tight and didn't even care that tears had blurred his eyes when Stef had made it plain he belonged in Bliss.

He wasn't sure he'd ever truly belonged anywhere.

"Is the baby all right?" Henry managed to ask.

Nell pulled back and then gasped as she seemed to come to a revelation. "Oh, Henry. I didn't think about the fact that you would be worried. The baby is fine. I should have thought about how you would feel."

"It's okay. You needed time. I'm going to respect that, but I would like it if you would text me when you get out next time."

"You can come." Nell straightened her skirt and walked back to grab her bag. "I'm sorry I was so emotional today. You're the baby's father. Unless you're planning to leave, and then I would prefer you weren't in our lives at all."

She'd gone cold fast, and that made him ache because Nell wasn't cold. Not ever. Even her anger was a warm thing that proved her rage came from a place of caring. But there was a harmful indifference moving her now.

"I told you I don't want to leave."

"I wasn't sure since the reason for you to be here is gone now," she replied.

"What does that mean?"

"Do you honestly think the Agency doesn't know?" Nell asked. "If the cartel knows, I would suspect the Agency knows. They might already have someone here watching you."

It wasn't anything he hadn't thought about. The trouble was he couldn't be sure how long the Agency had known, so he didn't know how far back to look. "That is a possibility. If I was running an op on a wayward agent, I would send in someone long term. An operative who could get close to the agent. But Nell, I don't want to leave. If they come for me, they come for me. If they do, you have to let them take me."

That seemed to stop her for a moment. "What will they do to you?"

He wasn't going into this with her. "It doesn't matter. If I tell you to run, go to Stef's. He'll protect you. You let them take me. No arguments. If they come in the front, you walk out the back, go to

Seth's, and call Stef. He knows what to do."

"Maybe you should run."

"If they know about me, they know about you. Running would only leave you unprotected. And honestly, I don't want to run. I ran from them and found this place. I don't want to leave Bliss. If you can't forgive me, I'll rent a cabin of my own and I'll find work, but I have no intentions of leaving Bliss. I'll admit I thought about the fact that I might not be a good father, that maybe I should let you find someone who knows how to be a dad."

She turned and walked into the kitchen, but not before he caught a sheen of tears in her eyes. "I think you'll be a good father." She picked up the kettle and started to fill it. "So you came here to get away from the Agency and the cartel, but you decided you liked it?"

"I came here because I fell in love with you." He was tired. A weariness threatened to overtake him, but he couldn't exactly go to bed. He didn't have one anymore. "I've got some research to do. I'll be at my computer if you need me."

Nell looked back at him. "Research?"

"Seth and I have been trying to piece together what happened after I left."

"What happened with the cartel you were watching?"

He nodded. "After I left there was a bunch of fallout. Apparently some money and a shipment went missing and that started a mini war inside the organization." He probably shouldn't talk about this, but she looked interested. It was the most eye contact they'd had in days. "After the fallout cleared, the cartel in Colombia started working with one in Mexico."

"I thought they were always at war."

"No, it's actually often very businesslike. Don't get me wrong. There was bloodshed, but the man who runs the Jalisco cartel obviously wanted the infrastructure associated with the weakened Colombian cartel. The trouble is the same man who took over now has a connection to someone I used to work with."

"Another operative?"

"She was a trainee at the time." His heart twisted at the thought of Kayla Summers. "She was one of my worst mistakes. Not because she was bad. She was excellent, but..." The last thing he needed was for

117

her to find out how ruthless he could be. "You don't need to hear this. Uhm, I can go work at Seth's if you would rather be alone."

She seemed to think about it for a moment. "Are you worried she's in trouble?"

"Yes. I don't like the pattern I'm seeing, and I don't like what I've found out about the man who took over my job. I fear he's manipulating the situation, and now he's got Kayla involved, and weirdly enough, a Hollywood action star."

Nell's chin came up. "I'd like to hear this story, Henry."

"I don't come off looking good." He wasn't sure telling her this particular story would help his cause, but at least she wasn't kicking him out.

"You wanted to tell me before. I'm ready to listen."

"I wanted to tell you a breezy version that makes me look noble for choosing love," he replied, a wistful tone to his voice.

She grabbed a mug and placed it on the counter. "Well, I want the real version. This feels like something you're going to have to deal with, and I'd like to know why."

He'd been thinking the same thing—that he might have to insert himself into this situation. "I'm not sure how I would handle it. I can't exactly walk in and announce myself. I would have to be sneaky, and I have no connection to some Hollywood actor."

It was obvious to him that the Agency was using the actor to get to the head of the cartel and likely to put Kayla into whatever place they wanted her in. The easiest thing to do would be to inform the actor of who his "friend" really was. If he could break the relationship between the actor and the man he didn't know was a criminal, then Kayla would no longer be in danger.

But somehow he didn't think an email would do the trick. He needed to get into Josh Hunt's circle, but without Kayla knowing about it.

The kettle started whistling. "Of course you do. There's always a connection. That's the funny thing about our world. There's only a few degrees of separation between any two people. The key is finding the connection. Now tell me the story."

It was the most assertive he'd heard her talk in days. Well, besides yelling at him in the parking lot. "All right. But like I said, I'm not the

Happily Ever After in Bliss

hero of the story. It all started when I discovered the MSS agent I'd been going up against for a couple of years had a twin sister here in the States. It was then that I realized I could have a double agent if I played my cards right."

He continued, and for the first time in weeks, she actually listened to him.

119

Chapter Six

She couldn't have written that story if she'd tried.

The next morning Nell sat at her computer contemplating the problems Henry had laid out for her the night before. When he'd been with the Agency, he'd found out about a young American woman named Kayla Summers and her twin sister, who worked as a spy for her home country of China. He'd manipulated the situation so Kayla had believed her sister to be dead and had taken her place at MSS, while her husband had taken the other twin and had the best of both worlds.

He was ruthless. Or at least he used to be. She'd watched the guilt he felt play out on his face as he'd told her the story. He'd lied and manipulated and placed a young woman in a position she shouldn't have been in, one that could have led to her horrible death.

Would he have ever seen how wrong that had been if he hadn't come to Bliss? Would he still be out there, still pulling strings and playing games? Had this place truly changed him? Or was it one more manipulation meant to make John Bishop's life more comfortable?

She'd managed to shove those questions aside briefly as she'd worked on the problem at hand.

"So Kayla is now the bodyguard for Joshua Hunt. I can't say I like his movies. The romantic comedies are good, but I don't love action. It's filled with white male rage." She wasn't sure what they had to rage about, but they did it a lot.

"It's not my favorite either. They often get things wrong, and that's not how gun fights normally go. It's way more boring. It's better to snipe your opponent." Henry looked up from his laptop. "Sorry."

It was actually kind of nice for him to be honest. "I take it you've sniped a lot of people?"

His eyes went back to his screen. "Probably more than my fair share."

She didn't want to find him fascinating. The night before she'd sat and drank her tea while they'd eaten black bean soup and he'd told her the whole story of Kayla Summers going from college student to CIA double agent. Now the young woman was with a security firm, but Henry believed she was still doing side work for the Agency. She was currently the bodyguard for a Hollywood star who had connections to a drug lord.

Henry thought the star had no idea he was dealing with a drug lord. Or the Agency. He feared that someone was using his former protégée in a way that could get her killed.

"I've thought a lot about this. I think you should go and deal with it."

He looked up, frowning. "I'm not sure how I would deal with it. I can't walk in and announce I used to be with the Agency and I think you're in danger. Oh, and your bodyguard is also Agency and I'm definitely worried she's in danger, and hey, she thinks I'm dead and so does her boss. Could you keep that secret?"

Put like that it did sound silly. But she'd lain in bed and all she could think about was the fact that those poor people didn't know what was coming for them, and Henry could help. He'd explained that he didn't trust the man who'd taken over his job. Someone who went by the name of Levi Green. Henry was worried Green was manipulating the situation and potentially working with the head of the cartel.

His old world was shadowy and dangerous, and he'd worked in shades of gray.

It was so hard to think of her husband in that world. And yet she also wanted to know more. That world had shaped him in so many ways, ways she hadn't contemplated.

"The actor is working on a film about a DEA agent." She knew how to look things up, too. "Joshua Hunt is known for meticulously researching his characters. He's probably planning on meeting with a DEA agent."

"Yeah, I read an article about how he always tries to have a consultant on set."

It seemed to be the easiest solution. "Why couldn't that consultant be you? You know about those things. It would be simple for you to answer his questions and then suggest a meeting before you go to the set. You could meet with him and show him what you've found out."

"I'm not a DEA agent."

She shrugged that off. "But you could be. You're good at playing a part."

His jaw tightened. "Nell, this isn't a part I'm playing."

That's what he kept telling her. He claimed he wouldn't leave Bliss if she decided to end the marriage she still wasn't sure was legal. "You used to go undercover, right?"

He sighed. "Yes. I did. I often went undercover."

She bit back all the questions that sprang to mind. It wasn't the time to be the curious writer. "Why don't you go undercover as a DEA agent?"

"Because I'm not a DEA agent. And I don't know one. Even if I did, how would I ensure Hunt would pick me?"

"He doesn't pick. He asks whatever agency he's researching to send someone. You might not know a DEA agent, but Nate and Zane do. He came to visit them last summer."

Henry leaned forward, nodding. "I remember that. He was roughly my age."

"If you could ensure Nate's friend gets picked as the liaison, then you take his place and you warn Hunt." It seemed fairly simple to her. "You can even go down to the set. It's in Mexico, not far from the state of Jalisco."

Henry had explained that he was certain that was where it would all go down.

"I could figure out what's going on and if I need to intervene further." Henry's expression had turned distinctly thoughtful. "I would have to go to California, and then possibly to Mexico. I don't want to leave you."

He would be off on a mission. It was so hard to think of her Henry that way, but she had to wrap her brain around it. "Will you be able to live with yourself if something happens to Kayla Summers?"

The hollow look was back in his eyes. "No."

"Then we have a plan. We need to talk to Nate." Nate would put them in touch with his old buddies at the DEA, and if they needed more influence they had Stef, who could talk anyone into anything, and Seth, who could simply go in and change the records and suddenly reality was whatever Seth wanted it to be. It was good to have a plan.

"Nell," he began.

She shook her head. "I think you should do this. I don't like the idea that you lied to that young woman so she would do your dirty work. You have to make it better."

"Will you forgive me if I do this?"

She sighed. He was trying to make this far less complicated than it was. She couldn't simply turn off her hurt and suspicions. "Henry, it's not about forgiveness. I can forgive you but I can't go back to the life we had before. You're not the man I thought I married. Can you understand that?"

"No. I am the man you married. I don't know how to prove it to you. I changed my whole life to fit into yours because you're everything to me." He stood and started pacing. It was something he did from time to time, but now she caught the predatory grace to his movements. "I never protested a damn thing in my life before I met you."

A flare of anger lit inside her. He wanted to argue about what he'd had to give up? "I've never been anything but honest with you. You knew exactly who I was when you married me. You never asked me to be anyone different. I don't know what I would have done, but you didn't even give me the chance to try to bend for you. So don't come back and tell me I'm some kind of tyrant who forced you into this. Do you even like tofu? Do you eat meat when I'm not around? I'm not going to judge you for it. I just want to know."

He stood and crossed the space between them. "I haven't had a bite of meat since the day before I came home to you. I do not miss it. I love your food. I love eating the way we do because it makes me feel healthy and it makes you happy. I know you think I've used you as a cover, but our marriage is the best thing that ever happened to me. Loving you is my whole world."

She wished she could believe him. "I need…"

"Time," he finished for her with a sigh. "And me being out of Colorado would give it to you. If I leave you'll have to go and stay with Stef."

She stood up and faced him. "I'm not leaving my home."

"Then I won't go. I can't be certain they won't show up while I'm gone."

"You don't know for sure anyone's coming at all," she pointed out. "You won't know until you figure out what the situation is. You can do it by going to Mexico yourself, or you can turn yourself over to the Agency." It was the only solution she'd come to. He needed to know what was happening or they would be in this perpetual state of fear and anxiety. They wouldn't be able to figure out if they could move on until they could breathe.

He moved to stand in front of her. "I can't leave you here alone with no one to protect you. I won't be able to work if I don't know you're all right. I'll spend every second of my time worried about you."

She didn't like the fact that he was so close. It would be far too easy to put her arms around him. "I don't want to be at Stef's. I want to be home."

"Then I'll call the Agency and I'll admit that I'm alive and inform them of what I think is happening. I'll agree to go into custody but only if they give you protection."

He was good at putting her in a corner. She loved Stef and Jen, but they had a pretty full house between the two of them, their newborn son, his father, Sebastian, and stepmom, Stella. There was a housekeeper, too. Jen and Stella would ask her all sorts of questions. Stef would push her to talk to a therapist. They would all mean well.

She wanted to be in her cabin. She wanted some quiet.

She had an idea. "If I hire a bodyguard, will you let me stay here?"

He stood in front of her, suspicion plain on his face. "It can't be Irene. I know she says she can build a circle of protection around people, but all that salt and chanting will not stop a bullet."

Did he think she was foolish? "The circle of protection is spiritual, and no, it doesn't work since she put one on me a long time ago and we're in this situation. I was thinking of someone else."

"Who?"

"I should talk to him first." She didn't want Henry to put pressure on the poor man. He'd been through enough, and if he didn't want to do it, she could ask Irene. Irene, while she was a spiritual jack-of-all-trades, also worked at the Dairy Queen in Del Norte and knew a surprising number of interesting people. Or she could use someone Henry might be more comfortable with. "If it doesn't work out, we can call Seth. He certainly has contacts."

"You'll accept a bodyguard?"

She wasn't going to be the character who was too stupid to live. "Yes. But I need to be home. I need the comfort and peace I find here."

"All right, but I get to interview this person."

She wasn't sure that interview would go well. "I'll go and talk to him."

Henry frowned. "You're going up the mountain, aren't you? I don't know about that. He's...different."

"There is nothing wrong with being different. He had his heart broken. I think he'll be perfect."

"He has to take a shower," Henry complained.

This new Henry was on the judgmental side. "His cabin doesn't have running water."

"Once I spent three months in a desert waiting for a bombmaker to make a dead drop. I never smelled as bad as Michael Novack."

Yes, very judgmental. And she didn't want to know about the bombmaker and the desert. Not at all. "Nevertheless, I'm going to hire him. He used to be a US marshal. Protecting people was his job."

"And now his job is growing facial hair and drinking whiskey." Henry groaned. "Fine. But I'm going to drive. There's barely a road to where he lives."

She got her purse. She hoped Michael Novack liked tofu.

* * * *

Henry parked the Jeep outside the...would he call it a cabin? At one point it probably had been, but now it was more of a shack, and there was another tiny shack outside. The man had an outhouse.

125

Michael Novack had shown up roughly a year ago when he'd been on assignment to protect Alexei Markov. He'd come to town with his partner, a woman named Jessica, who hadn't bothered to mention to her lover that she was on some bad guy's payroll. She'd died trying to kill Alexei, Holly, and Caleb, but only after drugging her partner so he couldn't stop her.

Novack had not taken the news well.

"I think it's charming." Nell always saw the sunny side of things, including the rundown shack in front of them.

Henry thought it was a menace, but she likely didn't want to hear that from him. "I think you should let me go talk to him first."

"Why?" She looked so pretty sitting next to him in her cotton skirt and shirt. Her belly had the slightest swell that he wanted to touch and cup and protect. It wasn't that pregnancy had made his wife more beautiful. She was always beautiful. It was that pregnancy had reminded him of how delicate and precious life could be, how much he treasured every moment with her.

"Because a wounded animal can be a dangerous one." He didn't want her to even get out of the Jeep. The ground wasn't close to level. It was late summer, so there could be any number of animals out and about. Then there was the man himself.

The door opened and Michael Novack proved Henry's point by walking out on the rickety porch wearing nothing but a pair of sweatpants, his big muscular chest on display, and one hand holding a rifle at his side.

Nell merely opened the door and waved the man's way. "Good afternoon, Michael. I hope you're having a lovely day."

Henry scrambled to get out of his side. He should have brought his own gun, but he hadn't wanted to upset Nell. It was the first time in days that she'd been willing to go somewhere with him, and he wasn't taking any chances.

Except this was all one big chance. He was trying to hire a bodyguard so he could go on one last mission.

Would Nell be upset if he died, or would it all be a relief?

"I'm having the same day I've had for a year," Novack admitted.

The man needed a shave. His beard was growing a beard. "We'd like to talk to you, but if this is a bad time we can come back later."

If he could put this off, maybe he should. It occurred to him that this man could be dangerous on a lot of levels. After all, his partner had kept secrets from him, too. The idea of the remarkably fit man watching over a woman as wounded as he was sounded like the plot for one of Nell's books. In this case, Henry was the bad guy, the obstacle the heroine would have to overcome in order to find proper true love.

Novack frowned. It wasn't like he'd been smiling before, but the expression took on a deeper tone. "You here to throw me out? I heard this is now some kind of nature preserve."

A few months before, a friend of theirs had needed them to help the town out by becoming the owners of a large tract of land a group of developers wanted to purchase from his company. Cole Roberts had come up with a plan that cost him, but saved the land from transforming from gorgeous forest to an outlet mall and all the stuff that came with it.

Roberts had trusted Nell to protect the land. It was a good thing, too, since Nell would have been the chief protestor of the development.

"Of course not. We would never do that," Nell assured him. She started walking toward the dilapidated cabin.

Henry moved in front of her. "Hey, let me go first. He's got this place trapped."

"Trapped?" Nell asked.

Novack sighed. "Who told you?"

"I don't need anyone to tell me. I can look around the ground and spot at least four places where you've laid out traps," Henry said. "It looks like they're alarms, but if you've got something set up that could hurt someone, then we really do need to talk. People hike out here."

"Traps?" Nell was looking around the yard. "Like for people? Or is he hunting? Because I can help him set up a garden if he needs food. Also, there are tons of edible plants out here. There's no need to kill animals."

"They're strictly alarms, Flanders," Novack replied. "I don't like being caught off guard, but I'm not trying to punish hikers or anything. I'm surprised you can see them. I wouldn't have expected a professor to know what a trap looks like."

He knew what it meant to sneak up on a paranoid target, and he knew how to set a hundred traps to protect himself. It was good to know there was one person in town who hadn't heard the stories about him.

"Oh, Henry wasn't a professor," Nell replied. "That was his cover. He was an assassin with the CIA."

Novack laughed. "That's a good one. What do you really need?"

"I was not an assassin." Sometimes her anger came out in little ways. He had to deal with her patiently, but he couldn't let her forget the truth. "I was an operative, and I managed other operatives."

"Did you assassinate people?" Nell asked in a prim tone.

He'd promised he wouldn't lie to her anymore. "Only people who deserved it. Bad people."

She snorted. "So you say."

"And it wasn't the biggest part of my job," he continued. "I mostly tried to stop terrorists from blowing things up around the world." He turned back to Novack. "I need to be out of town for a couple of weeks so I can settle some old debts. But I need someone to watch over Nell."

Novack's brow rose. "Someone wants to hurt Nell?"

Nell shrugged. "Probably. The activist's life is not for the faint hearted, but most of the people I anger are satisfied to call me bad names on the Internet. Henry, however, has many enemies, and they prefer to show their rage in person. He's killed all the ones who've come to town so far, but I prefer nonviolent methods."

They'd gone over this. "I told you, love, they are not going to listen to lectures."

She frowned his way. "You don't know. I haven't tried. I can be very persuasive."

"What kind of joke is this?" Novack asked. "Because it's funny, but I've got things to do today."

"Really?" Henry couldn't think of what the man needed to do. "Do you need to brood some more? Contemplate the dark turn your life has taken, perhaps?"

"I did have a book I was reading," Novack replied.

Nell sighed and sent Henry a look that told him snark was not appreciated before turning to the big man. "Michael, we're not pulling a prank. And I do know that there are people in the world who would like to hurt me to get to Henry. I was hoping you could stay with me while Henry's gone."

"Why would anyone want to hurt Henry? Look, I could believe that the professor here might have worked some desk job," Novack began.

Nell turned to Henry. "He's not going to believe you. You have to show him."

He was going to get killed. He could see it easily. At least then Nell might forgive him. She would probably feel sorry for him. She would bury him in the backyard and grow organic tomatoes over his dead body.

"Show me what? You going to send the professor to assassinate me?" The thought obviously amused the former marshal. "I'd love to see that happen. It might make the last year worth it."

If there was one good thing to come of all this mess, it would be proving everyone who thought he was weak wrong. They saw the sandals and the tofu and saw vulnerability. They should know he'd always been able to protect the woman he loved. He was on Novack before the marshal could move. The other man barely had a chance to gasp before Henry had taken his rifle and had him on his belly, his own gun pointed at his head.

"Hey," Novack complained.

Nell simply stepped onto the porch. "See. He's good at that. How about I make us some tea and we can talk? I do need a bodyguard. We can work out payment, and perhaps you can fix up your cabin. And the good news is I'll cook all the meals so you don't have to worry about eating well."

Novack's hands came up. "All right. I believe you. Now tell me what's going on and I'll tell you if I can help. As you can see I'm out of practice."

Henry backed off and Novack pushed himself off the porch. "I need you in practice if you're going to guard my wife. I'm not joking. If someone shows up, it'll be a serious situation. Nate's been informed and he'll check in while I'm gone. I can't promise how long it'll take."

He handed back the rifle.

Novack stared at him as though reassessing his whole opinion. "Okay. Nell's a nice lady, and it's not like I'm doing anything else. I don't like the thought of someone trying to hurt her. I'll do it. Is she serious about the cooking thing, though?"

He could prove something else, too. Everyone thought he suffered. "She's an excellent cook. Maybe you need to broaden your horizons, Novack. It'll be good for you."

Henry just hoped it wouldn't be the end for him.

* * * *

Nell stared at the closed bedroom door and wondered if Henry was sitting up on the sofa or if he'd managed to get some sleep. He would leave in the morning. She and Michael would drive him to the airport where he would board a plane for Los Angeles. He had everything he needed to be Josh Hunt's new DEA contact. In the end her plan had worked perfectly, and now she knew a whole lot about forging documents.

Not that she would do anything with it. She hadn't written in weeks, couldn't even consider working on the story she'd been developing about a young woman who falls in love with a man who isn't what he seemed.

That hit far too close to home.

He was right outside and she couldn't quite open the door between them. How would she feel if this was the last time she saw him?

She forgave everyone. Why couldn't she do the same for him?

There was a slight knock on the door, a timid sound as though the knocker was certain he wasn't welcome.

"I'm trying to sleep."

He hesitated for a moment. "I'd like to come in and talk to you."

It was stupid, and she knew she was being stubborn, but she couldn't help herself. "I've locked the door."

The knob turned easily and then he was standing in the doorway in his pajama bottoms and T-shirt that showed off his lean strength. "And I have an enormous amount of experience picking locks. This one is nothing, love."

She stared at him, wishing she didn't find him so sexy. "I thought the lock was really my will."

"I'd like to pick that apart, too. I don't want to sleep on the couch. I want to be with you."

She wanted nothing more than to wrap herself up in him and

pretend nothing had happened. "Then you should have told me the truth the first time."

"Do you honestly want me to go without letting me touch you one more time, without letting me top you? You're anxious, Nell, and I won't be here to calm you down. Michael will protect you, but he can't put his mouth on you until you cry away every bit of stress you have. He can't let you ride his dick until your eyes roll to the back of your head and it no longer matters what's going on in the outside world. Let me do that for you one more time."

Because he wasn't sure he would come back.

Every word was like a stroke to her skin, and her body didn't care a bit about his lies. Her body was already warm, and that deliciously antsy feeling had come over her. She loved it. It was the kind of thing that would be frustrating if she didn't have such complete faith that all her needs would be met.

"I don't want you to leave," she admitted.

"Then I won't." He pulled his shirt over his head and tossed it to the side. "Nell, if you ask me to scrap this whole mission, I'll do it."

She stared at him for a moment, taking in the beauty of his body. "You have to save that woman."

She didn't like to think about how ruthlessly Henry had upended Kayla Summers's life. It seemed utterly foreign to her that the man who volunteered every time he could, who'd helped her put together a food pantry and shown up every time a neighbor needed him, could have lied and manipulated the way he had.

His expression went stony as he stalked across the room. "Then that's what I'll do."

So often lately she found herself in the presence of the other Henry, as she'd come to think of him, the Henry who always looked hungry when they got ready for bed, the one who never seemed to eat his fill. Perhaps John Bishop had always been with her. He'd always been the Dom side of Henry.

He reached out and shoved aside the blanket she'd been under and let his hands snake around her ankles. He did it slowly and with great purpose. "I'll do whatever you want me to, but I get tonight. Tonight I get your submission, and tomorrow I'm your soldier to command."

"I thought you were doing this for you."

"There's no me without you. That's what I can't make you understand. Yes, I need to do this, but I would walk away from everything if you asked me to. Nothing is more important than you." He began to pull on her ankles, dragging her down the mattress.

She wanted to believe him. There was a part of her that did believe him, but a dark place had opened up inside her, a place she hadn't even known existed, and she couldn't deny it.

"You have nothing to say?" Henry looked over her, his jaw tight.

She shook her head. She didn't know what to say. She could tell him she loved him, that she would be missing half her heart when he was gone. She could say how sad she was that they hadn't been in sync for weeks.

She could tell him how hollow her life felt since she'd learned what shaky ground it had been built on.

His hands moved up her legs, squeezing lightly, and she moaned at the sensation. It had been too many days since she'd felt hands on her. Not just any hands. His strong ones. She loved how big his hands were and how she could feel the power in them when he stroked her.

"Feels good?" He moved up to her thighs, shoving her gown up as he traveled. "I can make you feel so much better." He drew her right leg up and took her foot in his hands. He squeezed and kissed the arch of her foot, making her shiver.

"Yes." It felt so good. Too good. It was precisely why she had Henry on the couch for now. She couldn't think when he was touching her. When Henry took control, all that mattered was being close to him. The world fell away and for tonight, she let it.

He would be gone in the morning, and she would have to think far too much.

He nipped at her foot, giving her the bare hint of his teeth. It sent her straight into that lovely place where she didn't have to think at all. He'd introduced her to this world and he was the tour guide, taking her down intimate paths she'd never imagined. Henry had been the one to prove to her how physical a being she was.

"I talked to Stef," Henry murmured as he started to kiss his way up her leg.

"So did I. He was at the Trading Post today." She'd gone into town to gather some supplies for the week. Michael would be here in the morning, and they would have to find a routine that worked for both of them.

This nip was sharper than the rest and made her gasp. "Sarcasm is not welcome tonight. I talked to Stef about how he and Jen played when she was pregnant."

She'd liked that bite. "Oh, I just talked to him about the state of plant-based proteins."

Another bite sent a thrill through her, and she felt the delicious drug known as arousal start to pound through her system.

"You're a little brat. You want to push me? Because like I said, I had a talk with Stef, and Caleb says everything is going well. He told me if I was careful I should be able to do whatever I want to you. I want to do a lot of things to you, but tonight I feel like you need some discipline. Give me the gown. You know damn well you're not allowed to wear clothes to bed."

She did, but she'd felt vulnerable without him next to her. She'd hated it, but she'd put on the gown. If she took off that gown, she would be accepting the fact that Henry was going to sleep in their bed tonight. She didn't even want to argue with him. She wanted one more night of feeling safe before she would have to work through her problems. She sat up and moved to the edge of the bed. Henry gave her very little space, as though he was worried she might make a run for the door. She could have told him she had no thoughts to running away. She wouldn't run away from him. They had to find a way to get through this.

She pulled the gown over her head and offered it to her husband. She wore nothing underneath, and her body reacted to the cool air of the room.

"God, you're beautiful," Henry breathed. He moved in closer, so close she could feel the brush of his cock against her belly. He stood over her, reminding her of how big he was compared to her. Her big, strong husband.

She would never tell him that watching him put Michael Novack on his belly in the blink of an eye had done something for her, wouldn't mention that sometimes the idea of John Bishop got her heart racing. All that power hidden away. It had always been there. She simply hadn't seen it.

But it had been there waiting for the right moment to come out.

His hands went up to cup her head, gently stroking her hair as he stared down at her. One hand curled around her hair and gently tipped her head back. "You don't have to say a thing to me. You stay stubborn, brat. But I will not allow you to forget me. We might be apart for a while, and you might be thinking to make that a permanent punishment for me."

She wished he understood. "It's not punishment."

His hand tugged harder, forcing her on her toes. "Oh, I'm sure you've convinced yourself it's not. Know that I will grovel. I will beg and plead. I'll do anything to get back in your good graces, with the singular exception of giving you up. You can make me sleep on the couch, but I'll find a way into our bed. Always."

It was habit to think of a million ways to explain to him how the speech he'd made was anti-everything. She should be able to tell him no and he should be able to accept it. But he wasn't threatening to force her. He was telling her he would find a way to make her want him.

She always wanted him. Yes, it was habit to argue, but instinct made her drop her head back and offer him the long line of her neck.

"That's right. Don't fight me tonight. Give me everything." He leaned over and ran his nose from the crook of her neck up to her ear. "Everything, Nell."

Again, she didn't argue, merely sighed because she couldn't fight him on this. If he did find a way to get her alone, she might never muster the will to turn him away.

"Everything." It was an easy thing to promise since he already had her everything. Her heart and soul and body and trust.

If only she'd had the same from him.

"Turn around and place your palms on the bed. You should be happy you didn't add underwear into your new nightly routine. I can understand the gown, but you're definitely not allowed to wear panties. I want easy access to all your beauty, my love."

She shoved away the deep well of sorrow that threatened to steal the moment from her. She could cry and worry later. For now, she needed this. He'd never been anything but honest with her in bed. She could see that now. Sex was where that dark part of Henry got unleashed.

Nell turned and put her hands flat on the bed. She spread her legs because she knew the drill. He would spank her and touch her and make her crazy. He would have her begging, and she would be happy to do it.

She felt his hand cup her ass and squeeze lightly.

"When I get back, we're going to talk. We can't go on like this."

He wasn't wrong. She found herself in an odd place she couldn't seem to force herself out of. She couldn't simply break things off with him. That wasn't what she wanted at all, but she also couldn't go back to the way things had been. So she stayed silent.

The first slap of his hand made her gasp. It had been months since they'd truly played, months of worry and anxiety where they hadn't connected in the way that always felt best.

He spanked her again, a bit harder this time. She'd come to crave this kind of play. Henry had made her crave it, made her crave him.

Her hands curled around the comforter as he spanked her, peppering the flesh of her ass and lighting up her skin. He was careful, but then he always was. Henry was always in control when they played.

He smacked her ass and she breathed through the pain, allowing it to morph into heat and pleasure. This was what she needed to feel complete, to bring the two sides of herself together.

She would be so lonely when he was gone.

Another smack and she could feel the tears pulse.

Henry's hand cupped her, holding the heat against her skin. "Spread your legs wider."

She whimpered because she knew what he was going to do and she wanted it. She moved her feet further apart, holding onto the end of the bed and offering her husband access to her tender flesh.

She bit her bottom lip to keep from crying out when she felt the first touch of his hand between her legs. She could feel him standing behind her, two big fingers delving into her pussy and drawing out the arousal he found there.

"You didn't seem to get the point of my discipline, sweetheart. It's supposed to be punishment."

God, she loved it when he played like this, when his voice went deep and he acted out his fantasies with her.

"It hurts, Sir," she replied, sinking into her role.

"Where does it hurt?"

That finger of his was so close to her clit and the ring she had in her hood. All he would have to do was toy with that ring and she would go off like a rocket.

But he was a cruel Dom and he knew her body well. The finger dipped inside her briefly before stroking her labia, not even coming close to her clit.

"A little higher, Sir."

This was the game. He liked to hear her cry and beg, and something about his denial made the eventual orgasm so much stronger.

He stepped back. "I think you're trying to take something that should only be mine to give, brat." This smack was hard and made her clench her teeth. "I think you need something more than a spanking. Don't move or I'll start again."

Damn him. He was going to drag it out, make her wait. He was going to remind her that he was in charge and she got nothing until he was ready to give it to her.

She heard him moving behind her. The bathroom door opened and she wondered what he was going to do to her. Anticipation was all part of the game, but so was this terrible mind fuck he loved so much. He wouldn't tell her what he was going to do. He would simply do it and she would go through the experience. She would let go of the control she felt she needed ninety-nine percent of the time.

She took a deep breath and listened to the water come on in the bathroom, felt the air on her skin, the ache in her ass.

"Have I ever told you what seeing you this way makes me feel?" Henry asked, his voice dark and deep.

She wished she could tell him not to talk, that she didn't want to listen to him say what he loved about her. It would be disrespectful to their roles in the moment. She could use her safe word and stop the scene, but she couldn't take control of it and get her way. In that he had her in a corner. She wasn't willing to stop the scene. She wanted the physical, and that meant she had to take the words he would say since they hadn't exactly laid this out.

She loved his words. One of the reasons he worked for her as a Dom was the fact that he loved to talk while they played, loved to tell her she was beautiful and how much she moved him. Those words connected them every bit as much as the sex did.

"It makes me feel like I'm worthy," he admitted, moving in behind her again. "You are such an independent woman, and the fact that you trust me enough to give this part of our lives into my hands makes me feel more powerful than any mission."

She wasn't going to listen. The words could be said, but that didn't mean she had to let them sink into her soul the way she normally did.

"I can see you thinking, my love. You think if I lied about one thing, why couldn't I lie about this? If the premise of the love story is a lie, doesn't the whole thing fall apart?"

She felt a hand on her backside, pulling her cheeks apart, and she whimpered. He was going there? Of course he was. He'd told her he wanted everything, and he was going to take it.

Because he knew she wouldn't be able to deny him. He'd branded her. She understood that now. The nipple rings and VCH enhanced their play, but they also were things only Henry could see, only Henry would ever get to touch. They were reminders that her body belonged to him because she'd given it to him.

Henry didn't even have a tattoo.

That didn't seem fair.

She felt the plug against her and gritted her teeth. She loved this part, and it only proved how perverted she was. Or maybe it proved how deeply intimacy affected her. Maybe the sex reflected the relationship. What she loved about anal was that frisson that went up her spine telling her this wasn't what should happen, that this was slightly wrong. Except it wasn't. It was beautiful and required adjustment and work to make it glorious. It was something that got better over time.

"What you don't understand is that sometimes the lie is only there to protect the most precious truth." He'd lubed up that plug. She could feel it. This was something they'd done enough that she was trained to take a plug, had muscle memory of the pleasure this would bring her. He pressed the plug to her and gently rotated it.

She let a deep breath out and flattened her back, allowing Henry full access to her.

"The truth is I love our life so much, I would have done anything to protect it," he said. "Hate me for being a ruthless bastard. Hate me for doing whatever it took to keep you. But never think that my love is a lie. It was the only thing real in my life back then. It's the only thing that matters now."

She pushed back against the plug, needing the sensation. He could say whatever he liked in this place but she still needed time, and she would get it. For however long he was gone, she would take it and think.

"Henry, please." It wasn't a plea for him to move faster or to stop the physical act. It was begging him to not force her to do something she didn't want to do.

He ruthlessly moved that plug in and out, fucking her ass with it. "You please me on every level. And I'll stop. It's hard. There's nothing I like to talk about more than you. Ask anyone. I annoy them. But for now, I'll give you the only thing you'll let me give you."

The plug slid in, opening her and making her deliciously vulnerable. She let the sensation wash over her. She'd missed this so much. For weeks she'd needed to feel like a woman and not merely an expectant mother. "Please fuck me, Henry."

"You want me to fuck your little asshole? Is that what you want? I'm going to need you to be specific because it's been a while since I've felt that tight hole around my dick."

Those were better words. Sex words. She could handle those words. "I want you to fuck my ass, Henry. I want to feel you there. You seem to think I didn't miss it, but I did. I missed that big cock of yours. I missed it in my pussy and in my ass and in my mouth."

She'd missed his hands on her, moving slowly, caressing up and down her back in the early hours of the morning and late at night. She'd missed the comfort of his body next to hers.

And she'd definitely missed being his sub, letting go in the way she only could when he was close to her.

He pulled the plug and she heard him moving behind her. He would have brought out everything he needed because Henry was like a Boy Scout when it came to sex. Always prepared.

Or a ruthless operative. Had he tortured with the efficiency of a Dom, never having to stop to do anything so bland as washing up? He would have prepared for that. He wouldn't have to go back into the bathroom to ensure he could touch her anywhere he needed to. He would have everything he needed to ensure her safety and pleasure.

Then she felt the hard ridge of his erection against the seam of her ass as his hands gripped her hips and moved her into position.

"You'll take this from me."

She'd never taken it from anyone *but* him. He'd been her only lover. When she'd met him, she'd discovered how different he was from the other men she'd known. She'd realized how dangerous he would be, and she'd still taken the chance because no one had ever moved her the way Henry could.

"Yes. I'll take this." Maybe this was where they should start connecting. Sex had always been good. She might not be able to open her heart again, but he owned her body.

His dick started to breach her, discomfort quickly giving way to a familiar heat. She let her head drop forward, panting as he worked his way into her ass. So big. He felt huge in her ass, and even as she was stretched tight, she found herself pressing back, trying to take more of him.

One hand came around and she gasped as he touched her VCH, the pad of his finger running over it and making it press against her clitoris.

It was only a matter of time then. Between the cock fucking her ass and the way he was pressing down on her clit, she couldn't last long. She wanted it to take forever, to be stuck in this place where the pleasure built and built, but he was too good, knew her body far too well.

Her eyes rolled back as the wave of her orgasm hit her, stronger than she'd felt it before. It seemed to go on and on until Henry stiffened behind her and she felt heat flood her as he came.

He kissed the back of her neck before pulling away from her. She was about to tell him thank you and goodnight as politely as she could. That was the moment he maneuvered her into his arms, hauling her against his chest.

"Henry, what are you doing?"

He moved toward the bathroom. "I've got one night. I'm going to take care of you. I'm going to clean you up and then I'm going to eat your pussy until you can't order me out of our bed."

"You can stay." If she was honest with herself, she didn't want him to go back to the couch. "I'm fixing up the guest room while you're gone. Then you won't have to sleep on the couch."

"Then I'll eat your pussy every fucking night," he vowed. "I told you I'm not giving up. God, I'm going to miss you."

She would miss him, too, but the words stuck in her throat.

She would miss him.

She hoped she wouldn't miss him forever.

Fall

Chapter Seven

Three weeks. It had been three weeks since Henry had left, and she wasn't sure if she missed him or not.

Well, she was sure she missed her husband, but she didn't miss the problems they had. Life had settled into a comfortable routine, and there were even days when she managed to forget that he'd lied to her.

When she really thought about it, what she liked was the numbness she'd found, and she knew that was a problem. She just couldn't seem to find her way out of it. While Henry was gone, she didn't have to feel, didn't have to think.

Twenty-one days without him. Did she honestly think she could handle a lifetime of this?

The first week had been pretty easy. She'd spent her time changing the craft room into a guest room. Michael had driven her around in his big truck, picking up a mattress and bedding that Michael would use, and then Henry.

If she could hold out.

"I've checked the yard. If you want to sit outside for a while, it's safe enough," a low voice rumbled.

This was her life now. She had to make sure no evil was lurking before she did something as simple as sitting on her back porch watching the river go by.

Michael Novack took his job far too seriously. He shadowed her everywhere she went. He'd even stopped her from going to the ladies' room at Stella's until he was sure it was secure. She foresaw problems as she got bigger.

Right now her baby was only the size of an apple, but from what she'd read that baby would soon use her bladder as a trampoline, and then Michael was going to be in trouble because she wouldn't care that an assassin could be waiting for her. She would use that bathroom.

"Thank you, Michael. Would you like a cup of tea?" She poured herself a cup of ginger tea. For some reason she found comfort in drinking something before bedtime. It used to be wine. She and Henry would sit together side by side and enjoy a glass of wine as they went over the day's events.

What had his day been like? What was he doing even as she made tea and prepared for bed? Was he getting back into his former lifestyle? Was he surrounded by beautiful women, his heart pounding with excitement?

"I think I'll pass on the tea." Michael had shaved weeks ago, but his beard was already growing back in. They made an odd pair. Michael was a mass of muscle in jeans, boots, and a leather jacket most of the time, while she was most comfortable in her airy skirts and loose blouses and Birkenstocks. The weather was already starting to turn, the chill becoming clear in the air. "But dinner was actually pretty good. I didn't know I liked eggplant."

Most people didn't. It was a highly underused vegetable, in her opinion. She took her tea and started for the back door. "It's Henry's favorite. I'm glad you enjoyed it. I'm making pasta and veggies tomorrow night."

He followed her out, his footsteps resounding through the cabin. "I look forward to it. It's nice to have something homemade. I'm afraid I've been living off beans and canned chili for a while. Did Henry reach out to you today? I haven't heard from him in a couple of days."

"I'm sure he's fine." All he would tell her was his original plan hadn't worked out, and he needed to go down to Mexico. Talking to her husband was frustrating these days. She wanted to know what was going on, and he would simply tell her he couldn't talk about it. It had been her plan. She'd helped him, but now he was shutting her out. "I wonder if he's going to come home at all."

"Because of the dudes who showed up last week?" Michael eased himself into the Adirondack chair Henry always used.

It had been two men in black suits. They'd looked utterly out of place standing on her porch asking if they could talk to…Henry Flanders. The man who'd asked had to look down at his notes to remember Henry's name. His fake name. She was sure they knew John Bishop. But she hadn't pointed that out. She'd done exactly as instructed. She'd told them Henry was hiking in the woods, thinking about his life. Actually she'd told them he was on walkabout until he figured his ass out.

It was the kind of thing Rachel would have said. It had the men walking away quickly.

"I told him they'd come looking for him and that they were obviously federal officials of some kind." She sat back, sipping her tea thoughtfully. "I wonder if he's decided to hide somewhere else now that we know for sure the Agency is aware of where he is."

Michael was quiet for a moment. "I don't think so."

"He didn't send me a note today. He always sends me something. In email or a text, although I have to remember that his number changes all the time. He's using burners."

Michael chuckled. "I'm always surprised when you know so much about the spy stuff."

"I read a lot." She did, though much of her knowledge of the "spy stuff" had come from Henry. She'd always thought he'd done meticulous research, had used his training as an academic to answer her questions and make her work easier. Now she wondered what he actually did with his time since he knew probably everything she asked and didn't need to spend hours looking up the right caliber of a weapon or how to defuse a bomb. He'd probably defused a hundred.

"I think he loves you. I don't think you'll get rid of him so easily. You need to be less insecure."

She sat up and turned to stare at him because that had been rude.

Michael frowned. "You have the judgmental thing down, Nell. I'm sorry. I used to be better at this. Or maybe I just thought I was. You're feeling insecure, right? You're mentally going over every reason a man like Henry would have to marry a woman like you?"

She couldn't deny it. "We were an odd match in the beginning. It's occurred to me that I would be good cover. Who would think the great spy master would end up with a woman who protests pretty much everything he used to do? So, yes, I look back and wonder."

"You worry he couldn't possibly have loved you if he could keep such a big secret from you."

Nell sat back and realized this wasn't merely about her. Somehow it was far easier to talk when she understood Michael needed this, too. "He's a handsome man. I'm fairly ordinary."

Michael's head turned, a single brow rising over his eyes. "You're a lovely woman."

She was also a realistic one. "I'm not terrible to look at, but I'm not Laura. I'm not a gorgeous bombshell of a woman. I don't mean to reduce any person to their looks. That's wrong, but it's also foolish to ignore that attractiveness plays a part in relationships. I seriously doubt Henry had dated someone like me before."

"He probably didn't date at all. I would assume most of his relationships were transactional. It's pretty common when you're undercover."

"Have you worked undercover?"

"No," Michael replied. "I didn't do those kinds of jobs. Everything was upfront. At least it was supposed to be. But I guess I can understand that you question everything. I wonder why she picked me."

Jessica. His fiancée. Her heart ached for him. "Yes, I can understand that. Would it be horribly hypocritical of me to say she likely picked you because she loved you?"

That actually got his lips to quirk up. "Seriously?"

She was well aware of how hypocritical she sounded. But all relationships were different.

"I'm a natural optimist. It doesn't mean that I can't have moments of doubt when it comes to myself." Moments? It had been weeks and weeks. Weeks spent reexamining everything she'd done, every minute of their relationship. "Do you still love her?"

"I guess that's the hardest part. I don't know that I ever knew her. If I didn't know her, how could I love her?" He sighed. "And that's where you are, too. The difference is Henry is alive and he's out there. You have the chance to know him if you want to. Jessie…well even if she'd lived, I would have been forced to hunt her down and arrest her. That's the hard part. I thought we were living one life, but what she did was counter to everything I thought we believed in. Is that what you're worried about? You think Henry will get back into his old ways now?"

It was a genuine fear. She'd seen him focused on prepping for the mission he was on. She knew there had been a part of him that missed his old line of work. He'd seemed more animated than he had in weeks. He'd been on the phone with Seth quite often, and he tended to go quiet when she walked in a room. She'd read some of the notes he'd left on his desk. Notes with names like Ian Taggart and Tennessee Smith. Ezra Fain and Levi Green.

She wanted to ask which ones were the men he'd worked with, the ones he'd called friends. But she'd hesitated because when she asked, he always told her not to worry and shut the conversation down.

How hard had it been for him to sit at craft fairs and dole out homemade apple cider? He'd spent weeks making dreamcatchers with her. They'd sold them at the annual spiritual reawakening festival. Had he sat there thinking it was penance for leaving his job behind? Or had it made him realize he'd made a mistake and should get back to it?

Did she have any right to ask him to give it all up?

"I worry those men who came out here a few days ago will want to arrest Henry. But I'm equally worried that they came here to ask him to come back."

"That's a definite possibility if he's as good as I heard he was," Michael replied. "But I don't think he'll go. I think he's made his choice. Like Jessie made hers."

Nell hated the hollowness in his voice. "She was desperate. She needed money."

"There are other ways, Nell. So many other ways. No. She tricked me. She used me." He turned back to the river. "And that's how we're different. As far as I can tell Henry's only real crime is not talking about his past."

"And killing a whole bunch of people." How quickly everyone forgot. "And not telling me he killed a bunch of people. I think if he's going to go around murdering people he should at least check in with his wife."

"Fair," Michael agreed. "You're right about that. No secrets.

That's the only way to maintain a relationship. Everything has to be aboveboard."

"So you're thinking about a relationship?" It would be so much nicer to talk about Michael's potential future than to sit here and worry that Henry wasn't coming home at all.

He hesitated. "No. No, I'm not...I don't know."

"Is it Lucy?" She'd seen the way his eyes always followed the petite brunette. They'd had dinner at Trio a few days before, and Michael had been on his best behavior. He was often gruff, but he'd been quiet and kind to Lucy.

He frowned her way. "I am not giving you grist for the gossip mill. I know how small towns run."

"I am not a gossip. Mostly," she amended. "If you need to talk and you don't want anyone to know, I am a locked vault."

She'd been the keeper of many a secret.

"I kind of believe you. You're an odd duck, Nell Flanders."

"Hah, and there's another one of Henry's crimes. He could have picked any name. Literally any name in the vast sea of names and he picks one that makes me sound like I'm eight hundred years old. I'm not joking. I tell people online my name is Nell Flanders and they expect to meet their grandma." She'd thought about it a lot. She'd started taking an anger inventory, and that one had shown up after the guns in the shop but before lying about how he knew where to plant a bomb in a fictional building so it exploded properly. "He could have picked something noble sounding. Like Windsor."

"Then I would think you were an old British person," Michael shot back.

"How about something pretty like DuVernay? He could have been Henry DuVernay."

Michael's head shook. "Old French person. Let's face facts—the last name is not the only problem here. Nell is an old-lady name."

"Rude. It's a family name, according to my mother." Of course her mother had told her the family member she'd been named after had been a Fae princess, so there was that. "It's only old because people stopped using it. One day all old ladies will be named Britney or Ashley. I'm only saying, he could have picked a better name. And you can't hole yourself up on the mountain forever."

"I don't see why not."

"Because at some point in time you're going to get used to regular showers again." She'd noticed he'd taken one every day since he'd gotten here, and he seemed to luxuriate in them. She hadn't even complained about his water usage.

"Yeah, I do not miss my facilities. Or rather lack of facilities." He was quiet for a moment. "I think it's better I stay up on the mountain. There's a lot of temptation in town. Well, only one, really, and she's too young for me."

Lucy worked at Trio, but Nell had known her for years. Her family lived outside of town, and there had always been trouble around her father. The Carsons were a large family, and Nell had taken food and clothes to them more than once. Lucy had gotten out, but she still worried about her siblings. "She's an adult. She's twenty-six years old. She's not exactly a baby. How old are you?"

"Thirty-five."

"That's not bad at all. Henry's ten years older than me." She'd been so young and naïve when she'd met him. She'd thought she could change him. Had it all been an act or had she actually transformed the man?

"I'm not talking about numerical age. I'm talking about experience."

That had her spine straightening. "You want a more experienced woman? That seems rude. You know a woman is more than the sum of her experience in bed."

"Hey, don't protest me," Michael complained. "I wasn't talking about sexual experience. I was talking about getting the shit kicked out of you and being damaged. Lucy is sweet. She doesn't deserve to have to deal with a moody bastard who isn't sure he can ever trust a woman again. I don't know what I can offer her."

"It's not the Dark Ages," Nell pointed out. "Women don't tend to go into a marriage with the thought that all they'll bring into the relationship is childbirth and housekeeping. Maybe she can offer you something. Like indoor plumbing."

Michael ignored her completely. "Then there's the kid who's always around her. The walking venereal disease. He actually came out to my place and tried to warn me off her. Said she's his. You want to protest someone, protest that asshole. Acted like he owned her."

"Are you talking about Tyler Davis?" He was from Creede. He'd grown up with Lucy and River, and he often could be found around the women. He worked as an EMT and a nature guide with River's company.

"Yeah. He marched right up to my place and told me to stay away. Like I was going to do something. I just think she's nice." He settled back.

That was such a lie, but she wasn't going to call him on it. It wasn't like she hadn't taken to lying to herself.

She was worried about Henry, and not merely that he was going to get the itch to work with the CIA again.

She was worried that he might die and she would never know, that someone in the shadowy agency would decide she didn't need to know what happened to her husband. She would wonder where he was for the rest of her life.

"Nell? Are you all right?"

Michael's question brought her out of her dark thoughts.

She nodded. "I'm fine."

He sighed. "Even I know *fine* doesn't mean fine. He'll call. He's probably having dinner or something. He'll call before he goes to bed. It's going to be okay."

She sat back and prayed that he was right.

* * * *

Meanwhile in Mexico

The moonlight illuminated the field of bodies he'd left behind.

He was so not okay.

His wife would want to know how the mission went, and he would have to tell her that he'd fucked up the plan where he simply told the actor about his friend and then stepped away.

Josh Hunt hadn't taken the bait. He'd gone through with the mission, and it had all gone to hell.

He'd taken care of it, and everyone who should have lived had, and most of the bad people died, but the agency definitely knew he was alive now since he'd taken some shots at the one who'd gotten away.

"Yes, Ezra's at the hospital and Shane called Tag. He's going to want to move fast, so be ready. Tag and Ten will be here in the morning."

Henry moved back into the bushes as Kayla Summers walked out of the big house that he'd managed to turn into a morgue. He hadn't talked to her much after he'd burst through the window and saved the day. He'd snuck off and taken some data he'd needed. He would go through it all later, but he couldn't risk Kay taking it in.

She had a phone to her ear. Josh Hunt walked behind her.

That man was going to have miles of anxiety to use for his next movie role. He'd nearly died, but he'd been solid in a fight.

Kay looked good. She was as deadly as ever, but despite the horrors of the night, there was a joy about her. Likely because she was alive and in love. She glowed with love for that man and he for her. She had her happily ever after.

It might have cost him his.

"Yeah, we'll be back at the set by morning. See you soon." Kayla hung up the phone. "I made sure all the security camera footage was erased, but we need to move out. I don't want us to get caught here. If anyone asks, we came to the party but you had to get back to the set for an early call."

"Hey, baby, don't worry about it. I know how to sell a scene," Hunt said. "I wish Bishop hadn't taken off. I'd liked to have talked to him, offered him a ride out."

"Yes, me, too. I had a couple of questions for him, but I assure you he hasn't taken off yet." She dropped Hunt's hand and put her hands on her hips. "John, I know you're still here somewhere. If I had time, I would show you how good I've gotten at finding people. We will have this conversation at some point."

He felt his lips quirk up. She remembered his moves. He stayed silent because they couldn't talk here, and he wasn't ready yet.

Like Nell wasn't ready.

"I want to meet your wife," she yelled.

Nell would be fascinated by Kay. Nell would want to be her friend, and she would listen to all of Kay's crazy stories.

God, he missed his wife. He missed his life, but deep down he'd missed this too. Not the killing, but the puzzle of it all. That was what he missed. He'd gotten the data he needed. With the Jalisco cartel in ruins, he'd likely bought himself more time with at least one of the groups of people who wanted him dead.

"And thank you, John." Kay took her boyfriend's hand again and they walked away.

He took a deep breath and started to make his way to the car he'd hidden. He needed to get back to Mexico City before dawn. The police would view this entire clusterfuck as cartel related, and no one would think to look for Henry Flanders.

It was time to go home. But first, he had some old friends to see. They were still in trouble, and he might have something to give them.

Maybe a big group of mind-erased men would soften Nell up.

He pulled his cell and realized how late it was. He didn't want to wake her. He sighed and started the long march back home.

He hoped he was welcome.

Chapter Eight

"Hey, you want anything?" Michael loomed over her, the lights illuminating his big body. The picnic pavilion at the park was decorated with pretty streamers and twinkle lights. "I think someone brought those rice things. You know, they're like rice, but they're not rice."

She glanced over to the big buffet tables that dominated one side of the pavilion. The tables were loaded with pots and pans of delicious-smelling food that didn't seem to move her at all. Some of her friends were standing behind the buffet, reloading when needed. Stella had brought a plethora of pies, and she and her husband Sebastian were doling out pieces.

It was Bliss at its best. She was surrounded by friends and feeling incredibly lonely.

"Quinoa. It's Teeny's quinoa salad. But because she's married to Marie, she puts a protein in it, and not black beans or tofu. Nope. That pretty salad hides a bunch of chicken," she replied. It was the reality of vegan life. Most of the time she looked down at a perfectly good salad and it had a big hunk of meat in it. Or mayonnaise. "It's okay. I'll get some of Cassidy's beet and carrot salad in a bit."

She was sitting at one of the tables toward the back, kind of sticking to the shadows because she didn't want to answer the inevitable questions.

When's Henry coming home?

Where did he go?

Or the worst—*how are you doing?*

She was doing shitty, and that wasn't a word she was used to using.

"There's not a lot of protein in a beet and carrot salad." Michael sat down across from her. "Caleb wants to make sure you're getting enough protein. You've seemed tired lately."

She *was* tired. Tired of avoiding everything. Tired of hiding from the world. Tired of not feeling like herself. "I'm fine. My blood work came back and he said everything is great."

It had been the second appointment Henry had missed, though she couldn't blame him.

Except that she'd read the reports of the Jalisco Cartel being brought down. The reports were that rival cartel members had taken down the shadowy head of the system, but she knew the truth. Most of the dead people hadn't been killed with bullets. They'd had their necks broken.

Her husband had put in some work that night.

That night had been three days ago, and he still wasn't home. He'd waved her off by saying he had some loose ends to tie up. He'd explained that he'd gotten back in contact with some old friends and needed time with them.

It was everything she'd worried about.

"Maybe we should go home and I can reheat some soup for you or something." Michael had become as much babysitter as he was bodyguard. In the absence of a violent threat Michael had taken to combatting the dangers of low protein and potential high blood pressure. And the possibility that her walk along the river could lead to falling into the river and dying.

He was a sweet man, but he was also a lot. She was fairly certain that either Henry or Caleb had told him to watch her carefully, and he'd become a large and intimidating mother hen. Or hearing the baby's heartbeat had a profound effect on him.

"I don't want to leave."

Michael sighed. "You want to be here but you're not really here. You know that, right? Why don't we go sit with your friends?"

Because then she would be reminded that she was the single one now. Because she would watch Laura with Cam and Rafe, and Holly with Alexei and Caleb, and she would feel her isolation. She would have to smile when she didn't want to. So why hadn't she stayed home? She'd told Michael she had to come because she had the recipe for the apple cider they served every year. She could have given it to Teeny. Or Callie. Or anyone.

"I just felt like getting out of the house." It was where she was now. She didn't truly want to be home because it reminded her of Henry. And she couldn't quite make herself be a part of the world around her. She was stuck in this weird place she didn't understand and couldn't seem to break out of.

Michael sat back. "Okay. We'll go with that." He glanced around the picnic grounds. There was a nice-sized stage where a local band was playing cover tunes. Most of the citizens had brought out picnic blankets and were sitting on the big lawn listening to the music and enjoying the food and drinks. "What is this festival about? I mean, fall I get, but didn't the Big Game Dinner welcome fall?"

He did not understand how much Bliss enjoyed a party.

"No. The Big Game Dinner is a way to say good-bye to summer. Also to prove we're all carnivores at heart. It would be so much more meaningful if we let all the animals go free." She attended the Big Game Dinner, though under protest. And it wasn't like they could let the animals go free since they were all dead. "The Fall Festival is to say hello to fall. Though mostly it's kind of a big get-together for Bliss in between our tourist seasons. Winter Fest is all about big tourism and pumping money into the town. I like this one better. Though this year I swear we're going to…"

"Going to what?"

"I was about to say that this year Henry and I will win the snowman-making contest. Jen and Stef do this super artsy thing, but we practiced all through February," she replied.

They'd built a snow castle over the course of a week, warming each other up between sessions. She'd written and he'd researched and they'd made love and built snow castles. And vowed to avenge themselves from the last Winter Festival Great Snowman Competition.

"You're very competitive for a granola girl," Michael said with a chuckle. "Or is that Henry?"

Henry didn't seem competitive at all. He was absolutely the best poker player in town and yet she'd watched him scrub hands he could have won. He'd said it was because he'd known whoever he was playing against needed the money or needed a win.

Or had he done that so no one would question him?

"I think that's me." Henry wanted to go under the radar, for obvious reasons. "I've always been a little type A when it comes to some things. Not with sports. With academic things, though, and certain artistic pursuits."

"I can see you being incredibly studious," Michael agreed. "You were probably in your class's top ten."

She sighed, the wistful memory overtaking her. "I would have been my class valedictorian."

"Would have been?"

"We moved a lot." When her mom got nervous, they moved. Sometimes it was because she claimed she saw someone she knew from the old country. By old country she'd meant the faery world she'd come from. Sometimes it was because people looked at her funny and she worried the authorities would show up again and take her daughter. "At the high school I graduated from you had to be at the school for at least three semesters in order to qualify. I'd only been there two, so they didn't rank me."

"That doesn't seem fair."

She shrugged. She'd agreed. "I protested them. They didn't care. I was in a state that's not a great place for protests. Colorado is better. Not that most people listen, but there are fewer guns pointed your way."

"Cool. I'll remember that for the future. We'll keep the protesting schedule to Colorado for the time being. I consider any protest where you get completely ignored to be a successful one." Michael obviously wasn't terribly interested in social justice. He'd tried to talk her out of her protest of a neighboring school board who were trying to ban several important children's books from not only the school's library, but also the town library. He hadn't seen the point, but she'd managed to gather together a group of parents who were even louder than the ones who thought books about magical creatures would send their

155

children into satanic worship.

She'd only been ignored at that protest because she'd handed it over to the parents with more to lose. That was how most of her activism went. People didn't see the problem coming at them because they weren't paying attention or didn't truly understand what was going to happen. Nell pointed it out. The people who were affected took over, and Nell helped them fight.

Henry did, too. Henry could spot a problem a mile away. He was the one who'd found the problem with a township's water and connected it to a nearby company's use of chemicals and utter disregard for EPA regulations. He was so sexy when he was connecting dots.

"Hey, Miss Nell, how are you doing today?" Mel Hughes walked up wearing his normal uniform of jeans, a T-shirt, and a trucker hat lined with tinfoil, his girlfriend at his side.

Cassidy Meyer had her steel gray hair in a long braid, one hand in Mel's and the other holding a big insulated tote.

Nell could remember when the tin foil routinely stuck out of the hat. Since Mel had started dating Cassidy Meyer, she'd taken over the management of his hat shields, and most of the time no one would know Mel was protecting his brain from alien death rays.

"We missed you earlier." Cassidy smiled so much more these days. Years ago Nell had Cassidy's tiny cabin on what she liked to call her "rounds." She'd identified people who lived alone and visited them. Sometimes only once because they truly wanted to be alone. But Cassidy had been isolated, and she'd welcomed Nell.

Nell had mentioned that Mel knew a lot about aliens, too, and now Cassidy was a part of the community.

Couples made each other better. The ones that truly worked did. They shored up the deficiencies in the other. Holly smoothed over Caleb's rough edges and helped him navigate social functions. She helped Alexei with his college work. Both men lifted up her confidence and supported her in everything she wanted to do. Stef Talbot gave his wife all the help she needed, and in return she'd softened the hard lines of his life and helped him relax.

Henry had given her a place where the world had been safer than it had been before. He'd given her companionship and unquestioning support. He'd thought like she did.

Except that had been a lie.

"I'm great," she replied with a smile she didn't feel at all.

Mel's expression dimmed. "I can hardly believe that. Henry's not here. Hell, I haven't seen you without Henry hovering somewhere close for six years or so. You said he was off on some retreat?"

This was why she should have followed her first instinct and stayed home. "He had some business to deal with. I'm sure he'll be home soon."

Ah, that was why she hadn't stayed in the cabin this evening. She'd sat there for two nights since he'd called to tell her he needed a few more days. She couldn't simply sit there and wait for him to decide to come home.

She couldn't be that faithful woman waiting for her man with a good meal on the table and a baby in her belly.

"It's weird that he would leave like that." Mel sat down across from her and leaned in. "Are we sure he left of his own accord, if you know what I mean?"

She softened. Of course Mel would be worried. She reached out and covered her hand with his. "It wasn't aliens. Michael and I put him on a plane. He's been in touch. He's okay. He's just…busy."

"I heard that some of the men in black came to visit you." Cassidy kept her voice low and shifted her gaze around as though those same men would show up at any moment.

Nell shook her head. She needed to make them comfortable. "No, they were definitely from the government, but they weren't looking for aliens. They were looking for Henry, who, might I remind you, has taken the beet many times."

Cassidy sat back. "Yes, he has. He's a good one, your man. Even if he was with the CIA fellas."

Nell nodded. "He faked his death to get away from them. Personally, I think he should have put in a two-week notice, but everyone tells me I'm naïve."

"Hey, Nell, Mel, and Cassidy," a feminine voice called out. Lucy Carson was walking by the pavilion, a big box in her hand. It was almost too big for her to carry. Yet she stopped and her voice went breathless. "Hi, Michael. How are you this evening?"

"Uh, good. Fine. Uhm, I'm working." The words came out of his mouth with all the grace of a truly horrendous pratfall.

Lucy's brows rose, and even in the low light she could see the young woman flush. "Oh, of course. I'm working, too. Bringing some supplies from Trio. Well, y'all have a good night."

Nell groaned as Lucy walked away. Cautiously. Like any minute that big box was going to drag her down. "Michael, help her. Mel has staved off whole alien invasions. He can take care of me."

"And I stabbed my ex-husband," Cassidy added with a smile. "I have a knife on me right now."

Michael practically leapt to his feet. "I know that shouldn't make me feel better. I've been here too long. Please don't let anyone murder her." He ran off after the dark-haired woman. "Hey, Lucy. Let me help you."

"I would never let anyone murder Miss Nell." Mel was shaking his head. "Henry would have my hide. Besides, I took an oath to serve the human race and protect them all. Now you need to know that Henry couldn't have simply walked away from those CIA fellas."

She knew she shouldn't argue, but she kind of wanted to. "Plenty of people retire from the CIA. They also leave and go to other jobs. They're not immediately murdered because they took a job interview somewhere else."

"Not at Henry's level they don't," Mel replied. "I did a stint in the Marines and I worked with the Agency from time to time. I got brought in when they couldn't explain something. Then I would get the alien and either negotiate for it to leave or sadly, put it down."

"It's not sad when you put down a reptilian." Cassidy opened her bag and started pulling out her portable food containers. "I mean I'm sure it's emotionally awful for the reptilian, but they emit this gas on death, and it's a lot like nitrous oxide. There you are having won the fight of your life and you can't stop laughing."

"The point is if what Henry says is true and he was in charge of dangerous operations, then they might not let him go so easy," Mel continued. "If he knew too much about something that could get some politician in trouble, they might not let him go at all."

The thought sent a shiver up her spine.

"Here, honey. I brought you some dinner. I heard what they were putting out on the buffet and worried about you." Cassidy pushed a bento box her way. It came complete with a reusable spork. "I saw that they assigned the salads to Teeny and Gemma and knew you might need something to eat. It's some of my beet and carrot salad, some quinoa and black bean bites, and a vegan brownie made with figs. I was real careful. There's nothing with a face in this."

"That brownie is surprisingly good," Mel said.

"And it's got a lot of fiber. Once you've been probed, you need fiber," Cassidy continued. "Now it's my first time making it, so…honey, I didn't mean to make you cry."

Cassidy reminded her so much of her mom. She was a woman who viewed reality differently than the people around her and had been so often ostracized. They called her crazy and thought to put her away, but she was kind and good and didn't hurt anyone except her abusive ex. And apparently reptilians. "It's nice of you. I was going to ask if you brought the carrot and beet salad. It's one of my favorites."

Cassidy beamed her way. "Well, I'm so happy you like it. You eat up, sweetie. You barely even look pregnant."

The tears were worse now. "I know. I'm only a couple of weeks behind Rachel, and she yelled at me for being too skinny."

She knew Rachel hadn't meant it like that. Rachel was on baby number two and had shown quickly. She was not handling it well. Rachel kind of snarled at everyone. Nell knew Rachel viewed it as a compliment, but to Nell's ears it was one more thing she wasn't doing right. One more thing she couldn't control.

Cassidy moved to her side of the table. "Honey, you're perfect. Rachel is mean when she's pregnant. I blame the Harper sperm. See, everyone thinks it's just Max who's got a bit of the devil in him, but they never got pulled over by Rye Harper when fleeing a potential alien abduction. That man can be every bit as unreasonable as his brother."

Nell pulled a handkerchief out of her bag. She washed them a lot lately. "Thank you. Most people don't go to this kind of trouble for me."

Cassidy gave her a hug. "Well, then most people don't notice all the things you do for them. It's not trouble at all. It's just being neighborly. Now, Melvin, I need to take the rest of this to the buffet. You watch after our sweet girl."

Yep, she needed to get control or she was going to lose it. She forced herself to tamp the emotions down, though the tears didn't quite stop. "Thank you."

Cassidy gave Mel a wink and took off with the rest of her food.

Nell tried one of the quinoa bites. It tasted like love. "She's so nice."

"Yes, she is," Mel agreed. "Lots of nice folk around here. Don't take it poorly that they can't get the vegan thing down."

She shook her head. "I don't expect anyone to cook for me. It's just my mom did, and this reminded me."

"Your momma was a real sweetheart. Had some strange ideas about faeries though. See, a lot of folk mistake aliens for faeries," Mel began and then stopped. "That wasn't what I wanted to talk to you about."

She sniffled. "You wanted to talk to me?"

"Yeah. Cassidy and I have been talking about you and Henry. It's not right that he left you. Your momma isn't around, and you didn't have a daddy."

Technically speaking she had, but she understood what he was saying. She should take a stand against the patriarchy and tell him that a woman could take care of herself. But everyone needed a family. Man. Woman. She bet aliens and faeries needed families, too. "Thank you, but he didn't leave me willingly. I told him to go. I kind of forced him to go."

Mel frowned at that. "Huh. I didn't think about that possibility. Well, then maybe I should have a talk with you. Henry doesn't have a daddy either."

"He lied to me."

"You are a young lady of strong principles." Mel continued on like he'd had both speeches prepared. "I understand that, but sometimes in a relationship your partner screws up, and you have to decide what's more important."

"It's not that simple. I know everyone thinks I should forgive him and move on."

"I didn't say that," Mel corrected. "From what I hear it wasn't like Henry told you. He tried to keep on hiding it."

"He claims he was going to tell me, but then I walked in when I shouldn't have. I think I would still have felt betrayed even if he'd confessed to me."

"And how would you have felt if he'd told you right after you met?"

She'd thought a lot about what would have happened if he'd been honest all those years ago. "I don't know. I hope I would have given him a chance."

"I've known you a real long time." When Mel wanted, he had the dad stare down.

She sighed. "Fine. I probably would have protested him. I probably would have used his job like a wall to protect me. I don't know. I was very attracted to him. I might have tried to sway him to my side."

"But you did," Mel began. "Sway him to your side. I've known about Henry for a long time, too. I figured it out pretty quick. I know I always talked about how I would protect the two of you if the invasion came, but the truth is, I would have had Henry watch my back."

A little hurt went through her. "You knew but didn't tell me?"

"In the early days I only suspected. He knew a whole lot about firearms, and he moved way too well for a professor," Mel explained. "By the time Nate and Zane and Rafe and Cam showed up, Henry was better at hiding that side of himself. Laura was too wounded to truly look at him. And Rye was a small-town sheriff. He didn't know what a true predator looked like. I watched him real carefully in the beginning, but there was only one thing I knew besides the fact that he'd either been military or Agency."

"What was that?"

"I knew that he loved you. That whatever had been in his heart that pushed him into that darkness had been replaced with love for you."

She wanted to believe him. "But he's very good at acting."

"That's what I'm telling you. He's not as good as he thinks he is," Mel replied. "Not if you know what to look for. Has he done anything besides this to make you think he doesn't love you?"

"No, but he's killed like a hundred people, and he knows my stance on the death penalty."

Mel shrugged. "Which is why he didn't tell you in the first place, honey. Do you still love him?"

That was an easy question to answer. "Yes, but I worry I don't know him. I worry that I only think I love him because he was the first man to pay attention to me."

"Sometimes you get lucky. I didn't. I had to try a couple of times before I met a woman who could love me. I had a fiancée back in my military days, but that ended real poorly, if you know what I mean. And then there was the alien queen," he said with a sigh. "Royalty is hard."

And sometimes it was difficult to find the kernels of wisdom that lay in between Mel's alien stories. "Most people don't get lucky. Most people do have to kiss a couple of frogs before they find their prince. What if Henry's a frog?"

Mel's gaze went somber. "And what if you're folding the first minute you run into real trouble?"

That wasn't fair. "I've had trouble in my life, Mel."

"Good. Then you know this is a dent in your bumper and not a complete loss. It feels like real trouble, but it's not. You know a real marriage doesn't stop because you wrote the words happily ever after. Sometimes there's happiness and then not. Sometimes you don't solve all your problems with a handy kidnapping. Sometimes it takes just holding on until you get through the storm."

She felt her eyes widen. Was he saying what she thought he was saying? "What are you talking about?"

Mel stood. "Those books you write. I told you. I see more than you think I do. And don't worry. Laura won't figure it out. She knows something is up, but she hasn't narrowed it down. And I will not apologize for liking romance novels. Cassidy got me into them. They're soothing, and yes, sometimes they are arousing."

Mel knew? "There's nothing wrong with that." She shook her head. "How long have you known?"

"Oh, I figured it out a while back. Got interested in how you afforded things, since Henry left all his money behind. His money, his career, his apartment. His past." Mel tipped his hat her way. "You think about what I said. You want some big revelation to sweep you up, but sometimes real love gets fixed by giving something time, by letting the day-to-day world bind you together again. If you do the work, maybe you can find your way back. Now, I'm going to get some dinner. I think he'll take care of you for the rest of the night."

She glanced behind her and then she was on her feet because

Henry was walking their way. He looked big and safe and alive. He had his duffel over his shoulder, so he hadn't even gone to the cabin to drop off his bags. He'd come straight here to look for her.

He stopped and stared at her like he wasn't sure of his welcome.

"Follow your instincts, Nell." Mel waved Henry's way. "You spend a lot of time in your head. Do what your heart is telling you to do. Start there and give all of this time. I have faith in the two of you."

Her instinct told her the man she loved was alive and he was home and they could figure out the rest later.

The father of her child was standing right there looking like he would die if she rejected him.

Some stories didn't pan out the way she thought they would. Life was like that, too. She didn't have to say yes or no right now. She just had to say what was in her heart.

She'd been in this very pavilion the first time he'd come back to her. She'd cried then, too. No matter what happened, she would always be happy to see this man.

Through her tears, she ran to him and into his open arms.

* * * *

He couldn't take his eyes off her.

Henry closed the door to their cabin and locked it while Nell stood in the living room looking like she couldn't quite figure out what to do.

He'd done this to her. Nell was assertive. Nell was sure of herself and her beliefs, and his lies had knocked her for a loop.

But had it only been his lies? Or had this been a perfect storm of his lies and the one thing he'd ever seen intimidate his wife—becoming a mom.

"Are you hungry? I didn't know you were coming home tonight." Nell turned back to the kitchen. "I still have some of what Cassidy made for me. And there's leftover soup."

"I ate on the plane." Young Taggart had done well for himself. He and Tennessee had come in on a private plane, and they'd been willing to drop him off in Alamosa. He'd caught a ride from there from a friend who owed him a favor. Young Taggart? His former student was a man with a wife and three kids. He was also the one who pointed out that

Nell was dealing with more than just Henry's past.

Pregnancy is not this easy-breezy woman thing. I mean they make it look that way, but it's a serious change in life, and it hits them emotionally. You've got a war on two fronts, brother. Don't forget to deal with both.

She stopped and nodded. "Okay."

"I had a sad salad," he admitted. "It was a private plane, so I was lucky the galley had vegetables. I'm afraid that was a plane full of carnivores." He caught the light in her eyes and put a hand up to ward off what he knew was coming. "I've already bought a carbon offset. I know private planes are a problem, but baby, I couldn't wait to see you. I wanted to come home. I've missed you so fucking much."

That moment when she'd run into his arms…it had felt like the world was right again. And now they were back to cautiously circling each other.

"I missed you, too," she admitted. "So they're all going to come here and stay at Seth's place?"

He'd told her Taggart's plan while they'd driven back to the cabin. He hadn't wanted to stay at the festival. He wanted to be alone with her, wanted to be honest with her. He didn't want to sit on this or tell her in the morning. "Yes, and I'll let you read the file I have on them. Tag calls them the Lost Boys. They have no memory of their prior lives due to being experimented on."

"And they're coming here to look for a CIA black site?" There was so much judgment in that question. "On national forest land."

"Yes. But I didn't start it and I never worked there. It was another department," he said quickly. "That doesn't make it right. But baby, it's closed down now and if you protested it, you would probably get arrested and sent to somewhere that would be hard for me to get you out of."

"But you could…"

"I would move heaven and earth, but let's protest after the boys get the data they need."

"Of course. They've been through enough," she replied. "They're getting in soon?"

"A couple of days from now." He'd told Tag that they were welcome in Bliss, but he wouldn't lie to his wife. "Seth's cleared it. He,

Logan, and Georgia aren't planning on coming back until the holidays. I think the op itself will be a week or two tops. And, my love, it's classified. They have to have cover. We're looping in law enforcement, but around town they'll have to maintain cover."

"I don't like lying." She was quiet for a moment. "I'll avoid town for a while. I don't feel like interpretive dance right now."

It was how she protested lies and being asked to lie. She danced. She was such a gorgeous weirdo, and he loved her with his whole heart. "I'm sorry. I can tell them not to come."

She shook her head. "No. I understand the need. There have to be all kinds of intelligence agencies after those poor men."

"Yes, starting with our own." He had to think about how to reach out. Apparently someone had come looking for him. "But the good news is I don't think we have to worry about the cartel."

A prim look came over her face. "Because you killed them all, Henry."

"That was self-defense." He wouldn't have been able to win their hearts and minds through careful dialogue. "I need you to tell me if you want me to defend myself. If I have to choose between your love and respect and my life…"

Her eyes rolled. "Don't be dramatic. Of course you should defend yourself. I would defend myself. It's just—it was a lot, wasn't it? You're sure you didn't accidently kill someone who was like a janitor?"

"I promise I left the janitor perfectly alive. I only killed people who tried to kill me." And unfortunately he'd let one get away. Levi Green could still be dangerous to all of them, but he thought the threat from the cartel might be gone.

"All right." She went quiet for a moment. "I'm going to be honest. I know you want my answer right this second."

Not if the answer was *get out of our cabin and out of my life.* "No. I want your answer when you're ready to give it to me."

Tears filled his wife's eyes. "I think I'm going about this wrong. Mel accused me of treating this like one of my books."

"Mel knows about the books?" That was news to him.

"Yes. Apparently Mel knows a whole lot about everything. He says he knew about you back when we first got together."

He doubted that. He was really good at undercover. He probably could have been an actor. But that wasn't the important thing now. And honestly, her work might be part of the problem. Or rather her lack of work. "What does he mean you're acting like this is a book? I know how serious this is for you."

"He said I might be looking at this whole thing like a romance novel where one specific thing happens and there's a resolution. He might have said that's not how a real relationship works. I mean it does sometimes, but that's not the end of the story. We're not just happy forever. We have to work, and I haven't been working lately."

"You don't have to work for our relationship. I do. I'll do all the work I need to do," he promised.

She shook her head. "We both need to work. I said I needed time to think, but that hasn't helped. I don't know that I can trust you again. I don't know that I can go back to the way we were."

His heart constricted. He had no idea what he would do without her. "Nell…"

"So we need to find a new normal," she continued. "I think we should keep living together and sleeping together and being together, at least until I have this baby. That should give me enough time to decide if I want to continue with the marriage. But I have some rules."

That was months away, and he could work some magic in those months. He could convince her. "Yes."

She stopped. "You don't want to hear them?"

"I don't need to. I'll do anything to keep you. I'll do anything for another chance."

"You can't lie to me again. Not about anything." She frowned. "Well, not anything important. You should tell me I look pretty even when I'm as big as a whale."

He moved in, closing the space between them. "You are always beautiful to me."

The tears started to fall and he knew she was softening. That was his wife. She couldn't hold out forever, and if he was in her bed, he would be back in her heart in no time at all. But he would pay any price she wanted. There was no question he'd done the wrong thing. He wasn't sure he would take it back because he'd needed her to love him, to accept him.

Or maybe he should have had more faith in her.

"You have to be yourself in front of me, and not only behind my back," she continued.

Another step and he could almost reach out and touch her. His cock tightened because he'd missed her every moment they'd been apart. "You might not like that part. I'm ridiculously territorial when it comes to you, and I hide that well. You joke about my possessiveness, but you haven't truly seen it yet. And don't tell me it's about not trusting you. I trust you. I could catch you in bed naked with another man and I would ask you what happened and believe what you told me. But you are my treasure. You are the one thing in this whole world I've loved with my whole being. I am a dragon hoarding your every smile." He reached out and brushed her tears away. "Your every tear."

She sniffled. "See. I should point out that you can't own a woman, but I just want you to kiss me now."

He pulled her into his arms, the curve of her belly nestling against his torso and making him want to strip her down and see every change the pregnancy had wrought in the weeks they'd been apart. "Baby, I'm a caveman at heart. I love you so much and I won't ever hold you back, but deep in every man's heart when he truly loves a woman he's possessive. It's all about how we handle that instinct. So I'll play it however you like. What are the other rules?"

He would agree to them all.

"I think we should go into counseling."

He could do that. "Okay."

"Alexei is working on his degree and he's got time."

Alexei Markov as a marriage counselor? It was going to be surreal, but a former Russian mobster was better than Crazy Irene, who would likely force them into sage rituals to cleanse their marriage. "Of course. It would help him, too."

"Irene tells me there's a ritual to help cleanse all bad vibes."

He managed to not wince. When he'd married Nell, he'd accepted the different people she brought into their lives. So different. "Absolutely."

"You have to talk to me about things. You have to trust that I'll handle your secrets," she continued.

"I'll tell you anything you want to know."

Her mouth went prim. "I think I shouldn't be the only one who has body modifications in order to sexually please my partner."

"It's about more than sex," he started and then realized what she was really saying. "You want a mark on me because they're my marks on you. All right. I'll talk to Austin about getting a tattoo. Anywhere you like."

"I want you to get a Prince Albert."

She wanted him to pierce his dick? He closed his eyes and took a deep breath. It wasn't that he was against the idea of something on his body that let Nell know he was thinking of her.

His dick was always thinking of her. Always.

"Oh, Nell, I love those nipple rings. I love how I can twist them and play with them," she taunted. "I pierced my vagina for you."

No, she'd pierced her hood. That had very little feeling in it. Still, he said he'd do anything. "I'll set it up with Austin." But as long as they were doing painful things. "I have one condition."

A brow rose over her eyes. "What's that?"

This was a gamble, but one he had to take. "You have to write. You haven't written in months, and I think that's part of the problem."

"I haven't felt like it," she admitted. "You know sometimes I get blocked."

"I don't think you're blocked. I think you're avoiding it because writing is how you process the things that happen to you. I want you to write whatever comes to you. Not the next book in the series. Don't worry about money or readers or anything. Just write and let it all out. That's my only request."

"Okay, but I can't promise you it will be good." She looked up at him. "I did miss you."

It suddenly didn't matter that his dick was going to go through hell. He leaned over and picked up his wife. "Let me show you how much I missed you."

He carried her to the bed and vowed he would be right beside her no matter what.

Chapter Nine

Late September

Nell sat on her front porch, a thousand thoughts running through her head. Normally she would sit on the back porch and watch the river flow by at this time of the afternoon. In a bit she would go and start dinner. This was the lovely time when she and Henry would sit and talk about the day.

Henry had spent most of the day at Seth's with all his new friends, and she couldn't even drink. She'd seen him in the morning and he'd been all peppy and eager. He'd barely downed a piece of toast and a half a cup of coffee before he was running out the door and going to Seth's for what he called a "debrief" on yesterday's debacle at Mountain Adventures.

She sighed. At least River knew what her new clients were looking for now. That was one lie out of the way.

Even when Henry had come home, he'd gone straight to his computer because he was certain there was an Agency "plant"—as he'd put it—somewhere in Bliss.

So here she was sitting alone and thinking. Had she made a terrible mistake? Should she have told him to get out and stay out?

It kind of hurt to see him so content when she was so…restless.

She'd spent the last two weeks doing exactly what she'd promised. She'd welcomed Henry into their bed. They'd made love most nights, and the nights they didn't, he'd told her stories about his time with the Agency. He'd prompted her to talk about her mom more. He'd give her an Agency story if she told him one from her childhood.

Yeah, that made her restless, too.

Off in the distance she heard the sound of shouting, but that wasn't surprising these days. Those men who'd been experimented on seemed determined to play out some sort of second adolescence. They played pranks on each other most days, and they were far too invested in their own bodily functions.

"Hey, sorry. I looked for you on the back porch." Henry stepped out and had a mug of tea in his hand.

"I wanted to change it up a bit." She kept her eyes on the lawn.

He sighed as he sank into the chair beside her. "I'm sorry I worked all day."

She had to be patient with him. "There's nothing to be sorry about. I worked all day, too."

"But we usually work together. We have a routine to our days, and I've screwed that up. I'm not trying to. I can tell Ian that I need to be here."

Ian Taggart was an overly large man who'd apparently been Henry's student at one point. He'd obviously learned how to kill people, how to run a mission, and how to speak sarcasm. Though she would admit the man had a certain amount of charm, and he'd managed to choke down the black bean burger she'd served him the night he and Henry had sat up and talked about the old days.

"I know you're trying to help those men. I get it. I'm fine."

"It won't be long now. They're going to go into the woods soon, and then I'm out of it," Henry promised.

There was more shouting from somewhere beyond the cabin.

Would he truly be out of it? "I thought you were going to have to talk to the Agency at some point."

"I think if they were going to arrest me, they would have done it by now," he said with a confidence she didn't feel. He turned her way. "What do you think of Heather Turner? She moves well, right?"

He'd been watching how the gorgeous blonde moved? "Well, I suppose she could be a model."

He frowned her way. "Or an Agency plant. Love, I wasn't talking about her level of sex appeal. I was talking about the fact that she moves very fluidly. And she doesn't make a lot of sound. Have you ever noticed that? And she's weirdly absent whenever Ian or Ezra are around. Not the boys. She's cool around them, but then the boys wouldn't know her even if they'd met her before. I haven't said anything yet, but I think I'll talk to Ian about it tomorrow."

"Okay." What was going on over at Seth's? Was that smoke?

"How about we watch a movie tonight? There's a new documentary about water pollution," he offered.

"Sure." So she would know that her daughter or son wouldn't be able to find clean water.

"I'm trying here, Nell," he said with a sigh.

"I know."

She gasped as a man ran by, sprinting as fast as he could. Tucker. She thought that man was Tucker.

Henry was on his feet in a second and down off the steps. "Get inside, Nell."

Her heart started to race because something bad was about to happen. Had the Agency come for them all? Was it the cartel Henry thought he'd gotten out from under? All she knew was Tucker was terrified.

And then she saw the small creature racing across the yard. A badger chased after Tucker, all claws and teeth. That small animal was the definition of irritation.

Outrage sparked through her as Tucker managed to turn and run the other way.

"Did you smoke that badger out of her hole?" Nell asked, her hands on her hips.

"I'm sorry. It was a prank," Tucker yelled. "I didn't think it would chase me. Sasha said it would be okay."

Sasha was standing at the edge of the property line, laughing his ass off.

Lexi Blake

Yeah, she wasn't happy with Sasha either. "Okay to smoke a poor animal out of its home?"

"How long will it chase me?" Tucker asked, still running.

She expected Henry to go to the young man's aid.

Instead, he shook his head. "At least a mile or so. If she catches you, she'll probably take a toe or two. You should keep running. And take another way to come back because she will remember you. She'll lie in wait for you. You know what they say."

"No, I don't," Tucker said with a little cry as he tried to avoid the badger's claws. "I don't know anything."

"Badger never forgets," Henry said. "Good luck."

"Come on, Henry," Tucker pleaded.

"Nope. You poked the badger. You get the badger. I've been that badger and I would bite your ass, too." Henry settled back into his chair.

"You're really not going to help him?" It was surprising.

"I'll help the badger," Henry admitted. "Poor thing was probably taking a nap and that asshole thought it would be fun to smoke him out. Well, who's having fun now?"

"Not me!" Tucker took off, running by the river now.

"Go, Badger, go!" Henry yelled. "Little asshole. We're going to teach our kid not to be a dumbass."

She smiled his way. "Yes. Yes, we will." She sat back. "Maybe we could watch a comedy."

It would be good to laugh.

Henry reached for her hand. "That sounds fun."

Another man ran by. Robert. "I'm coming, Tucker!"

"Or we can watch them instead," she said, flipping her hand over to slide her fingers between his. "What do you think will happen when they see Maurice? He was down river a little while ago."

"What the fuck is that?" Tucker screamed.

Henry's lips quirked up. "And he's still there. Yeah, this should be fun."

Henry's hand tightened around hers, gently pulling her toward him. She found herself sitting on his lap and couldn't argue with him. It felt too good. When his hand came over her belly, she sat back and waited for the world to entertain her.

172

* * * *

"How does this be making you feel?" Alexei Markov sat back in the office he shared with Caleb in the pretty cabin they'd built the year before.

"It made me feel like Henry was going to kill someone," Nell replied primly. "And right in the middle of the festival."

Henry bit back a groan. What had happened at the Festival of Spiritual Rejuvenation was inevitable the minute Nell had demanded he not hide his instincts anymore. "I wasn't going to kill him."

"Good, Henry, this is good." Alexei had a notepad in front of him. "You were only going to hurt man who touches her belly. See, this is progress. I have same impulses. Man touches my woman and I wish to kill, too."

Nell frowned his way. "You told that man if he didn't take his hands off me you would pull his bowels out and wrap them around his throat. That would kill him, Henry."

Henry shrugged. "Maybe. Maybe not. I was willing to find out."

It had felt good to make that fucker flee. He was off the leash when it came to protecting his wife, and she was conveniently forgetting the fact that after she'd yelled at him for his caveman like tendencies, he'd had her skirt flipped up and his cock deep inside her in the back of the store she'd set up to sell her vegan bread to Squatchers. Yeah, he'd had a mating call out of her pretty mouth really quick.

But he was smart enough to know that if he wanted to take advantage of the fact that his caveman side got her hot, he shouldn't point it out to her.

"I could have handled it. I've always handled it in the past," Nell insisted. "Do you remember last spring when that tourist was incredibly rude to me?"

Henry felt a feral expression come over his face. "The one who hit on you and then called you a whore?"

"I explained my position to him and he came back and apologized after he thought about my words." Nell gasped and sat up straighter. "You talked to him, didn't you? Henry, did you beat that man?"

He hadn't had to. He was good with words. "No, I merely

explained what would happen to him if he talked to another woman that way, he pissed himself, changed his clothes, and then properly apologized." It hadn't been the first time he'd dealt with a man who'd gotten handsy with his wife. Sometimes tourists thought country girls were there for their entertainment. Henry liked to put them straight. "If it helps it wasn't just you I did that for. I caught some asshole being aggressive with Hope and handled it for her, too."

Her voice went low. "Did you kill him?"

She could be a little overly dramatic. "No. I told you. All I had to do was point out a few hard truths and we came to an agreement. See, I learned that from you. I talked to them."

His brat's eyes rolled. She was asking for it again. She asked for it a lot lately. "I tried to teach you to find common ground with people we don't agree with."

"We did find common ground. I was willing to tear his penis off and stuff it down his throat, and he decided to do whatever it took to get me to not do that," Henry shot back.

"I meant common ground on an emotional level."

The man had cried. "He was very emotional about his penis."

She looked to Alexei. "Could you tell him how wrong he is about this?"

"I am actually only here to facilitate communications between two of you. That's what a therapist does," Alexei replied. "As friend, I tell Henry he is good man and I will help with taking of penises."

Nell stood. "I'm done with marriage counseling now. I should have known a male therapist would agree with you." She turned and walked out.

Alexei looked crestfallen. "I might not be cut out for this part of therapy. I am better in bar. Shouldn't you follow her?"

"She'll go to the bathroom and then she'll find Holly and yell about me some more." Then he would collect her, head home, and plant his face in her pussy. He'd found that was a good way to get her to forget her annoyance. Then he would cook dinner, rub her feet, and fuck her again before they went to sleep. He would cuddle her close all night long.

All in all, not a terrible day.

"You don't seem upset by this," Alexei said, one brow raised.

Henry sat up. "I'm always upset when she's angry with me, but it's good for her to get it out. A couple of weeks ago she wasn't talking to anyone. Now she tells everyone who will listen what a liar I can be. She even interpretive danced our entire fight in a drum circle at the festival."

Alexei's lips quirked up. "And you watch this?"

"Oh, yes. It was for a group of witches. I'm pretty sure there are a couple of hexes on me," he admitted. But she was writing again. He'd woken up one morning last week worried because she wasn't in bed with him. He'd found her at her laptop, typing away. He was fairly certain he was the bad guy in this one since it was about a young activist caught between a manipulative CIA agent and the too-pure-to-be-an-actual-man owner of a nature preserve.

At least the heroine was attracted to the CIA agent.

He kind of wanted the CIA dude to murder the nature guy, and then he would show the heroine the joys of anal sex.

"And then he told the man he would kill him," Nell was saying as she and Holly walked by. "He's entirely too invested in murder. I blame that Taggart man. He's a bad influence."

"You know what happens when boys play with their friends," Holly said with a sigh. "I'm glad Alexei's old mob friends don't come visit."

Alexei stood and frowned. "I have no mafia friends. They all assholes."

"All my CIA friends left the Agency, so it's pretty much the same," Henry admitted. "I figure she's going to be at least an hour. You got a place where I can take a quick nap? I've got another sageing scheduled for this evening. I don't care what they say. Sage is not soothing."

"Sure. Couch in library is comfortable," Alexei replied. "Come along. I will watch over our women while you get rest. If you want my nonexpert opinion, the two of you seem to be better. I cannot imagine she will hold this in her heart for too much longer."

Henry hoped so.

October

"Are you sure?" Nell leaned in, not wanting to let anyone else in on this secret of Holly's.

All around her Caleb's birthday party went on. Holly and Alexei had surprised Caleb with a party, and by "surprise" they'd told him they were having it, he'd said no, and they'd done it anyway.

Caleb Burke actually looked relaxed and happy, a beer in his hand as he talked with Henry, Rafe, and James Glen.

Nell and Laura had joined Holly in the kitchen. From here they could see the whole of the great room where most of the party was taking place. The big windows that led to the patio and the outdoor living space were open, and Nell could hear music and chatter.

Life had gone back to normal, and she felt okay with that. She rather thought this was what Mel had been talking about, allowing the rhythm of the days to flow and bring them back together.

So why did she still feel so far from him? There was an odd distance between them she couldn't seem to get past.

"You took a test, right?" Laura had an expectant look on her face.

Holly nodded. "I took three, and then Caleb ran the blood work. It's so stupid. I'm too old to do this. I have a grown son."

Joy spilled through Nell, bringing a warmth she hadn't felt in months. Holly was pregnant. Laura had a baby and now her other bestie would join them and they would be able to have playdates and a mom's group and she would have support.

Her mom hadn't had support. When her mom reached out to people they'd thought she was crazy, and she'd learned to stop talking, to stop relying on other people. Until they'd come to Bliss.

Her mom had met Callie's mom and it had been the first time she'd been able to open up to another person in years.

They'd come to Bliss and suddenly she'd been surrounded by people who made the world a warmer place, who somehow had become family.

"Nell, sweetie, are you okay?" Holly put a hand on her shoulder.

"I think this is one of those pregnancy things," Laura said. "She cries a lot. I usually hold her hand and fix a cup of tea."

She did. Laura fixed her a cup of tea and asked if she wanted to talk, and then listened to her for hours with no judgment.

Henry was already on his way over, as though he'd felt her emotion.

She wasn't her mom. She wasn't alone. Her mother had done her best. Her mom had loved her and tried her hardest. In the end her mom had given her the greatest gift of all, the one that came naturally to so many, but as in all things in her mother's life, she'd had to work for this gift, had to seek it out.

Her mom had found a way to give her a family, one that lasted long after she was gone.

She sniffled and wrapped her arms around Holly. "I'm so happy we get to go through this together. You're one of the best moms I know and I love you."

She felt Holly gasp and hug her close. "I love you, too. I don't know where I would be if I hadn't had you and Laura."

"Hey, I want in." Laura completed their circle. "I love you, too. I didn't know how good friendship could be until I met you two."

"You are going to be a wonderful mom," Holly whispered. "You and me and Laura, we're going to get through all of it together."

"And you two are having girls," Laura said. "I just know it. So Sierra can have her two best friends."

She looked up and Henry was standing there, staring at them. He wasn't alone. Caleb stood beside him.

"This is a woman thing," Caleb said with a nod. "It's one of those things where they're crying, but it's a good thing. I think they're bonding over babies. Did I mention Holly's knocked up?"

Henry turned and held out a hand. "Congrats, man."

Caleb shook it. "We're excited. I'm going to grab another beer."

Holly started to laugh. "Men."

Men, indeed. She noticed that Henry was still staring at her, the softest look on his face.

* * * *

Henry looked down at the saw, trying to go over all the steps in his head before he actually started that sucker up. He had the perfect wood and he didn't want to waste it with ten tries before he got the cut right.

After all, this was his gift to Nell and the baby girl she was carrying.

A girl. Taggart had laughed and called him a sucker when he'd told him. Max and Rye had simply shaken their heads and welcomed him into the club. Apparently girls were hard.

Daughter. He was going to have a daughter. What the fuck did he know about daughters?

He took a deep breath and grabbed his goggles. Safety first.

It had been weeks and not a hint of anyone looking for him. The Agency operative who'd been watching him for more months than he liked to think about had promised him her report would encourage the Agency to leave him be. Heather Turner's real name was Kim Solomon and according to her, he wasn't any kind of a security risk and considered it all a done deal.

Seth had told him he'd gotten not a single hit on his information in weeks.

They might be okay.

Things with Nell were going all right, too. At least he felt like they were. She wasn't ready to forgive him yet, but she'd stopped talking about what they should do about living arrangements after the baby was born.

They were floating through the days as though time itself could make them whole again.

Maybe it could. Maybe the simple act of living together, loving each other, could be the balm to the wound he'd given her.

He hoped she liked the cradle he was building.

"Henry!"

Henry's heart threatened to stop. That hadn't been Nell calling him in to dinner or requesting that he come and fix her laptop. No. That had been his wife calling for help. He dropped the wood he'd been working on and ran for the cabin, his brain already going to all the dark places.

"Henry, come quickly!"

He couldn't breathe. Time seemed to slow and he knew what he would find. He would find her bleeding and crying and asking him why this was happening to them.

He stopped short when he realized she was still upright.

She was standing on the back porch, her hand on her round belly, and he felt sick. God, they couldn't have come this far only to lose again. He wasn't sure how Nell would handle it. Maybe there was still time. "I'll call Caleb."

She shook her head, and despite the tears on her cheeks, a rapturous smile crossed her lips. "I felt her kick. I felt her. I've been so worried. Rachel talks about her baby moving all the time. I was supposed to be able to feel her by now, but I haven't. Until just now. I felt her. I think I've actually felt her before but I thought it was indigestion."

His knees buckled with relief as she chattered on excitedly, and he found himself hitting the wood of the porch, his hands still shaking. She was okay. The baby was okay. She was all right. He had to say the words over and over again in his head to make himself believe them.

"Henry?"

God, what was happening to him? The world had gone cloudy and he...was he fucking crying?

Nell dropped down beside him, her hands coming out to pull him close. "I'm so sorry. I didn't think about the fact that you would..."

Would think she'd lost another pregnancy? Would think that they'd lost again? He couldn't stop shaking. "I'm sorry. I'll be okay in a minute. I...I...just need to breathe."

She wrapped him up. "No. You need to let it out. You were so strong for me. You held me. Let me hold you. You want to show me that you're really the man I fell for? Then be in this moment with me. Don't push it aside. It was horrible and we got through it. It's okay to feel it now."

The tears wouldn't stop. In that moment, he'd known he would do anything for that child in her belly. Anything for their daughter. When Caleb had told them they had a daughter coming, Henry's world had tipped again, and he had so fucking much to lose. So much. He had the whole world to lose.

Nell rubbed her cheek against his. "I'm here with you. I'm with you."

And that made it okay. He let the tears fall because he'd been walking a tightrope for so long. He had to be strong for her while every day he worried. He hadn't had a father. Would he even be good at it? Would his past bring hell down on his family?

Did he even deserve a family?

"Of course you do," Nell whispered. "You deserve all the love I have, Henry. I'm sorry if I made you feel different."

He'd said that out loud? Why couldn't he stop crying? He never cried. "I'm so scared of losing…"

He held back. He didn't want to put her in a corner. So he kept the final word inside.

You. I'm so afraid of losing you because you are my whole world.

Nell sniffled and then gasped, a smile brightening her face once more. "She moved again. Give me your hand. Feel her."

She moved his hand to her belly and shifted so she was sitting in between his legs, cradled by him. He let his head rest against hers and felt an odd peace.

"She's not doing it." Nell's frustration came out through her tone.

"Shh, it's okay. She will. We have to be patient." Being close to her…it was everything.

She was quiet for a moment, his hand on her belly, the late afternoon light soft around them, and despite the chill in the air, there was warmth between them. "You'll be a great dad."

"I didn't have one." He hadn't had a dad or siblings, and when his mom had died, he hadn't had anyone at all. "Bill was the closest I had, and I didn't let him in until much later in life. What if I don't know how to let her in?"

Nell's hand came over his. "Did you know how to be a husband?"

His mom hadn't dated when he was young. Most of the homes he moved in and out of later on had absent dads, or in one case an abusive one. "No."

"Who did you learn from?"

Those stupid tears were back in his eyes again. "I learned from you."

He'd learned by watching her, by caring so much he'd studied so he could give her what she needed. His love for her had led him.

"Then we'll learn how to be parents from her," Nell said softly.

And then he felt it. He felt something softly move under his hand. "She moved."

Nell leaned back.

They sat there as the first snow began to fall.

November

"Max, if you say one thing about my wife's tofurkey casserole and she cries, I will kill you. I will not do it humanely. I will make it hurt," Henry vowed.

Stef Talbot snorted and let them all in, his hand on his son's back. "This is on you, Max. Take one for the team. Come on, Logan. Your Thanksgiving dinner is still milk. Henry, I'll be sure to get a slice of Nell's berry crumble."

Max nodded, his eyes lighting with what looked like hope. "Yeah, I could do that."

But then his problem wouldn't be solved. And Max deserved it. Besides, it wasn't that bad. Of course he hadn't actually eaten turkey in years, so maybe he didn't understand, but he didn't care. "No. It has to be tofurkey casserole."

Nell had wanted to insure she had a protein to eat, but he knew she would also like it if they weren't the only ones to eat it.

Max frowned. "But it's wrong. It's so wrong. Why would I eat tofu when there's a perfectly good turkey who sacrificed to get in my belly?"

"Get it all out now." He wasn't going to listen to Max make fun of tofu.

"I don't have to taste it, do I? I can hold my nose and swallow it as fast as I can and then stuff my mouth with a real turkey leg, right?"

He pointed Max's way. They had to get this all out before they joined the rest of the group celebrating with Stef and Jen. It was most of Bliss. "Who helped you fix your truck after you dinged it up when Rachel told you to put the snow tires on but you didn't?"

Henry'd had to go out in the cold, help Max haul that sucker back to Long-Haired Roger's, and then convince Roger not to call Rachel, even though everyone else in town would have.

Max went a little pale. "I would have taken the lecture if I'd known my other penalty was fake turkey. Come on, man. Do a guy a solid."

Nell was nervous about Thanksgiving. Nervous about her welcome here. They typically went up the mountain for the weekend and celebrated with the gang up at Mountain and Valley.

But Mountain and Valley was an adults only resort, and their baby girl would want to play with her friends on the holidays. Neither he nor Nell had deep connections to Thanksgiving. There had been no big family get-togethers in their past, and they'd decided that while they would absolutely explain about the destruction of indigenous people and that history shouldn't be eradicated with a piece of pie, she could enjoy a holiday with a basis in family.

Max wasn't going to make his wife cry today by making fun of the food she'd brought.

He narrowed his gaze. "You remember when Rachel thoughtfully made raisin pie?"

Max sighed. "I'll do it. How you managed to choke that down I will never understand."

The things they did for their wives…

* * * *

"I've been pregnant for five hundred years," Nell said.

Rachel sighed. "Girl, same. Max, you get Rye and tackle those dishes. All the pregnant ladies are watching a movie."

"But baby, the game is coming on. I already had to…" Max's eyes went wide when he saw Nell sitting next to Rachel on the couch. "Yes, baby."

He turned on his heel and strode right back to the kitchen.

"What did Henry do to make him eat that casserole?" Nell asked because she'd seen tears in the poor man's eyes.

Rachel sat back. "Whatever it was, he needs to tell me. So you and Henry good? Or are you still signing that postnup thing?"

Stef's lawyer had drawn up a document that gave her everything, in the event of a divorce. All the money, the cabin, the Jeep. "I tore it up and told him if he ever presented me with something like that again, he would sleep on the couch for the rest of his life."

Laura had Sierra Rose in her lap. "Thank god. I was worried when I heard he'd done that."

"I think he was trying to make a point," Holly added.

The point had been made and rejected. "Anything we made, we

made together."

"So you're going to share the fortune you made off dreamcatchers at Woo Woo Fest?" Laura asked.

She loved her friend, but sometimes Laura was nosy. She hadn't given up on trying to figure out Nell's secret. "Yes. We made them together. We should share in the profits."

Laura groaned. "You're never going to tell me."

"Come on. She can't. According to the rumor mill, Henry brought a ton of cash from his days working for the CIA," Rachel replied, a light in her eyes. "It's why the cartel might come after him."

Jen nodded. "That's what I heard, too."

She knew a trap when she saw one. Now was the time she should leap to her husband's defense and tell them all the truth. She simply nodded. "I heard that one, too."

Callie was sitting on the big comfy chair, one of her twins in her arms. Nate was walking around with the other. "Told you she wouldn't fall for it. You keep those secrets, girl."

Or maybe it was time to come clean about everything. Henry had always told her it was up to her when or if she ever wanted to talk about her writing. It felt so good to be writing again. At first it had been a chore, but then somewhere along the way, the words had started to flow and the plot had begun to change. It might be fun to talk about it now. "What secrets? Like I'm a bestselling author of truly filthy romance and Henry helps me with them? I mean dirty, and by dirty I also mean beautiful. They are also carefully researched by a man who knows how to study. That secret?"

Somehow she didn't need to keep that secret anymore. She and Henry had other things that only they knew. Only they knew what it meant to love the other. Only they knew what it meant to live their lives.

The whole room went silent.

It was good to know she could still shock her friends.

And it was good to know that she and Henry were going to make it through.

Winter

Chapter Ten

Nell stared at the windows of Stella's Diner, the snow forming a lattice pattern on the glass. It was dark outside and the lights from the café illuminated the snowflakes. She loved the winter. Oh, she complained about it when she had to slog through the snow, but there was something infinitely soothing about watching the world get blanketed in white, in cuddling up on the couch with her husband while they talked about what to name their baby.

They'd narrowed it down to Daisy or Poppy. She smiled at the thought because she'd teased him by demanding they consider Freedom Justice Flanders or Liberty Suffrage Flanders. She'd watched her poor husband try to figure out how to maneuver his way out of those names without upsetting her.

It was then and there that she'd given up any anger she'd had with him. Mel's words had truly sunk in over the course of long months spent simply living with the man. John Bishop might still be in there, but he loved her, too. John Bishop hadn't become Henry Flanders to get away from his past. He'd done it because he'd finally found a future he wanted. A future with her.

And their child, who was definitely going to be a Poppy.

She turned her attention to Henry, who sat across from her, his eyes moving down the tablet in front of him. He was reading intently, his finger turning the virtual pages.

Her latest book. The one she'd started almost as a way to flip off her husband. She wouldn't have said it at the time, but she could be more honest now. She'd started the book firmly intent on having the spy be the bad guy who tried to rip apart her young, idealistic lovers. The handsome but lying spy was supposed to ruin everything. He was supposed to be the conflict they had to get over. And he was going to die because that was what writers did when they were upset with a person. Kill them off in inventive ways.

Over the course of writing, the damn thing had become a ménage because somewhere along the way she'd realized that she loved John Bishop, too.

She loved all of the man, and the book he was reading was her way of telling him.

"Hey, Henry," a familiar voice said. "I was wondering if you could come out and help me with the plumbing in the guest bathroom."

Cade Sinclair stood at the front of the booth, still wearing his big overcoat.

"No," Henry said, never once looking up.

She gave Cade a smile. "He absolutely would love to, but he's not willing to talk about it at the moment. He's involved in his book."

"I told you I got us a repair manual." Gemma joined her husband, sliding her hand into his. "Jesse can totally handle it."

Henry kept his eyes on the page. "Jesse knows cars. He's terrible at plumbing. I'll be there tomorrow. Go away."

She'd gotten used to Bishop's growly nature. It came out only at times when he was super involved—usually with her—and she had to admit it did something for her.

"Thanks so much, Henry," Gemma said. "The last time Jesse tried to fix something we ended up turning the water off for two days. Hey, Nell. Come on, babe. Jesse should be here soon. I'm starving."

Nell gave the pretty blonde a wave as she led her husband away.

"When did Henry get so scary?" Cade was asking.

Gemma snorted. "He was always that way. You just didn't see it."

Henry huffed, a gruff sound, but went on with his reading.

Nell stretched because her lower back was aching. It had been all day, but she'd been running on the high of finishing her book that morning and having Henry be so engrossed in it.

She got a good kick to her kidneys, and then something moved across her belly. Probably a hand.

Had she complained about the baby not moving? Some days she prayed her little girl would take a nap. Her daughter was obviously practicing to be a gymnast. Or an acrobat. And she loved to get super active the minute her momma tried to get some rest.

She put a hand on her belly as though she could soothe the baby with touch. Christmas had been a lovely time. They'd been holed up in their cabin, happy and warm.

Seth, Georgia, and Logan had come home for the holidays. They'd celebrated with Teeny and Marie and Georgia's brothers. Seth had treated Henry like a father figure.

It had been so good to spend time with family, but she was also happy to move into a new year.

Winter was when she'd first met Henry Flanders. Winter was their time.

The door opened again and the Harpers strode in with their newest member in tow. Rye held a baby carrier in one hand while Max had a bundled-up Paige in his arms. Rachel pulled her coat off and hung it on the coat rack, waving as Stella moved from the kitchen to the dining room.

"Stella, I need a meal that isn't a casserole." Rachel waved to all in the room, which this time of year was mostly locals. "I thank you all for the lovely dishes we have been surviving off of since Ethan was born, but I need French fries."

"Go on," Henry said under his breath. "You know you want to. We've still got a couple of weeks. Go get some baby love in. I'm almost done and then we're going to talk."

That last was said with a bit of a growl that let her know he'd gotten at least part of the message. She did want to see the baby though. She pushed herself out of the booth that she wouldn't be able to get into soon.

She meant what she'd told Rachel on Thanksgiving. It felt like she'd been pregnant for at least seven years. And it also felt like yesterday.

She stretched to try to get that ache in her back to ease. It was getting harder and harder to ignore. "I hear promise in your tone, but I'm afraid the only play you're getting tonight is to rub my back."

His eyes came up, his gaze going soft. "I can do that right now. We can head home and I'll rub you everywhere you need."

"Finish the book." She leaned over and kissed him. "I want to talk about it."

She turned and walked over to greet the Harpers and get a good look at that sweet baby.

Rachel gave her a hug. "It's good to see you. I've decided if we have any more kiddos, we're definitely doing this in the summer. Winter deliveries are the worst. That storm we had kept everyone away. I forgot how nice it was to have help."

"What am I?" Max asked as he settled in. "Chopped liver? Paige, sweetie, defend your dad."

Paige giggled and tried to climb over the booth.

Rye had the new baby out of the carrier and cuddled in his arms. "Hey, you want to meet this guy?"

Her heart did a flip. "I do. But just let me see him. I'm so clumsy these days."

Rachel took her son. "No, you're not. You're moving toward the finish line and getting nervous about everything. But it's all worth it. I promise."

Nell gazed down at that perfect face. Ethan looked like his dads, with a cap of golden-brown hair and bright blue eyes. He yawned and got that half smile babies had that made every woman in the room feel maternal for a second.

"He's precious." Nell reached out and gently stroked the baby's head, careful around his soft spot. "How are you feeling?"

"Well, I'm getting by. It's been three weeks, so I feel somewhat human again. That one was nine pounds," Rachel pointed out. "Paige was only eight and a couple of ounces. Those men of mine can't make regular-sized babies. Arc you still planning a home birth?"

She had the tub ready and everything. "My midwife says everything is good to go."

She'd found a midwife in Creede and carefully laid out her birth plan. Even Caleb thought the woman was solid. She'd worried that Henry might put his foot down had Caleb objected, but Caleb and

Naomi had sat down with the midwife and proclaimed her of sound mind and good knowledge.

Which Nell would usually have said infantilized her, but she had originally planned to go with Irene, and after she'd been arrested for using her Dairy Queen job to launder money for a biker gang, Nell had to sit back and rethink a whole lot of her positions.

It was probably why the sage hadn't worked.

"Okay, but I need you to remember something." Rachel got serious. "I really need you to hear me, Nell."

She was likely going to get a lecture on how she should deliver in a hospital. "All right."

"You like to plan and you like to be in control," Rachel began. "And I hope that it all goes exactly the way you want it. I will be there in the women's circle with soothing music and aromatherapy, and I will cheer you on as you give birth in a bathtub. I'll love that baby and I'll be so happy for you."

Tears sprang to her eyes. "Thank you."

"But, Nell, if it goes wrong, I need you to remember the one thing I've learned about being a mom."

"What's that?"

"There is no one plan," Rachel said solemnly. "There is no one way to do this. Pregnancy, childbirth, being a mom. You're going to have a thousand different voices telling you to do it this way or that way. Or they'll tell you you're going to ruin your baby if you need something for the pain. The only thing that matters at the end of this isn't that you did it perfectly. It's that you and the baby are alive. Okay? Can you promise me, because I've been worrying about you."

All that mattered was that her daughter made it into the world safely. She nodded. "I promise."

"And if you need it, take the drugs," Rachel said. "It's okay. If you end up in the hospital, it's okay to ease your pain. It's okay if you need a C-section. Everything is okay as long as you and your baby are fine at the end of it. And anyone who tells you different is going to have to deal with me."

Nell managed to smile through her tears. "I will remember that."

Rachel gave her a half hug. "And know that we will all be here for you. We're going to get you through, and then we'll get Holly through.

And then we're going to hit up the Richie Richs for that school they've promised us."

"Oh, Henry and I are homeschooling," she replied.

Rachel's lips kicked up in a grin. "Well, you're always going to be welcome at our little school. Like I said, there's no one way."

"Hey, sweetie. Hal's got your burger ready," Stella said with an indulgent smile on her face. "This one is black bean, and he thinks it's his best yet."

Warmth poured through her. Hal had been trying out all kinds of new vegan recipes the last few months, and she knew it was all about her. It was kindness and caring. "I'm always thrilled to try his new recipes. I'm going to the bathroom first. Baby girl is jumping on my bladder."

She turned and felt a rush of warmth between her legs. Embarrassment flashed through her. It had finally happened. She hadn't made it to the bathroom in time. Pregnancy wasn't all glowy. It was also about utter humiliation.

It was probably meant to prepare her for motherhood.

"Stella, I'm so sorry," she began.

"Oh, no." Rachel was staring down at the floor. "Nell, this is one of those times I just talked about."

"I can clean it up," she began.

Rachel shook her head. "No, you're going to be busy, sweetie. Henry!"

"I'll be there in a minute," he called back.

"You know he was way easier to get along with before he stopped hiding his grumpy side," Rachel said with a sigh. "Henry, Nell's water broke. It's go time, buddy."

Her back seized and she held on to Stella. "No. It can't have. It's not time. I have two more weeks."

Henry was next to her, lending her strength. "Baby, it's going to be all right."

"Hey, we need to move." Rachel calmly directed her husbands to clear out. "This is the birthing booth. It's surprisingly comfortable, but I'll warn you they will not give you snacks."

She couldn't be...she wasn't ready. She wasn't at home. She couldn't have her baby here at Stella's, no matter how much she loved this place. "I don't want to use the birthing booth."

Pain wracked through her and she moaned, holding on to Henry's hand.

"Yep, that's a contraction." Rachel had passed off Ethan. "Has your back been hurting all day?"

Tears made everything watery. "Yes."

"Okay, so you've been in labor for a while." Rachel looked over and Gemma had joined the small crowd.

"Jesse's going to get Naomi. We saw her at the Trading Post before we came here, and I put a call in to Caleb. He's on his way," Gemma said.

"I want to go home. I need my midwife." Her hands had started to shake.

Henry's arms went around her, holding her from behind. His head nestled close to hers. "I don't know that she can get here from Creede tonight. We've got a bad storm blowing in."

"It's worse to the north of us," Rye said. "They've already got a foot of snow, and it's coming down hard. Why don't we take her to the clinic? Gemma, does Nate still have a key?"

Gemma had her bag open. "I've got it. I'm at the station house more than Nate, so I keep it with me. It's the closest safe place."

Everything was speeding up, going far too fast for her to handle. "I want to go home."

"And maybe we get to the clinic and Caleb says you're still hours away," Rachel reasoned. "Then I promise we'll get you wherever you want to be."

"If Caleb says it's safe," Henry whispered.

Her poor husband was trapped. He would want so badly to please her, but he would be scared, too. Losing her was his biggest fear.

She had to breathe. She couldn't breathe.

Henry moved in front of her, looking down into her eyes. "Look at me. Forget everything else and listen to me. We can do this. We're going to take it one step at a time, and the first thing we're going to do is meet Caleb at the clinic."

She managed to nod. "Did you finish the book?"

He smoothed back her hair. "It doesn't matter now. All that matters is you and our baby."

But she wanted him to know. "The spy lives and they all get married and live happily ever after."

He leaned over and kissed her forehead. "I was the spy and the other guy, you know. Even when you were mad at me, I was still the hero, too. And you are everything to me."

They could do this. They would do it together.

Although it would be nice if Henry had to take half the pain because it was…way more than she'd dreamed.

She took a deep breath and let Henry start to lead her out.

* * * *

The baby's in a good position, but I don't feel comfortable sending you home. I know she wants to be there, but I've got a feeling. I'm making the call to stay here.

She didn't want to stay here. Here was cold and too bright. She wanted to be home.

It's going to be okay. Just breathe.

Henry's hand clung to hers as the hours passed. Hours? Sometimes it felt like minutes. And then time would slow and the world seemed foggy and unreal.

Except for the pain. Something was wrong. She shouldn't have done this. Why had she done this?

Because we love each other. Because we wanted a baby. Because I talked you into it.

She shook her head. She couldn't put this on him. She'd wanted it, too.

Why did Caleb have to keep pushing her? Why couldn't he leave her alone? Didn't he know she was dying here?

Hey, it's going to be okay.

She was sick of everyone telling her that and she told Laura.

Use that anger, sweetie. Let it fuel you.

Hours floated by. Hours and hours, and she didn't take the drugs. She could get through this.

Just hold my hand. Break it if you need to. I won't let go.

She floated on pain and hope. She held on to her husband. Laura was there, too. She'd brought her familiar blankets, and the lavender oil that always calmed her down. There was a whole group of friends waiting outside, reminding her that home wasn't a place. It was a group of people. It was love and kindness and caring. It was a feeling she could feel no matter where she was in the world.

And somewhere in those hours when she cried out and held on, when she pushed and panted and rested back only to do it all over again, in that time, she felt her mother with her. As surely as she felt Henry's hand in hers, she felt her mother's love in her soul.

She would make mistakes. This child she was giving birth to would feel the brunt and bear the burdens of her mother's flaws. And she would feel her mother's love even after she was gone. Her daughter would have only to reach out and it would be there, a well of love and light she could draw on. Like Nell could in those long hours. No matter what, her mother had loved her, had branded her soul with that love, and it couldn't be destroyed by anything so flimsy as death.

That was what it meant to be a mother.

So when the time came, when her daughter's heart rate dropped and Caleb announced he had to go in, it was simple to say yes. To throw away every plan she'd made. To toss it all off without a single regret and say yes to anything that saved her child. Then she was the one lending Henry strength before Caleb gave her the drugs that would allow him to perform the surgery.

I'm so sorry. Nell, if we could have gotten to the hospital...

But she wasn't sorry. Regret might come later, and she might look back and wistfully wish it had gone another way, but now only one thing mattered. As the darkness took her, she sank into warmth and believed that they would be okay.

Chapter Eleven

Henry Flanders felt years older, and so young it hurt. Older because that night two days before had been beyond rough. He'd thought he would lose them both, and a black void had opened in front of him.

But then he looked down at the tiny girl in his arms, her chest against his, and he felt like the whole world was new. He'd shed his shirt because Nell had told him their daughter needed to be skin to skin. She'd told him a whole lot of things when she'd woken up and gotten to see their daughter for the first time. He was planning on doing anything she asked of him because that night had been…the worst and best night of his life.

Yesterday had been okay. Nell was still in pain from the emergency C-section, but she was determined to do everything she could to get back on her feet. Holly had come up to the clinic three times a day to take Nell for a walk. Holly had been through it and promised Nell that moving might be painful, but it would save her so much more discomfort down the line.

So he'd watched his wife gingerly move around, trying to recover.

God, if only he'd been able to take that pain. He'd never felt as helpless as he had in that moment when Caleb had told him Poppy's heart rate had dropped.

The door came open and Caleb strode through, his clipboard in hand. He glanced over at the machines that monitored Nell's vitals. "Has she been sleeping all right?"

"Yes, but she's ready to get out of here and go home." He'd already talked to her midwife, who'd promised to come out as soon as the roads cleared. Until then, Caleb could easily make it to their place. He wanted to give her something…anything.

"She can go home this afternoon. Everything looks good. Little Poppy there is perfectly healthy, and Nell's moving along nicely. She's going to want to get off the meds before she's ready," Caleb started.

"No, I'm not." Nell yawned and winced. "I'm going to do everything you tell me to, Doc. This sucks, and I don't think that turmeric tea is going to take away the pain. But it will help with inflammation."

"You're being surprisingly reasonable," Caleb said.

"Well, I am stapled together," she admitted. "I've thought a lot about the fact that what happened to me wasn't natural."

"It was perfectly natural," Caleb said with a frown. "Was I supposed to let you…"

She forced herself up with a wince. "No. That's what I'm saying. Without that surgery I would have died, so I will follow the traditional medicine world in this case. I can't take care of her properly if I'm in pain. The drugs don't make me loopy."

"When they do, you'll know it's time to get off them," Caleb said. "About two weeks should do it, but until then, it's best to stay ahead of the pain."

"I'll make sure she gets everything she needs." And he knew what she would want. He eased out of the chair as Poppy started moving. It was like she knew her mom was awake and she could get where she wanted to be. "You want to hold her?"

That brought a smile to his wife's face. "Yes. I want to see if she'll latch."

"Naomi's on her way in. She's the expert." Caleb moved to the door. "Like all things with this whole parenting thing, be patient. You'll find your way. Henry, you should go back to your cabin and get things ready for your girls. You haven't even had a shower in days."

He hadn't been willing to leave them. He'd slept on a cot beside her bed. It wasn't like this was a big hospital where they had a nursery.

Naomi and Caleb had taken long shifts, and Tyler Davis had come in to cover when they needed a break. They'd had plenty of help, but this was his family and he wouldn't leave them for his own comfort.

Without a bit of self-consciousness, Nell shrugged the top part of her gown down and put their daughter to her breast. "You aren't going to be able to make fun of Michael Novack anymore, Henry."

Was he really stinky? That wouldn't do. But he didn't like the idea of leaving her here alone with Caleb, who was a great doctor but probably would get involved with something else and only check on her and not hover over her like she deserved.

The door opened again and all of his excuses fled. Holly and Laura walked in, carrying some flowers. They would absolutely hover over her. Her best friends would take care of her.

"Hey," Laura said, beaming. "How's our girl?"

He would be happy to share her with her sisters. That's what Holly and Laura were, and it was so good his daughter would have this marvelous family to rely on.

"I'm achy, and lactation hurts way more than getting my nipples pierced did." Nell's eyes went down to the baby in her arms. She'd had to take out the rings he loved so much and wouldn't put them back in until Poppy was done with nursing. "But I kind of don't care because of how beautiful she is."

Before Laura and Holly could take over, Henry slipped in and gave his wife a kiss. "I'll be back before three. I'll stop by the Trading Post and grab some food I can make for you. I want you to rest and love on our daughter for the next two weeks."

"You're going to spoil us both," she said with a dreamy smile on her face.

"You bet I am." It was all he wanted to do.

"I should warn you that I saw Gemma this morning. Jesse tried to fix the plumbing and now their bathroom is flooded," Holly said.

He sighed. "I'll go by after I hit the cabin. But I'll be back for you two." He kissed his daughter's forehead. "Love you."

He reached for his shirt, pulling it over his head and smoothing it down. Maybe he did need that shower. He'd barely left the room since Poppy had been born. He grabbed his wallet and his dead cell and left the room even as Nell, Laura, and Holly started talking and laughing.

She was in good hands.

He blinked in the light of day and bit back a yawn. The snowstorm that hit the night Poppy was born had passed and the roads had been plowed. It was a gorgeous winter day. He felt like he'd been slammed with a sledgehammer.

Nothing a couple of hours of sleep couldn't fix. Yeah, he wasn't sure when he would be able to do that.

"Yep, you look about right." Nate was striding down the sidewalk, a bag from Stella's in his hand. "Get ready. You are not going to sleep much the next couple of weeks."

He felt a smile cross his face. It was good to know all of this was normal. "I can handle that. And thanks so much for the diapers."

Callie had brought them a present of a dozen organic cotton diapers in various colors. He was going to have to learn how to clean those suckers.

"You're welcome. You should know that Callie had a bunch of the women around town over to make some meals for you. And Cade. They'll drop it all by as soon as Nell gets sprung from Caleb's tender care."

Cade was an excellent cook, and he'd been trying out some vegan recipes recently. "That's wonderful. We appreciate it so much. I would love to be able to focus on Nell and Poppy. And Caleb was…well, go easy on him. He wasn't expecting to have to do an emergency C-section and he's still calming down. He did not like being in a place where he could lose a mom or baby. And he's got Holly to think about now."

"I'll see if I can buy him a beer. You let us know if you need anything." Nate tipped his Stetson and walked on toward the station house.

Henry took a deep breath of crisp air. Snow covered the ground, making the whole world white and bright. The sun shone down and he felt like he'd finally made it.

His wife knew who he was, and the spy had gotten the heroine, too. While she'd slept he'd finished her book and the message had been clear. She loved all of him. She forgave him.

He got into their Jeep and plugged in his dead phone. He hadn't even thought about using it. He'd spent all his time fascinated with the two women who would hold his heart forever.

After the storm of Poppy's birth, the last few days had been peaceful. Poppy slept a lot, and so did her mom. He loved to sit in the rocking chair Holly had brought up and hold his infant.

Tonight he would place her in the cradle he'd made with his own two hands. They would keep her in their bedroom while she was nursing. He was going to redo the guest room as Poppy's room.

How odd it was to think of her spending her whole childhood here in Bliss. He'd moved so many times. So had Nell. The world had seemed a transient thing until he'd come here.

He was pulling onto his drive when the phone finally had enough charge and started pinging. A lot. He put the Jeep in park and glanced down at the screen. Had something gone wrong? He should have kept it charged.

He breathed a sigh of relief as he realized it was texts. A whole bunch of texts and missed calls. From Seth. Damn, he hadn't called Seth. He should have, but the days had flown by.

Henry, I've got some weird pings on you. There's a pattern coming up, and I don't like it.

He was probably being paranoid. Everything had been quiet. He moved to the second text.

I don't know where you are, but I need you to call me. I've managed to find one of the members of the cartel who got away. I think he believes that you know where the money and drugs that went missing around the time of your death are, and he wants it back. There's a bounty on the Dark Web. At least I think they might be talking about you. Call me soon or I'll call Nate Wright.

That had been thirty minutes ago.

He reached for the ignition. He would go straight back to the clinic.

"I wouldn't turn that engine over if I was you, Bishop."

Henry moved slightly and could see there was a man standing beside the Jeep, a revolver in his hand. He checked his other side and found yet another man there, a rifle in his hand. From his rearview mirror he caught sight of two more behind him.

They weren't playing around.

He could shove the door and take out the one to his left while he

199

brought up his weapon, and shoot the one on his right before he could get that rifle up. He would have to move quickly to evade the two behind him, but he thought he could manage it.

If he had a gun. But Henry Flanders didn't carry.

Henry Flanders was about to take a whole lot of pain.

"Get out of the Jeep," the largest of the men said.

He might have a chance to run. He knew the woods far better than they would. They likely weren't acclimated to the elevation. Yes, he could run down river and make his way back into town.

"Leave the phone."

The damn phone had gone dark, and it was still plugged in. He calculated the odds of being able to get the phone and get away and finally eased out of the Jeep, holding his hands up.

He would bet his life these were mercenaries and not from the cartel. They would need him alive to collect the bounty. Of course he really was betting his life, but he had to take the chance.

God, it was so much worse when a man had the world to lose. He couldn't be John Bishop, couldn't flip that switch on and turn down Henry Flanders's horror at the thought of not seeing his wife again, not watching his baby girl grow. Because John Bishop loved them both, too. He'd finally managed to be complete, and it could be the very reason he died.

He eased out of the Jeep.

"You sure that's the guy?" One of the men behind him sounded unsure. "He doesn't look like some dangerous spy. I want the money, but you know it'll go poorly if we offer the cartel the wrong guy."

Oh, he was about to show them.

That was when he felt something hit his thigh.

"Yeah, that's Bishop. I got the picture from a contact who's still in the CIA. Says he tangled with this guy a few months back," the boss said. "He told me not to fuck with him."

And he hadn't. The world was starting to go fuzzy because he'd taken a damn tranq dart to the thigh. He wouldn't be able to run. In a few seconds, he wouldn't even be able to think.

"He also told us we need to get in and out pretty fast or these guys in town will be all over us."

Henry hit his knees because his legs didn't work anymore. He tried to make them move, but he was so weak.

"Grab his feet. Let's get him out of here before someone comes along," a deep voice said. "We need to contact the cartel and get our money and disappear as fast as we can."

The world started to go dark and he thanked the universe that at least he would pay for his sins alone. At least they wouldn't touch his girls.

His wife and daughter. They would be safe.

It was all that mattered.

* * * *

Three o'clock came and went and Henry didn't show up.

By three thirty, Nell had called, and when he didn't pick up she knew something had gone terribly wrong. He'd said he would be back by three. He might have been ten minutes late or so, but not this long without calling her.

It was silly now to think she'd been worried he would leave without a trace. Henry would never leave her side. Not unless something bad had happened.

"I can go to your cabin and check," Laura offered. "I would send Cam, but he and Nate are working an accident over the pass, and they're not answering anything but emergency calls. Apparently it was bad. They called out three departments to help. But that accident happened before Henry left."

"He probably fell asleep," Holly offered. "He looked tired when he left. Newborns can wreck your sleep schedule. He probably thought he could take a nap and then his body was like nope, you are sleeping, mister."

Nell shook her head. "No. He didn't. He wouldn't. Something's happened."

She knew it deep in her soul.

"Someone pass me my phone. I turned it off so it wouldn't disturb Poppy," Nell said.

"Of course, but he's fine," Holly insisted as she grabbed the phone.

Laura was walking with Poppy in her arms, soothing the baby with motion. "Are you nervous about this? I think Henry's fine, but I don't want you to worry. I can call Rafe. He's at city hall, but he can go out to the cabin if we honestly think something's happened. Sierra's with Hope and Beth this afternoon. We've started a play group, but it's really so we can take afternoons off."

A sense of panic was crowding out everything else. Where was he? Had he fallen or had an accident? He wouldn't have gone over the pass so he wasn't involved in that accident, but the roads could be hard to navigate this time of year.

"Yes, please send him." She would far rather inconvenience Rafe than not help her husband if he needed it. If she was embarrassed that she panicked at the end of this, she would count that as a win.

Laura handed Poppy to Holly, grabbed her cell, and walked out into the hallway.

She was panicking for nothing. That's what she told herself, but some deeper instinct was at play. Something that told her this was not nothing.

This was what she'd feared since the moment she'd found out about Henry's past.

The phone came on and she saw Seth had called. A couple of times.

And knew she was right.

Hours later she still sat in the clinic's small room and wondered where her husband was. Afternoon had turned to evening and she prayed the calls she'd made earlier would come to fruition.

"Hey, Nate's on his way in." Michael strode through the door. "He's already been out to the cabin and ran it as a crime scene."

The minute she'd told Holly there was a bounty on Henry, Holly had called Michael Novack. It had been less than half an hour later that her former bodyguard had put himself back on active duty. He'd spent hours standing outside her door vetting anyone who came into the clinic.

"I'm glad he's working on it, but I already called someone." She'd known exactly what Henry would want her to do. This was beyond what Nate had done in the past. She knew he would try his hardest, but she felt better with her choice.

"I'll go grab our order from Stella's." Holly got up from her seat. Laura had been running around town trying to help out their overworked sheriff's department, but Holly had stayed right by her side.

"I can't…" She took Poppy into her arms. She had to eat. She fed their baby, and her fear couldn't take priority. "Thank you."

Holly nodded. "And I'm calling Stef. I think you should move in there for a while."

She wanted to argue, but it made sense. Talbot Manor had good security, and she would have help. There was so much she still couldn't do for herself.

"Tell him I'm going to need a room close to hers," Michael said. "And I'm going to want to look at his security."

"Wait, Jen and baby Logan are there." She hadn't thought about the fact that she could be putting the Talbots at risk.

Holly frowned her way. "Do not let Stef or Jen hear you say that. They won't let you go anywhere else. I would take you to our place, but we don't have the same security. What Stef does have is enough rooms for me to stay with you, too. Michael can protect your body and I'll hold your hand." Before Nell could protest, Holly was shaking her head. "Don't argue with me. I'll be back in a couple of minutes. This is going to be fine. If what Seth told you is true, they won't have killed him."

No. They were going to sell him to someone who would kill him.

How far away was he? Was he hurt? Was he praying she made the right moves to find him?

Holly pushed through the door, and it wasn't more than a moment or two before Nate walked in. His uniform was wrinkled and there were spots of blood marring the khakis, but that was from the accident earlier in the day.

He pulled his hat off as he approached her. "Nell, I need you to understand that I'm on this. I'm not going to stop until I find Henry. I'm going to call in some law enforcement from around the area so Cam and I can work on this. He's got contacts."

She forced back a groan as she shifted. This would have been so much easier if she hadn't been split down the middle and stapled back up. She patted Poppy's back as she looked up at the sheriff. "I appreciate everything you've done, and normally I would put this all into your hands, but I don't think you can solve this. If we don't find Henry in twenty-four hours, we have to suspect that he'll be taken out of the country. You can't work there."

"I'll do whatever it takes," Nate vowed.

She heard someone moving out in the hall and breathed a sigh of relief. He'd told her he would be here quickly, and it looked like he'd kept that promise. She was going to have to buy a whole lot of carbon footprint offsets, but for once she was grateful for private planes. "You won't have to because I called in some favors."

"I don't think he'll call it a favor," Michael pointed out. "I think he'll call it a family responsibility."

There was a quick knock and then a big man with sandy blond hair was walking through accompanied by another man with golden-brown hair. Ian Taggart was dressed casually and had a duffel bag over his shoulder.

Tennessee Smith carried one as well. She'd never met the man, but Taggart had told her he was in Dallas and wouldn't be left behind. Introductions were quickly made and Nate offered the former CIA agents use of the station house as a base of operations.

"Thank you, Sheriff Wright," Ian replied. "We've already got a line on the group that has Henry. I've got a couple of hackers, one who has some ties to people on the Deep Web, and we've identified a group of mercenaries who do work for some shady people. They're based in Colorado Springs, and we caught them on a few of the traffic cameras between here and there. We're working on real estate in the area where they could keep him until they move him out."

"It's harder here than in a city," Ten Smith explained. "But you need to understand that even if they move him, they won't kill him. From what we've uncovered, a couple of lower-level members of the Jalisco cartel believe the rumors that Henry knows where a fortune in drugs and cash is stored."

"He doesn't." Ian set his bag down. "From what I've managed to piece together, one of the partners used Henry's faked death to steal a shit ton of money and blame it on him. Henry's got no clue and that dude is now dead, so we're working with people who have no idea what's going on."

None of this made her feel any better. She held on to her daughter. "If Henry doesn't know anything, he doesn't have anything to barter with."

"Ah, but I actually consider it good news." Tag moved in front of her. "Henry is going to figure out what's going on. He knows how to play this game better than anyone."

"He's been here before," Ten added. "He's tough. He'll play for time and we will find him, and then we're getting rid of the problem for good."

"By putting them all in jail?" Nell asked.

Ten's face went still. "Uh…"

Ian nodded, an oddly angelic expression coming over his face. "Yep. Jail for all of them. We'll make sure of it."

Nell felt tears slip from her eyes. "I know you're going to have to kill them. It makes me sad. The whole thing makes me sad and scared, and I hope they don't have families that will miss them."

Taggart sat on the end of the bed, his expression more serious than she'd seen before. "They won't stop. I'm sorry. I wish I could make this world better. There is a time for you to work and a time to call me in. That's what Henry understands. You think I live for this, and deep down maybe I do, but I admire what you do, too. You do the work to make the world a better place, to make sure my kids have clean water and a government that gives a shit about them. I do what I do to make it safer for you and that sweet girl you have there."

He navigated the dark stuff so she could work in the light. It was what Henry had done for so very long. "Thank you, Ian. And you, too, Mr. Smith."

"Kay is on her way," Ten assured her. "She's on a plane, and I'll head back to Alamosa to pick her up. Mr. Novack, I've read your record. You're solid. Do you need backup? We can have a couple of guards up here tomorrow morning."

Michael shook his head. "No. I'm going to move her to the Talbot Manor this evening, and I want to keep a low profile. She's high value now."

Nell frowned. "I was high value before, too. I don't like my value being predicated on my ability to force my husband to talk. That seems demeaning."

Taggart snorted. "I can't wait for you to meet Kay. She's going to love you." He sobered. "Nell, you have the hardest job of all."

The room seemed to close in on her because she knew what he was going to say. "I have to wait. I have to be patient."

Taggart nodded. "Yes. I'm sorry, but I need you to know that I will do everything in my power to bring your husband home to you. I've been assured the Agency won't stop me from doing what I need to do, but they also won't actively help me. As far as they're concerned, John Bishop died and Henry Flanders is on his own."

But he wasn't. Henry had a family. John had a family.

And they would bring him home.

It was late in the night when Michael drove her to the Talbot Manor. She sat in the back of his SUV, Poppy tucked safely in the car seat she and Henry had selected after weeks of research.

This wasn't how it was supposed to go. They were supposed to go home as a family, and Henry had promised he had a surprise for her. They were supposed to spend their first night in their cabin together as a family.

"We're back to the same protocols we had before." Michael put the SUV in park. "You go nowhere without me. I mean it. You want to go for a walk around the grounds, I'm with you. This is more serious than it was before."

"I won't fight you. I can't even run." She'd never felt more vulnerable. She was recovering from a surgery and she had a baby to protect, and she didn't have Henry by her side.

"You won't have to. I promise I won't let anyone close," Michael vowed. He sat there for a few seconds as though trying to decide what to say. Or whether to say it. "Spending those weeks with you…they made me realize I have to move forward. I don't know how it's going to go, but I'm looking for a better place, and I've been told by my boss that I can work out here. I'm coming off my leave and starting my life again. I'm thinking of asking Lucy if she wants to go out with me."

"That's wonderful."

"I'm telling you because you should know how much you affect people."

She wrinkled her nose. "I'm afraid I annoy a lot of them."

"Only the ones who don't see why you do the things you do," Michael explained. "Why you do all those kooky protests and all that letter writing. You care about things other people don't. Or you care about them enough to do something. I just want you to know that I admire you. You let go of the hurt, and I want to do the same. I like Lucy."

At least one good thing had come from all of this. "I'm glad to hear it."

"And that damn Ty better understand that he doesn't own her." Michael opened the door and slid out. He opened hers, his face frowning in the moonlight. "I'll put that kid in his place if I have to."

"And if his place is on the other side of Lucy?" She felt compelled to make the argument. After all, it was Bliss.

Michael froze for a second. "Not happening. Not. Happening. Come on. Let's get you inside. I'll carry the baby. And take my hand. It's still icy out here."

"No need. I've got her." Laura was outside the SUV, wrapped in a parka.

That was when Nell noticed there were a lot of cars in Stef's big circular drive. "What's going on? Am I disturbing a party?"

Laura reached a hand out. "No, silly. We're here for you. You don't need to be alone. It's me and Holly on duty tonight. We're going to stay in case you need anything. We'll be here every night. The day shift is going to alternate between Rachel and Callie one day, and Hope and Beth other days. But Holly and I will be here every night until Henry's home."

She might feel vulnerable but she wasn't alone.

She took Laura's hand and eased out of the car, every movement painful but less than it had been the day before.

"But tonight pretty much everyone's here," Laura said. "We thought we would get you through the first night. We're going to have a sharing circle and everything."

Tears had started to fall again. "You hate that."

"But you love it," Laura replied. "Do you honestly believe that if we all send out our energy, that if we sit and think about him, he'll feel it?"

Nell nodded, far too moved to speak.

"Then he will feel us tonight. He'll feel our love and our hope and our strength. He'll know we're with him." Laura had some tears of her own. "And Cam found something when he searched your cabin. It was out in the shop."

Laura led her up the stairs while Michael carried the sleeping baby behind them.

"What was it?" Nell asked.

"I think Henry was planning on giving it to you today," Laura explained. She opened the door and led her inside the warm house. To her left was the front parlor, and it was easy to see that most of Bliss was out here tonight. "I don't think he would mind us bringing it to you. It was obvious he meant for Poppy to have it tonight."

Nell stopped and stared at the beautiful cradle. This was what he'd spent hours in his shop working on. He'd been lovingly making a bed for their baby.

Poppy would sleep surrounded by her father's love.

"I love it. Thank you for bringing it here," she said.

And then she was surrounded by them. The town closed ranks around her and she wasn't alone.

Chapter Twelve

"Y ou want to tell us where you hid those drugs, brother?"

Henry's head hurt, but then his fucking everything hurt. His mind was foggy. How many drugs had they pumped through his system? They hadn't stopped with the tranquilizer dart.

"Don't call me brother." He managed to get the words out as he took stock of where he was. He wasn't in the same place he'd been the two nights before when they'd loaded him on a plane. He thought it was the third day, but he couldn't be completely sure.

His daughter would be six days old if he was right. He'd had two days with her.

Did Nell think he'd left? It wasn't like he hadn't done it before. She knew how well he could dump one life for another.

No. Seth would have talked to her. Seth would have told her what he'd found.

"Or did you sell the drugs?" There was the sound of pacing. "I suppose after all these years you would have sold them, but I bet you still have the money. If you don't, then I'll simply have to make an example of you. We can't have employees thinking they can get away with stealing from the company."

"I wasn't a fucking employee." He shouldn't have to explain the finer points of being a CIA operative.

"That's not what my former bosses believed, but I'll give it to you. You're a hard man to find, Bishop." The man in front of him came into focus. He was roughly six foot, with lean corded muscle and some fairly impressive neck tats that told Henry he knew how to kill. He wore tactical pants and a black T-shirt. There was a big gun in his shoulder holster that Henry would love to get his hands on.

But Henry had no idea who this guy was. It had been years, and the man standing in front of him hadn't been in the inner circle at the time. "You know my name. Good for you. It's only polite to know the name of the man who's going to kill you."

"We're not there yet," the dark-haired man said with a chuckle. A deep scar ran across his face. "But I don't think we need introductions. You're not here to make friends, Mr. Bishop. I know you manipulated everyone before, but it won't happen with me. All you need to know is that I'm now the head of this organization. Thanks for taking out everyone above me a few months ago. I thought I would have to do far more to get to where I am."

The fog was starting to clear and he glanced around. He remembered the place. He was in Bolivia at a compound owned by one of the cartels he'd investigated. He'd gone undercover with them, and he'd witnessed some truly horrific crimes here.

Was this karma? Payment for his sins? He'd seen paradise, held hope in his hands, and now it would all be taken away from him.

Or it was one last fight. One more test to see if he deserved the life he wanted. He hadn't really had to fight the first time, but this last year had been one long battle for his marriage and his place in the world he loved.

Maybe this was the finish line. If he managed to fight his way out of this place, he wouldn't have to look over his shoulder for the rest of his life. If he took out these assholes, his family would be safe.

"You misunderstood me." Henry forced himself to sit up straight, to test the restraints he was in. His hands were fastened to a wooden chair by zip ties and his feet were bound to the legs. But the chair wasn't bolted to the floor, and that was a mistake. The mercenaries had been smart enough to bind his hands behind his back with cuffs he couldn't get out of. Hands in front was much easier to deal with. "I don't care what your name is. I was saying it's nice that you knew mine because I'm going to kill you."

Nell would have to forgive him. Maybe there was a version of a carbon footprint offset for his soul. He would buy a couple of those.

Another low chuckle came from the man. "Sure, you are. You don't even remember me. I guess you were too busy with the big guys to notice those of us who did the real work, but that's okay."

There was some talk around him. He used it to get some idea of what was behind him. Or rather who. At least two, both men. Another big guy stood behind the boss. They would all have guns. If his plan worked, Henry would have the broken chair, and it would take him a few seconds to get on his feet. He would have to time this carefully.

"Now, Bishop, let's talk about what you took from this business when you decided to conveniently die on us."

He'd taken absolutely nothing, but over the course of his stay with the mercenaries, he'd come to understand that money had gone missing. And a rather large amount of drugs that would have been sold for more money. With the cartel in chaos, money would be needed for this man to finalize his hold on the organization.

It wouldn't hurt to be the man who killed John Bishop either. It would give him a bunch of cred, and the Agency wouldn't even come after him. All in all, it was a good play.

Except he hadn't been the one to take the money. Of course if they knew that, he would be dead.

"I might be convinced to tell you where I put it." Lies were the only thing that might give him a chance.

A nasty smile crossed the man's face. "Yes, I think I'll find a way to convince you."

This was where they brought the pain. He'd already had some of it, though he actually thought the drugs were worse. At least with the pain he knew what was happening to him. Every time he woke up from the drugged stupor he'd been in, he had to wonder what they'd done, had to take a personal inventory of all his limbs because the cartel could be brutal.

"And I think I'll keep my mouth shut for the time being. You know it's been a long time since I was tortured for information. I wonder how long I'll last." He couldn't give them intel he didn't have. This was all a play for time. Someone would look for him. Even if Nell didn't think to call Taggart in, Seth would.

God, he hoped Seth would think to call Ian. He was afraid this was the kind of thing only Ian or Ten or Kayla could help him with.

It struck him that if he hadn't been forced to reconnect with his old friends, they wouldn't be able to try to save him. If all of this had gone down the way Henry had hoped—Nell never knowing about his past—he wouldn't be able to pray someone had called Tag. Tag wouldn't have known he was alive. Tag and Ten would have gone on with their lives believing John Bishop was a dead man.

Perhaps his wife was right and things always happened for a reason. No one on the planet was better at handling a curve ball than his wife. She might not like the circumstances she found herself in, but she always made it work.

If he died, she would find a way to raise their daughter, to make her strong and loving. She would stay in Bliss and…god, he hoped she found someone who could love her. It was odd because he was a possessive man, but in that moment she was all that mattered. Nell and her beautiful soul, the one who had sat with him in the courtyard of a nudist resort with the snow falling on her hair as she'd shown him there was another way to live. He could still picture her sitting there, her head tilted up and snow on her cheeks as she stared at the stars above and found meaning in them.

And he remembered the look on her face when all her plans had been wrecked and Caleb told her she needed a surgery she'd been desperate to avoid. She'd held his hand and told him everything would be fine. There had been such strength in her.

He wanted her happy, even if he couldn't be the one to make her happy. But she better pick right the second time around. She better pick a real Bliss man because he would be waiting to share her in the afterlife.

He heard someone coming up from behind and braced himself. The whack to the back of his head actually helped clear it a bit more. He wasn't a fan of pain, but it had its uses.

"Pay attention, Bishop. I'm going to show you how a real man gets information," the burly guy said.

The key would be picking his time. He had to wait until the time was right. Some of these guys would get bored and leave. When he was down to two or three, he would attempt to bust out.

Hopefully he would have enough energy to do what he needed to do. Then he would face something worse. He would face the jungle, and he didn't have any supplies. He didn't even have a passport or cash.

All that mattered was getting home to his girls.

"This is my friend," the boss said. "He's my go-to guy when I need some information. Do you know what it feels like to have your balls tased?"

Ah, they were going straight to the good stuff. "It's one of my favorite things in life."

"I was hoping you would say that. It's so easy to torture a man. Though I've found oftentimes a man like you doesn't respond to pain." The boss began to pace and the go-to torturer moved to the side where he'd helpfully gathered all his supplies in one place, a wheeled tray. It was good to know he was organized.

"Oh, I assure you, I'll respond." He couldn't not respond. At least he'd given Nell their daughter. He might not be able to manage a sibling after this.

The boss studied him. "I have no doubt we can make you cry like a baby, but that's not the response I need."

The more the guy talked, the longer Henry's balls stayed intact. "I might prove harder, although I am out of practice. Have you ever thought about starting smaller than the balls? You know sometimes it helps to warm a guy up before you go for the big stuff."

The boss stared at him for a moment as though trying to figure him out. It was easy to see this guy thought he was an expert. He was playing the big guy for the rest of his crew. Henry could work with that.

It was important to figure out what a man wanted in these situations and then to decide whether to give it to him or hold back.

He would howl. He wouldn't hold back. He would let this guy think he was going to break, that he was weak. Then he would let the "pain" take him out for a while. He would do it over and over again. He was excellent at pretending to be unconscious. He would lay in wait and when it was right, he would pounce.

"I don't like to waste my time." The boss paced in front of him. "I

213

know other men would try to see if they could get you to talk by beating on you or pulling out some fingernails. I think you're stronger than that. I was joking about your balls. I actually don't think that would break you at all. I've decided to go another way."

Henry went still. "And what way is that?"

A chill went up his spine at the man's smile. It was genuine pleasure. That man was enjoying himself and truly believed he had the upper hand. That smile meant trouble.

"You have a wife, Mr. Bishop. A pretty thing. Younger than you. Dark hair."

He could taste bile in the back of his throat. There was no way. "Try again. You can't get to her. She's protected."

No one in Bliss would have taken their eyes off Nell. She wouldn't have gone back to their cabin alone. She would have stayed with Stef, or perhaps allowed Seth to fly her out to New York and hide there. Nell would protect their daughter.

"Not as much as you think," the man said with a laugh. "She's a moron. She actually found the mercenaries and paid them to take her to where you are. Such a sweet thing. I can understand why you chose her. If you hadn't taken my money, you could have had a life with her."

He snapped his fingers and that was when Henry heard a woman crying.

Oh, god. He was going to be sick. What had she done? Had she thought she could talk to these men? He had to find a way to get her out of here. She wouldn't last. He wouldn't be able to watch her being tortured.

"I'll get you the money." He had no idea how much they were talking about, but he had to say something.

The boss's smile got deeper. "Yes, I think you will."

The doors came open and he could see a petite woman being dragged into the room. There was a bag over her head and her hands were tied in front of her. They'd taken her shoes, but he recognized that cotton skirt of hers. It was one of her favorites.

"Please don't hurt her." He started to move the chair and quickly felt big hands on his shoulders. "I'll get you whatever you want."

The boss pulled her against his body. "I bet you will. But first you'll watch me play with your bitch for a while. Here, honey. Why don't you go give your husband a kiss and remind him what's at stake."

"Please," she said, her body shaking.

Henry stopped. Something was wrong. And then he knew what it was. The bag came off her head and midnight hair spilled out.

"I just want to see my husband," the woman said, her voice quaking.

Kayla Summers.

Kayla was good. Like Hollywood actress good. She always had been, but getting married to a top-paid actor seemed to have refined her talent because she had tears running down her face.

"John." She stumbled toward him but he could see she was still in complete control. "John, I told them we would give back the money."

So they hadn't even bothered to get a real look at his Nell. He'd always said the cartels didn't do enough reconnaissance. They tended to fly by the seat of their pants when it came to these things, and it was about to bite them in the ass.

Kay wouldn't be alone.

Kayla hit her knees and made a spectacular show of fear. "I was so worried for you."

He needed to know what the play was. "How could you do this? How could you walk into their hands? You have to know it was foolish to come here."

She sniffled. "I thought about ten different plans, but this was the only one that could have worked. I had to talk to them, had to make them see they didn't need to kill you."

So Ten was somewhere around. "This isn't a game. You're not some fish they're going to tag and release, Nell."

She nodded, telling him Tag was here, too. "I know that now. We have to give them the money. It was a mistake to take it. If only we'd thought for five minutes, we would have known we wouldn't get away with it."

Five minutes and then Tag and Ten would do whatever they were going to do. Her hands were on his lap as she looked up at him, and he could see she was practically holding those bindings together. She'd already worked her way out of them and was trying her hardest to not let the bad guys know.

"This has been a bomb waiting to go off in our lives forever," Kay cried.

So he was waiting for a big boom.

The boss hauled Kayla up by her hair. "You were never going to get away with anything, bitch."

"Please don't hurt me," Kayla begged. She managed to cradle her hands to her chest as the boss held her against him.

"Your husband there was talking about how he thought we should go slow in the beginning." There was a cruel look in the man's eyes as he crushed Kay close to his body. "I think I'll honor his request. I wasn't willing to go slow with him, but maybe I will with you, sweetheart."

Henry had to stop himself from snorting. *Yeah, try that, buddy.* Kay knew exactly what to do with a rapey son of a bitch. He was sure this asshole had done shitty things to many women who hadn't had the means to fight back.

He was about to find out he was dealing with one who could.

"Please don't hurt me." Kay was gasping, her voice filled with fear.

He should probably try to make it look good. Although he had to say his first instinct was to simply watch her. She was spectacular, and as a teacher, he truly enjoyed his students doing well in the real world. Seeing them all grown up and able to emasculate a bad guy…it did something for his soul.

"Oh, I think you'll like the way I hurt you. What do you say, Bishop? You want to watch me do your wife?" the boss asked.

It was time for a little confusion.

"Do I have to? I think it's going to bore her. Kay, do we need to wait? Josh will kick my ass if I let that man even start to molest you," he said with a sigh because he'd already seen her move to get the gun.

She wasn't waiting.

That was the moment the ground shook and a loud boom went off in the distance.

Taggart really did like to blow shit up. He'd always been overly invested in explosives.

"What the hell was that?" The boss had dropped his hands from Kayla's body and turned toward the sound of some building blowing up. Likely his house. The man reached for his gun and came up empty.

"Looking for this?" Kay had her perkiest smile on. "Thanks. I couldn't bring a gun with me. I thought I'd just take yours."

Kay turned and immediately fired off three quick shots.

"Don't forget behind you, dear." Henry was perfectly calm now. He trusted his former protégés. "He might not have a gun, but he's still bigger than you."

Kayla's eyes rolled. "Like that matters." Without looking, she kicked back and caught the jerk right in the balls. She turned and faced him down. "We're going to have a long talk about treating women like pawns, asshole. I don't simply exist so you can rape me and make my fake husband tell you something he doesn't even know. Also, eww, he's like another dad to me."

"Older brother, please." He wasn't that old. "And thank you for believing me about the money and the drugs."

Kayla gave him a bright smile. "Never doubted it. You did it all for love. It's so romantic."

Then she turned and fired two bullets into the man on the ground.

"I thought you were teaching him a lesson." He could breathe again.

Kayla shrugged. "He wasn't smart enough to learn."

Another explosion rocked the ground.

"You should probably let me out," Henry said. "More could be on their way."

She shook her head. "We're good now. The boys will take care of everyone else. Ten's having so much fun. He found a flamethrower. Tag's blowing shit up all over the place. They'll be here soon. Oh, your little girl is divine, John...Henry. She's the sweetest thing ever. I swear if we had my phone I would FaceTime her right now. I promised Nell I would keep her up to date, and the last time I was able to DM her was right before I let the mercenaries take me. They wouldn't even let me keep my phone. Assholes. It's okay. Ten promised he would get it back after he killed all of them. The case is Chanel. Josh got it for my birthday, so I don't want to lose it."

Kayla could talk a mile a minute.

"I don't think we should call Nell until we get clear of the compound."

"I know what it's like to have to sit and wait to find out if the person you love is okay." Kayla frowned down at the restraints. "They also didn't let me bring in a knife." She gasped and then Henry jumped at the sound of a shot so close to him. "Dude, stay dead. I hate it when I only halfway kill them. Eww, I also hate having to search dead bodies for the things I need. Do you think there's a kitchen nearby? Or did Tag already blow that up?"

"Kayla, focus." He so wanted out of those restraints.

"What the hell?" a deeply Southern accent said. Ten Smith strode through the door wearing all black, and he'd obviously ditched the flamethrower for an AR-15. "You're out of practice, man. I remember a time when you would have smashed that chair and gotten yourself on your feet in no time at all."

"Well, I'm a lot older now, and it hurts to break a chair around your body. I leave that to you youngsters. Although I would again point out that I'm not that much older than you." Henry felt that way sometimes.

Tag jogged in, a huge grin on his face. "Hey, Henry. Smart of you to wait until someone showed up with a knife. Breaking a chair hurts. Damn, this was fun. I would stay away from the heavy white cloud that is currently hovering over the warehouse. I think it's cocaine. It's pretty when it explodes."

"Yeah, I gotta admit. I missed this," Ten said with wistful grin.

"You know what I miss? My wife." If he let them, his former students would likely start a new team and tour the world blowing things up. "I thank you so much. Can I go home now?"

Ian pulled out a really big knife. "Sure thing. But my services come at a price. You're going to have to find me a cabin. Charlie likes Bliss. She wants a summer place. I like the crazy shit that happens there, and I'm trying to raise free-range kids, so it all works out."

Henry frowned. "They don't like it when Texans buy up all the land and turn the whole place into a vacation…" Having Tag around might be fun. It would be good to see him handle Marie when she got in a bad mood. "Sure. Why not. The more the merrier."

The smile was back on Ian's face. "Cool. Hey, maybe we can do this more often. Like a reunion." Another boom went off. "Sorry. There's probably a couple more where that came from. We should leave. Someone's going to show up soon."

He started to work on Henry's restraints.

"I thought we killed them all," Ten replied.

"There's always more." Kayla took the super sparkly phone Ten held out. "Oh, I missed you so much. Smile, Henry."

She knelt down beside him and took a quick shot and started typing.

"Are you seriously doing a social media post?" Ten complained.

Henry's hand came free, and then the other. "She's sending Nell an update. Tell her I love her. Tell her I'm coming home."

"I will," Kay agreed and then frowned. "Nell's happy you're coming back but she wants to know if those are reusable restraints."

He turned to her.

Kay smiled. "She didn't say that. She sent me prayer hands and the crying emoji and a heart. I think that's for you. When we're safely away, you can call her."

She was only a phone call away. She was safe. Their baby was safe. Henry stood up and stretched his back. "Let's go home. As for the reunions, they better be somewhere nice. I am too old for this."

Another boom went off.

Ten frowned Tag's way. "Did you have to use all the C-4?"

Tag shrugged. "Didn't want to waste it."

Henry followed them out, happy to be going home.

* * * *

Patience sucked.

"I don't understand why I couldn't go." Nell rocked in the nursing chair Stef had brought in when Nell had tried the one his wife, Jen, used. She'd learned quickly that Stef overcompensated for feeling helpless. He'd stuffed his kitchen with an overabundance of ingredients he thought she might use. He would be drinking almond milk for a long time.

It was his love language, and she'd stopped trying to tell him she didn't need anything. Besides, she loved the rocker. It was soothing, and she spent a lot of time in it. She wasn't even going to ask where it had been made or about the company's protocols concerning the environment. It wasn't that she was giving up on making the world a better place. That was more important than ever, but she was giving herself a break. The chair worked, and it would be an indulgence that got her through the day.

Like Rachel had said, anything that worked was okay.

"Because you've got a massive list of things you can't do for the foreseeable future, and sitting in a car for an hour there and an hour back is definitely one of them," Holly said. She stared out the window of the room Nell and Poppy had been given.

It was a full-on suite because the Talbots didn't do tiny guest rooms. Michael had been staying on the couch in the living area despite the fact that there were other rooms available. He'd taken his job very seriously. Either Holly or Laura had stayed with Nell, helping her out in the first full week of being a new mom. It had been exhausting because even when she should have been able to sleep, she would sit there in the dark and think about what was happening to Henry, wondering if he was even alive.

"I can sit in a car." She looked down at Poppy in her arms. Her daughter was sleeping since it was midafternoon and she seemed to like to sleep through the day and demand milk all night long. Though at least she'd managed to get Poppy to latch properly. That had been hard work, and worrying that her baby was getting enough to eat had briefly distracted her from worrying about her husband's life.

"You're not supposed to drive for a few weeks." Holly sounded like she'd been told exactly what to say, as though Caleb had prepared her for this argument. "Or be in a car as a passenger for a long period of time. There are bumps in the road and the seatbelt would be uncomfortable. Henry wants you safe." She turned Nell's way. "They should be here soon. Are you worried?"

"About what?"

"About how you're going to feel when you see him?" Holly moved to sit on the bed across from Nell. "I know you had made up when he was taken, but you'd also been through something traumatic. That can bond two people in the moment. Have you realized you're still mad at him?"

She'd thought a lot about this in those hours when she couldn't sleep. "No. I forgave him and I have to move on. I can't keep going back to it, so no, I'm not still mad at him. I'm torn because I hate the fact that I want those people to never come after him again, and there's only one solution and I sent it out in the world. I did it to protect my husband and my child, and I have to live with it."

"You think those men will kill the people who took Henry?" Holly asked. "That Kayla woman seemed nice. I'm worried about her going into such a dangerous mission."

She'd gotten to know Taggart. Tennessee Smith, not so much. But Kayla was a doll, and she'd kept Nell informed on every part of the mission that she possibly could. Those phone calls from Kayla Summers had been a lifeline.

"Oh, I'm fairly certain Ian was ready to burn down the entire cartel," she admitted. "And that's what bothers me, but I'll get over it. Having to make that call...I know it's not the same, but it's a bit of what Henry had to do over the years. It's hard to make those calls, but they're necessary."

"It haunts you even when you know you would do the same thing a million times over," Holly said. She'd been the one to pull the trigger once, and Nell wouldn't change a thing.

"It doesn't change my mind that a nonviolent world is the best world, but there are times when it's necessary." She would do anything to protect her child.

There was the sound of tires crunching in the snow and Nell felt her heart flutter.

Holly was on her feet in an instant. "They're here. Give me Poppy and get up carefully."

Holly should be studying nursing because she'd been all over her like one. Nell could already feel tears welling as she looked down at her baby. "Daddy's home."

Poppy gave her that smile that everyone claimed was actually gas, but Nell knew better. She passed her over to Holly and got to her feet as quickly as she could. Holly had been right about moving as much as possible. She was already walking better, and it was a good thing because she really wanted to run.

Tears were pouring down her face because she could feel him. She wasn't sure why or how, but she could feel him close, and it was like she was warm again.

Stef was opening the door and then Henry was walking through, and he only had eyes for her.

"Nell. Nell, baby, I'm so sorry," he was saying as he moved to her.

She shook her head and then she was in his arms. "No. I'm sorry. I should have understood. It doesn't matter. You're all right."

She laid her head against his chest and listened to his heart beating.

Henry stroked her hair. "I thought I wasn't going to see you again. You did so good, baby. You did exactly what you should have."

She sniffled and pulled back because they weren't complete. Holly came forward and then Henry's eyes went wide and he held out his arms.

"God, I thought I wasn't going to see her again." He took their daughter into his arms, cradling her gently.

"She missed her father," Nell whispered.

"John Bishop has a kid. I never thought I would see the day." Tennessee Smith stood in the hall, a smile on his face.

He wasn't alone. They'd dropped Kayla off in LA, but Ian and Ten had chosen to stay and take Henry all the way home before making their way back to Dallas.

"I'm Henry Flanders," Henry insisted.

This was what they needed to get right. "You're both, and you need to feel free to be both, Henry. You're the sum of all your parts, and ignoring the John Bishop part of your life didn't work for us. You have to be okay with all of yourself, or how can we teach the same to Poppy?"

"I can work on that. I want her to be happy." He drew Nell close. "I want you to be happy."

He said it in an almost questioning way, as if he would walk away if she told him that was what it took for her to be happy.

That was the furthest thing from the truth. She needed him—all of him. "Seeing you safe makes me so happy. Having you home makes me the happiest. Don't ever leave again."

His lips kicked up. "I didn't mean to leave this time."

She glanced over at Ian. "Is it over?"

The big man gave her a nod. "We had a good talk and everyone's agreed that Henry knows nothing."

Everyone thought she was naïve. "Did you at least kill them in a humane fashion?"

It was Ian's turn to grin. "If by humane you mean did I kill a dude, take his balls, and turn them into a chew toy for my dog, then yes." He brightened. "Hey, when you think about it, I reduced human garbage. I reused some body parts and I totally recycled because there's a bunch of ground that got some human fertilizer."

She wasn't sure Ian got the point, but she smiled anyway.

Henry winced. "Sorry about that, baby."

She wasn't. "Can we go home now?"

He kissed her forehead. "There is nothing I want more."

She sighed in relief. It was time to finally bring their daughter home.

Spring

Epilogue

May had come and she was back where she'd been before, although this time she wasn't the one lying in a hospital bed, staring down at a newborn.

"I can't believe I have a baby." Holly stared at her daughter. Little Amelia Burke-Markov had a single curl of dark hair on the top of her head. She was adorable, and her two dads already doted on her.

Of course one of them had delivered her despite the fact that he shouldn't have. Caleb had upgraded both of the rooms in the clinic that was now rated as a small hospital.

"She's so beautiful."

Life seemed beautiful right now. Poppy was sleeping through the night and she and Henry were…they were playing again. Oh, they often got interrupted, but they weren't going to let that part of their relationship go.

After all, they'd learned that they could get through anything as long as they were together.

The door opened and Laura walked through, Sierra in a sling around her body and a bag from Stella's in her hand. "Did you hear that big guy who helped save Henry bought Hiram's old place?"

Henry had made that happen. "Yes, Ian's not planning on staying here all the time, but he's bringing his family up this summer. He's got

226

two girls and two boys. His wife seems nice. They got a membership to Mountain and Valley."

She missed going up to the retreat, but that time would come again. She had no doubt. For now she would sink into being Poppy's mom and enjoying this time of her life.

Laura set their lunch down and frowned Nell's way. "I heard he's already put in for a permit to build on to the cabin."

Nell gasped. "That cabin is a historical landmark."

"No, it isn't," Holly corrected. "It's kind of rundown."

It was lovingly used, and Ian should be able to see that. "It is the home of the first mayor of Bliss and should be honored as such. And if you believe Hiram, it's where the great battle with the bear was fought. Now you know I firmly believe we should leave bears alone, but that fight with one of nature's most magnificent predators formed many of the stories about Bliss over the years. How could he even think about changing a thing?"

"Well, he bought it and it's his property, and like I said, a little rundown," Holly began.

Laura shook her head. "No. Let her run with this. Come on. Don't you want to see Nell take on the big bad ex-CIA guy?"

"The last time she did, she tamed him and now he wears Birkenstocks with socks and eats tofu," Holly pointed out.

"Sometimes my feet get cold." Henry was standing in the doorway. He had a sling wrapped around his body, their baby tucked happily inside. He took her wherever he could, always gentle and loving with their daughter. When he worked in his shop, he would bring her bouncy seat out and talk to her the whole time. "What's this about Ian renovating Hiram's old place? That's a historical landmark."

Laura's lips had turned up in a mischievous grin. "Not technically. I think we'll have to have a town hall to discuss it."

Nell stood, a fire coming back into her that she hadn't felt in forever. "And I shall protest Mr. Taggart. But we should also have his wife out to our club. I've heard she's shot many a son of a bitch, and she makes excellent lemon tea cakes."

"Then she'll fit right in," Holly replied.

"Are you ready, baby?" Henry asked. "We've got that protest at the Stop 'n' Shop. I've put Poppy in her *Fight the Patriarchy* onesie."

Then they were ready to go.

"I'll be back tomorrow," she promised because she didn't let a day go by without spending time with her sisters.

"Go get 'em, Nell," Laura said.

It was time to make the world a better place. A more blissful place. As a family.

Lucy, Michael, and Ty, and all of Bliss will return in *Far From Bliss*.

Author's Note

I'm often asked by generous readers how they can help get the word out about a book they enjoyed. There are so many ways to help an author you like. Leave a review. If your e-reader allows you to lend a book to a friend, please share it. Go to Goodreads and connect with others. Recommend the books you love because stories are meant to be shared. Thank you so much for reading this book and for supporting all the authors you love!

Bayou Dreaming
Butterfly Bayou, Book 3
By Lexi Blake
Coming December 1, 2020

New York Times bestselling author Lexi Blake's heartfelt contemporary romance set in Louisiana's Butterfly Bayou.

Roxanne King left the big city looking for a simpler life, but after years of proving herself on a SWAT team in New York City, being deputy in a sleepy Louisiana parish is something of an adjustment. She's settling in, but she knows she made some mistakes in the beginning--Zep Guidry being the worst of them. Zep drifts through life on his looks and Cajun charm. Roxie learned the hard way he's not for her.

Zep is a man who knows what he wants, and what he wants is Roxie. He's just not sure how to get her. They spent one hot night together a year before and now all the lovely deputy seems interested in doing to him is arresting him. He's not used to a woman he can't charm, but Roxie seems immune. He's determined to win her back by any means necessary. Including becoming the kind of man she desires.

And when Roxie's past comes calling, it might be the opportunity Zep needs to show Roxie that the town bad boy might just be the man of her dreams.

* * * *

The door opened and Lila walked in. "I've got good news and bad news. You do have a concussion, but it's minor and my brother says the rest of your brain looks great. So you'll be fine, but I either need to send you to the hospital for observation for the day or someone needs to stay with you."

"I'll be fine." She wasn't about to go to the hospital. No way. "Just give me some instructions and I'll be out of your hair."

"No, you won't. You'll be completely in my hair because, like I said, I need to know someone is watching you for the next twelve hours," Lila explained. "I can do that by driving you an hour and a half to the hospital, checking you in, and then having someone pick you up late in the evening. Or you can have a friend stay with you today. I would tell you to hang out here at the clinic, but we're closed this morning. I'm going to Noelle's science fair. If we can ever trick another NP to come down here, well, we'll still be closed sometimes."

It was weird since hospitals didn't close in New York, but this clinic was the nearest thing they had to a hospital in Papillon. Lila would definitely insist on driving her since she wasn't even letting her lie on the couch by herself. There was no way Lila would let her get behind the wheel.

"I swear I'll be cool," she promised. "I'll sign one of those forms and everything will be okay. I don't mind signing it."

"You want to sign an AMA?" Lila's eyes had widened slightly but not in a surprised way. Nope. Roxie knew that look. It was the "dumbass said what" look.

"You're not leaving against medical advice," Armie declared with a frown.

She didn't have anyone to call. She quickly went through the short list of people she knew well enough to ask for a favor. She pretty much only knew the guys she worked with. She worked and then went home. She got the occasional beer, and sometimes she hung out with Lila. That was the sum of who she might be able to ask.

Major was working. He would have been called in to take over the rest of her shift and his own. Armie would be at his daughter's school event. Vince would be working with Major, and the fourth deputy, Chris, had recently hired on and was moving today.

The door opened and Zep walked in, Daisy on a leash, though she obviously wasn't trained. She squirmed and strained against the leash the minute she got in the room.

"Sorry, I wanted to make sure you were all right before I head into Houma," he said. "Also wanted to give you the chance to say good-bye to Daisy."

If she didn't find someone to "watch" over her, Armie would likely do it himself. Or they would have to spend their whole day driving back and forth to the hospital. He would miss his daughter's science fair, and it wasn't some elementary event where they showed off homemade volcanoes. Noelle was in her senior year of high school and competing for scholarships.

Also, she might save the puppy from having to go to some horrible shelter.

She looked at Zep. She knew what she was about to say was a mistake, but she didn't see that she had any other choice. She was desperate. "I need someone to make sure I can wake up every couple of hours."

Zep stopped and looked around as though trying to make sure she was talking to him. "You want me to call my sister or something?"

His sister and her husband, Harrison Jefferys, owned a B and B, the nicest one in town. That could be the solution. She could check in for the day and sleep on the couch in the great room. She'd heard their family dog was almost like a nanny to their little boy. Maybe he could be a nurse, too. "Does she have any rooms open?"

Armie huffed and Lila started shaking her head as though they both knew she planned to ask a dog to help her out before she'd ask the human male in the room.

Zep nodded as though that was what he'd expected. "Sorry. I was talking to Sera and Harry last night and they're completely booked. They've got a big family coming down for the week. From somewhere back East."

Then she didn't have a choice. She closed her eyes and wished the ground would swallow her up. It would be easier than doing what she had to do now. She sighed and opened her eyes because the ground was still firm beneath her. "Would you do it?"

The slowest, sexiest smile crossed his face. "I can definitely wake you up, darlin'. Though I'm more used to putting pretty ladies to sleep. Wait. That came out wrong. Never mind. I can do it."

She already regretted the choice.

About Lexi Blake

New York Times bestselling author Lexi Blake lives in North Texas with her husband and three kids. Since starting her publishing journey in 2010, she's sold over three million copies of her books. She began writing at a young age, concentrating on plays and journalism. It wasn't until she started writing romance that she found success. She likes to find humor in the strangest places and believes in happy endings.

Connect with Lexi online:

Facebook: https://www.facebook.com/authorlexiblake/
Twitter: https://twitter.com/authorlexiblake
Website: www.LexiBlake.net
Instagram: https://www.instagram.com/lexiblakeauthor/